Julie Corbin is Scottish and grew up just outside Edinburgh. She has lived in East Sussex for thirty-three years and raised her three sons in a village close to the Ashdown Forest. She is trained as a nurse and combines running the medical department in a boarding school with writing novels.

Her psychological thrillers have been described as 'creepy and gripping' (*Closer*) and 'remarkably assured . . . suspenseful narrative' (*Daily Mail*).

She speaks at writing events, book groups and libraries, and runs writing workshops for beginners and more experienced writers.

Visit Julie's website at www.juliecorbin.com and follow her on Twitter @Julie_Corbin.

Your Best Friend

JULIE CORBIN

HODDER &
STOUGHTON

First published in Great Britain in 2024 by Hodder & Stoughton Limited
An Hachette UK company

2

Copyright © Julie Corbin 2024

A CIP catalogue record for this title is available from the British Library

Paperback ISBN 978 1 529 37122 2
ebook ISBN 978 1 529 37123 9

Typeset in Plantin Light by Manipal Technologies Limited

Printed and bound in Great Britain by Clays Ltd, Elcograf S.p.A.

Hodder & Stoughton policy is to use papers that are natural, renewable
and recyclable products and made from wood grown in sustainable forests.
The logging and manufacturing processes are expected to conform
to the environmental regulations of the country of origin.

Hodder & Stoughton Limited
Carmelite House
50 Victoria Embankment
London EC4Y 0DZ

www.hodder.co.uk

For my sons Michael, Sean and Matthew

Prologue

She's running through the woods, gulping cold air that stings her throat and makes her cough. She feels him behind her and her heart doubles its speed but her legs can't go any faster. When he catches hold of her hair, she screams, yanks herself free, then pushes back into his chest. He grunts several times, sounding so much like a pig that she has to stifle the hysteria wedged tight against the fear in her chest. She pushes him again and he loses his balance, slithers down the bank to one side of them. There is the crack of twigs, the dull thump of thighbone and elbow, the scrape of flesh on stone, and all the while he's cursing, howling her name into the darkness like a wolf to the full moon.

Seconds of falling, and then a loud splash as his body comes to rest in the stream.

She waits, her heart ticking, her knees shaking. A huge shiver passes through her. Wide-eyed, she holds her breath and listens, tuning into sounds beyond herself: the soft shuffle of small mammals and insects, the breath of wind trailing through the leaves and lifting single strands of her hair.

When she's satisfied that enough time has passed, she follows his fall down the bank, not sliding as he did, but carefully placing one foot in front of the other, stretching out blindly to grasp hold of tree roots and rocks to keep her steady.

She reaches the bottom and blinks into the gloom before spotting the body-shaped lump in the stream. She shivers again when she imagines him crawling towards her, silent as a snake, to wrap his hands around her ankles and pull her underground. But as she edges closer, she sees that he can't crawl, that movement would be impossible. His limbs are twisted, his pelvis raised at one side, the angle unnatural. She feels sure his left knee has popped from its socket. There is the dark stain of blood on his temple. His eyelids flutter open then close again as he hovers in the space between the conscious and the unconscious.

The air is heavy here. *Off the beaten track.* Where dangerous possibilities lurk. She feels this significance move through her in a wave of heat. Here, chance and opportunity collide. No one is watching.

With quick, rough hands she digs aside the pebbles beneath his head. An inch more depth and his head drops further back, his ears, his cheeks and finally his nose and mouth sinking under the water. He breathes in the stream and coughs. Startled, his eyes open fully this time and she catches his panic, her indrawn breath caught short as her hand flies to her throat.

Should she? Shouldn't she?

She stands away from him, watching as he tries to lift himself up. He almost manages, gives a growl of desperation when he fails. She hesitates for a split second before placing her foot high up on his chest, leaning in until all of her weight is over this one foot. He gurgles, tries for the last time to lift his mouth to the air, his bloody-knuckled hands failing to grasp the shoe pressing down on him.

When he's quiet, she watches him for a full, unconscionable minute before blowing on her hands to warm them. Then she retraces her steps back to the village, the moon's glare highlighting her flushed cheeks.

Lydia

My stomach was in knots. The agent had a list of five couples interested in renting our house and the first was due to arrive any minute. 'They'll snap it up!' the agent had said to me earlier that afternoon, her tone determinedly upbeat. 'It's exactly what they're looking for!'

I'd spent two weeks putting off all viewings by inventing important meetings, a plumbing catastrophe and a strange smell in the basement. The agent had offered to show the house while I was at my meetings, contact a plumber on my behalf, spray air freshener in the basement. I refused all offers of help and told her I would call her back ASAP. I didn't call her back, and so she had bypassed me completely and spoken directly to Zack. He was genuinely perplexed. 'What's going on, Lydia? Why didn't you tell me about these issues? What am I missing here?'

'I didn't want to trouble you.' He was staying weeknights at his mum's house in Sussex. She'd recently been admitted to the hospice where she was receiving end of life care. 'The smell was easily sorted but I didn't want prospective renters sloshing through water from a burst pipe,' I told him.

'What pipe? When? How?'

'The Patersons had the same issue,' I said quickly. *Since when had lying come so easily to me?*

'Who are the Patersons?'

'They live at number twelve,' I told him. 'We went round there last year for a curry?' I could almost hear his brain ticking over. 'She made the most delicious samosas.'

'Oh yeah, I remember now. And they had a cinema room on the top floor.'

'Anyway ...' I took a breath. 'They were about to begin a similar extension to ours and we talked about the plans.' I exaggerated a story about their builder who had referenced ground level issues and an ancient stream that ran beneath the street. '... so it's probably to do with the angle of the pipes, the plumber thinks. And with all the rain we've been having ...' I trailed off.

Fortunately, Zack had other things on his mind so he didn't pick over the details. 'The sooner you and Adam join me down here, the better,' he'd said. 'I miss you.'

'And I miss you,' I'd replied.

It was true – I did miss him. But that didn't mean I wanted to move to Ashdown Village. I'd agreed to do it because I never really expected it to happen. And now, here I was, dragging my feet, hoping for a reprieve. Not because I didn't care about Paula. She had always been a wise and supportive mother-in-law, and I was closer to her than I'd ever been to my own mother. Every day since she'd been admitted to the hospice, we'd messaged each other. I'd send her photos and videos of Adam and his friends, links to articles I'd read on the internet that I knew she'd enjoy and funny videos of animals or toddlers. She never made me feel as if I was letting her down by not visiting. But life was all about timing, wasn't it? And she did have a terminal diagnosis. She could pass away at any moment; that wasn't what I was hoping for – it was simply the reality.

I knew that these were thoughts I couldn't voice. I would be too ashamed to say them out loud. Zack was a good son; that was one of the many reasons I loved him. To know that his wife was anticipating his mum's death? That would break his heart, and make me the worst sort of person. Someone who puts herself before others. *A selfish bitch.*

I picked Adam's jacket up off the floor and hung it on one of the hooks by the front door. He wasn't happy at his London school and had gone to Sussex with Zack for a trial day at a school close to the village. He was excited at the thought of moving out of London. 'It'll be great living in the country, Mum, won't it? And we can see Grandma more.'

Adam adored his grandma. Zack's dad had passed away just after Adam was born and his mum had come to stay with us, often for months at a time, caring for Adam while Zack and I were working. I loved that they had such a close bond. Losing her was going to be hard on him.

I went through to the living room and half-heartedly plumped the sofa cushions. The room was a mess. As a rule, we weren't tidy people and with Zack barely here, I'd given up all pretence of clearing up. There were empty wine glasses and coffee cups all over the surfaces. A thin layer of dust was accumulating, and the room smelt stale. I hadn't baked any bread and there were no fresh flowers on the mantlepiece. It struck me that the house had never been so unwelcoming, and I was hoping that the couple coming for the viewing would hate it.

The bell rang and I opened the front door. 'Sorry.' I kicked several pairs of shoes out of their way. 'There never seems to be quite enough space in the hallway.'

Mandy was all smiles as she introduced them both – 'Hi! I'm Mandy and this is my husband Fergal' – I didn't return her smile, my head was too full of noise.

'This is *so* lovely!' Mandy said, stepping onto the black and white floor tiles and stretching her arms out either side of her. She was classically beautiful, a modern Grace Kelly. The sort of woman whom everyone looked at twice. 'Much more room than we have at the moment.' She walked to the bottom of the stairs, her ponytail bouncing with each step. 'I *love* the shape of this stair-case.' There were books, shoes and clothes on practically every step but she saw past it all, her eyes following the graceful curve upwards.

'Any downsides to living here?' Fergal asked me. He was small and bald with a pointy chin. People would have looked at them both and said he was punching well above his weight but I knew better than to judge any book by its cover.

'When you have visitors, it'll be really hard for them to park,' I said. Then shook my head. 'Impossible, in fact. It's a nightmare.'

'It's like that all over London though, isn't it?' Mandy replied, undaunted. She pulled at Fergal's upper arm. 'Don't you just love the cupola?'

He followed her eyes and stared up two flights to the dome-shaped glass ceiling, and the blue sky beyond. 'Wow,' he said. 'That's quite something.'

'It makes the house hard to heat,' I said. 'Our bills have doubled in the last few years.'

'We can wear layers,' Mandy replied. 'I love a cash-mere sweater.'

'Let's go down to the kitchen.' I ushered them ahead of me. 'I'm afraid it's smaller than some of the others in the street.'

Mandy paused twice on the staircase to reference small details that caught her attention before gasping as she entered the kitchen-diner. 'It's so perfect,' she breathed. I watched her eyes mist over. She turned to Fergal, and they discussed entertaining 'in a space like this' with 'all this natural light.'

'It's south-facing, isn't it?' she asked me.

I nodded. My arms were folded and I used my foot to nudge a binbag of empty wine and spirit bottles, pushing the bag into the recess between the fridge and the breakfast bar. *Had I really drunk that much in a week?* Mandy walked past me into the garden, and I prodded the bag a little more, the bottles clinking loudly. I gave Fergal a meaningful glance, as if to say this will happen to you if you live here.

'Hydrangeas!' Mandy called out, chirpy as a cheerleader. And then, 'I've always wanted to live in a house with a walled garden.'

I let them both linger over the magnolia tree and pots of hydrangeas before taking them upstairs. We'd seen two of the bedrooms when Mandy said, 'The agent told us there's a good chance you'll list the house.'

'Sorry?' I swallowed awkwardly, my mouth dry.

'That you'll most likely stay in Sussex and put the house up for sale?'

'No.' I shook my head. 'No, no, no!' I repeated, more forcefully this time. 'The house will only be rented out for a year and then we'll be moving back.'

'Oh.' She smiled, her expression uncertain. 'Okay.'

I stood in the hallway while they wandered through the master bedroom. Why had the agent said that? If Zack had told her we'd sell the house within the year then that wasn't what we'd agreed. He had been travelling back and forth for almost a month when he bumped into one of his old school friends. 'Remember Crofty?' he'd asked me. 'It was great to see him again.' They met up for a game of golf and the next thing Zack was convinced that we should move back to his home village. He was all for putting our house on the market at once. 'What's stopping us?'

'Our lives are here! And you're making it work, living in your mum's house during the week. Upping sticks and moving, that would be—'

'Not really, Lydia,' he interrupted, a sad frown on his face. 'There's barely room for me at Mum's. The house is full of stuff. You know what it's like.' I nodded. His mum was a bit of a hoarder. 'All the travelling up and down. And I want Adam to spend as much time with Mum as he can.' His voice wavered. 'She's the only grandparent he has.'

I'd already suggested that she come to live with us but she needed specialist nursing care. So I agreed to the move – what else could I do? Especially as Adam was all for it. But I didn't want to completely let go of the house.

'We'd sell this place overnight, Lydia. You know that,' Zack had said wearily.

'But buying and selling can take months! It's all the stuff that goes with it. Lawyers and surveys and toing and froing with one thing and another.'

'Okay,' he acknowledged. 'Let's rent ours out and find something down there.'

That was our agreement.

Mandy and Fergal finished their tour of the bedrooms and I took them back to the front door.

'We love your home,' she said to me, her eyes wide with sincerity. 'We'll speak to the agent straight away.' She joined her hands as if praying. 'Please consider us. We promise to look after it.'

'I will. Thank you.' I closed the door behind them and ran downstairs to the kitchen. I took a bottle of vodka from the freezer and a shot glass from the cupboard. I poured three shots one after the other, swallowing the liquid with a shudder, before collapsing onto the floor next to the binbag, my knees pulled up to my chest.

How could I have let this happen? I thought I'd been so clever. I thought I could erase my past with omissions, deflections and the odd well-timed lie. But here I was about to go back to the worst place in the world and there was nothing, short of leaving my husband and son, that I could do about it.

You could be honest, a small voice whispered.

Imagine that? I poured another shot of vodka and knocked it back. By now the alcohol was swirling in my blood and I felt relaxation spreading through the muscles in my arms and legs. The voices in my head were quieter; the pain in my heart subdued.

I drifted off with my thoughts, remembering how Zack and I met, one Thursday evening in a too-trendy bar in Camden, the place heaving with rowdy twenty-somethings. While his date was on her mobile and mine had gone to the loo to hook up with his dealer, we got chatting about how out of place we felt – we were both in our early thirties and neither of us were drinking – and then I asked, 'Where are you from?'

'A village south of Gatwick. You won't have heard of it.'

'Try me,' I said, never for one moment expecting him to say ...

'Ashdown Village.'

I froze. My breath stopped. Ice spread through my skull. Zack didn't notice my reaction because he was distracted by a crowd at the end of the bar who were playing drinking games. When he looked back at me, I was able to draw breath and paste a smile on my face. 'Gone are the days when I could drink like that.' My breath stopped again but this time it was for a good reason. He held my eyes and an understanding passed between us – *I've found you. You're mine.* 'Of all the bars in all the world,' he said. We both grinned and then laughed. I felt a flood of relief, from terror to safety in the blink of an eye. 'Do you fancy going somewhere quieter?'

We abandoned our dates and left together. When a few weeks later he 'introduced' me to his home village I kept my smile on full beam and my fear locked down. And when we became a couple, I always found reasons to invite his parents to our house. They loved visiting London so were more than happy to make the journey, watch a show, stay overnight and visit the less tourist-heavy streets.

Years had passed and it was far too late to be honest, not without causing Zack to question everything I had ever said. I was going to have to tough it out as best I could.

My mobile rang and I looked at the screen – Zack. 'Hi, love.'

'Mum, it's me. Guess what?'

'What?' I smiled at the excitement in Adam's voice.

'The school's amazing! They play games every afternoon. There are *four* pitches and my form teacher said I'm good enough to get into the football team in the village.'

'That's great news, Adam!' I was two people: the mum who was pleased that her son was happy and the woman who was sacred witless of returning to a place she'd sworn she would never live in again.

'And because it's only the second week of term, the teacher says I can easily catch up with the work.'

'Okay.' I didn't want to burst his bubble and say that we weren't thinking of moving there until November at the earliest.

'And I met Jenny who's been helping Gran at the hospice. She invited us back to her house and it was really brilliant. She has loads of Lego and a big garden where the deer come in.' Zack had told me about Jenny. She was a volunteer at the hospice and had taken Paula and Zack under her wing. And now, by the sounds of it, Adam too. 'Dad wants to talk to you.'

'Okay, love. I'll see you tomorrow.'

'Good news on the rental!' Zack said without preamble. 'It'll be ready in a week. Two months earlier than we thought.'

Fuck.

'Adam's really happy about it, and so is Mum.' He left a pause for me to fill. 'Are you there?' he asked.

'Yes, I heard you.'

We'd spent one long Saturday viewing houses and I'd found fault with all of them. Finally, I had to give way when we looked around one that both Zack and Adam were enthusiastic about: it had generous family rooms, was in a prime location and with an established garden big enough for a mini football pitch. I couldn't argue with any of it but still I'd tried. 'It's very modern.' I pointed to the spread of glass and huge cement blocks. 'I'm not sure I like it.'

'Easy to heat and to clean. Everything works. It'll make a change from a Victorian town house.'

'I like our house.'

'You can like both, Debbie Downer!' Zack had said, exasperated. 'It's not as if we're buying it.'

I'd given in when the owner said they wouldn't be moving out until the beginning of November but now here we were with a date. *Next week*. I poured another vodka shot.

'How were the couple who came to view our place?' Zack asked.

'Nice.'

'Do they want to rent it?'

'I think so.' And then I remembered. 'They also seemed to think they'd be able to buy it at some point soon.'

'Well, it's likely we'll find somewhere permanent down here, isn't it?'

'No. I'm not … I'm not.' I tried to catch hold of a reason but the booze was clouding my mind. 'I like our house! I've never wanted to live in the country!'

'The pollution, the rush, the expense, the traffic noise – London has so much to offer,' he said dryly.

'We live in a quiet street. We have lovely friends.'

'Why can't you see this as an opportunity, Lydia?' He lowered his voice. 'For fuck's sake! Do you think I want any of this? Do you think I want my mum to be dying?'

'Of course not, I—'

'Stop making this such a battle.'

'I'm trying,' I said quietly. 'I really am.'

We said our goodbyes and my hand went up to my neck but there was no clothing there to loosen. The tight feeling was lodged inside my throat, a lump that wouldn't dissolve no matter how much liquid I used to wash it away.

I was on a runaway train with no way for me to get off.

Tess

The numbers. They just never seemed to add up any more. Or to be more accurate, the debit column was always hundreds, sometimes thousands of pounds greater than the credit column.

It was five years since she'd started her company – Maids of Honour – nothing to do with weddings, which she knew caused some confusion, but she was really stuck on the name and people soon got it. The honour referred to the cleaning products they used – everything was bio-degradable and planet-friendly. She cleaned houses for a living. It wasn't glamorous work but, until recently, it had helped pay her share of the household bills. Now, with only one salary and her dad's pension, making ends meet was nigh on impossible.

She felt the baby kick and her hand automatically strayed down to her pregnant belly. She would have to take out another loan to tide them over until she could grow the business. It wasn't fair to ask her dad for more money. He would dig into his savings if he knew she was desperate, but he was helping her out more than enough as it was. Why in God's name hadn't she and Steve got life insurance? Because they had thought they were invincible, that's why. They had never imagined that either of them would die. They were only in their forties! It was inconceivable.

Until it wasn't.

Steve had died seven months ago, but Tess felt like she'd been grieving for years. And at the same time, it was as if it had only happened yesterday. Every day was a fearful, endless grind: dragging herself out of bed, getting dressed, going through the motions of home and work, trying to find meaning in day-to-day activities. Trying, and failing, because every action and every thought led back to Steve.

She was thirty-eight weeks pregnant, and while she felt blessed to be carrying his baby, she was dreading giving birth. Steve got her through Bobby's delivery, cheering her on when she felt as if it was all too much … *Could I have more gas and air? Could someone please, please just knock me out and pull out my son because I'm not strong enough to do this? …* Steve had coaxed her on, breathing along with her until Bobby was born and they became a family. But this baby, their daughter, would be one of those children who'd never know her dad. She'd be familiar with him through photographs, video clips and memories that were shared with her, but she would never truly know him. She wouldn't experience the warmth of his smile, his hand holding hers as she walked into school, the joy of being thrown up into the air by a dad who would always catch her.

Tess blinked back tears and refreshed the spreadsheet, but it made no difference. Takings were down, not just because they'd lost some clients but because two of her six-strong cleaning team had left and she hadn't had the energy to interview for replacements. Vanya had kept things ticking over, and Tess was grateful for that, but a business didn't run itself.

'I need a strategy,' she said out loud. For the umpteenth time she wished that Steve was here, beside her, her life partner for ever and a day. Before he passed away, in one of their lighter moments, they joked about her getting a T-shirt that said, 'What would Steve do?' As far as parenting went, Steve was far more confident than she was. He seemed to know exactly how to pitch it. The balance between keeping Bobby close and tossing him in at the deep end was something he instinctively got right. 'I know what I'll do,' he'd said to her one day after a chemo session. 'I'll write you letters.'

She asked him not to, because she felt that the very act of writing the letters was an invitation to death, an admission that he was giving up. But he wrote them anyway and left them in a shoebox for her. There were over twenty of them. Some of them dated for future birthdays, others had titles such as *Being a parent* or *When you're unsure what to do next*.

There wasn't a letter titled *Strategy for Maids of Honour*, but she didn't really need one. She could hear Steve's voice saying, 'Word of mouth will get you so far, Tess, but every now and then you'll need to put an ad in one of the local papers.'

'Sound advice,' she muttered. She would advertise in the local magazine, the free one that was delivered to all the houses in the village. She needed to make the advert eye-catching, punchy. She couldn't afford to invest in a whole-page spread, so a standout font and bright colours were vital. She began to design the copy on her laptop, losing herself in the task until she heard the front door open and close, and her dad came into the kitchen.

'What are you doing still up?' He bent to kiss her cheek. 'You should be resting.'

She glanced at the clock on the wall. It was gone eleven. 'I've been carried away doing this.' She turned the laptop screen towards him. 'I need to drum up some more business. A quarter-page ad in the Ashdown Village magazine could work. What do you think?'

Her dad's lips moved silently as he read the copy. 'I think that's brilliant, Tess! Most people can't resist a bargain. Twenty per cent off sounds like a winner to me.'

'Thanks, Dad.' She closed the lid of her laptop. 'How was your evening?'

'The usual. Snooker and a pint. Old blokes shooting the breeze.'

'I thought you were going on a date?'

'So did I.' He looked bashful. 'But she didn't show.'

Her dad hadn't had a permanent partner since he and her mum had separated, way back when she was ten. When Steve was alive, they had encouraged him to find someone new. Now, though, Tess knew she was being selfish, but it would be the worst sort of timing if he suddenly fell in love. 'Dad …' She stood up and gave him a hug. 'Whoever she is, she's a fool. You're a gift for any woman.' She drew back and smiled at him. 'Mind you, I don't know what I'd do without you.'

'You and Bobby and that baby in there are my priority for now.' He looked down at her pregnant belly. 'Catch some sleep while you can. If this baby is anything like Bobby was, you'll be waving goodbye to an undisturbed night for at least three years.'

'Oh, God! Don't remind me.' Tess rolled her eyes. Bobby didn't sleep all night until he was almost four. She and Steve used to spend hours pacing the floor or trying to tire him out with games, searching for reasons for his wakefulness. Was it them? Were they really hopeless parents? The health visitor had assured them that wasn't the case. Some babies were just like that. Tess was praying she'd have better luck second time around. All the more important when she was an older mother with no partner. At times she felt all of her forty-six years, and some.

She said goodnight to her dad and climbed the stairs. Before she went into her own room, she checked on Bobby. His bedroom was compact, his bed pushed up against the wall so that his Lego models could have free rein on the floor. She stepped over the pirate ship and a line of warriors on motorbikes and found him curled up in his bed, the duvet completely covering his head. She pulled the duvet back a little and stroked his hair then kissed his warm cheek. His eyelids half opened and his lips formed a smile before he was sound asleep again.

Her own room was usually tidier than Bobby's except she was sorting through her belongings in preparation for the new baby who would sleep in a cot next to her. The floorspace was covered with boxes and bags of old clothes that she'd hauled out of cupboards, stuff that she'd amassed over the years. Some of it could go up into the loft but she was determined that at least half of it should go straight to the recycling bin or to a charity shop. It was a work in progress.

She kept the shoebox containing Steve's letters close to her bedside table, and counted six more boxes, none of them containing shoes. She picked up the nearest one to her and looked at the label. The edges were curled and peeling, the writing illegible. She opened it up and found all sorts of mementos that she'd kept from her childhood: a concert ticket stub, an essay she'd got 95 per cent for, a postcard from when she'd gone to Wales with Lydia's parents.

Lydia. Tess smiled at the memory of their friendship. She was her one true friend back when they were in their teens. Tess would never forget the first time she saw her and suddenly, the whole world shifted on its axis. She couldn't believe it when Lydia had wanted to be her friend. The sun had finally risen on her life! She was someone! Lydia Green had singled her out!

Not for the first time she wondered where Lydia was now and how she'd spent her life these last thirty years.

1991

They first met when they were both thirteen. Lydia arrived in Tess's class on a damp, winter's day when the sun was low and the air chilled. It was Tess's third year of attending the girls' grammar school, a red sandstone building with four fairy-tale towers, one at each corner. First day back after the Christmas holidays, and Miss Humble, the headmistress, was standing at the door to welcome them. Her nose was sharp, her eyes narrow and cold. Her mouth was a thin, straight line made for mockery. Tess half-smiled a good morning and scurried past her to her form room while Miss Humble's eyes narrowed in on a girl who was wearing make-up.

Her classmates embraced the cliché of female stereotypes. At one end there was Elizabeth, a kind, gentle, straight-A student with blonde hair, blue eyes and one of those faces that seemed always to be smiling. She walked with a bounce in her step, as if the ground was softer on her than it was on the rest of them. Tess wanted to hate her but she never could. It would have been like hating the sun. 'Hi, Tess. How was your Christmas?' Elizabeth asked her.

'Great thanks.' She dumped her bag on the desk and tried to smile like she meant it. 'Lots of presents and family fun.' She circled the flat of her hand above her belly and widened her eyes. 'And way too much food!'

Elizabeth laughed. 'It doesn't show on you. You're lucky that way.'

'How's Tess lucky?' Karen asked. She was sitting on top of another desk, legs crossed, one foot revolving at the ankle, and she was thrusting out her boobs like there were boys in the room. She was at the other end of the girl spectrum – a regular little witch. She was where the spite took shape and the oil boiled.

'We were talking about Christmas,' Elizabeth told her, her tone upbeat. 'How was yours, Karen?'

Karen didn't bother to reply. She had little time for Elizabeth. Perfection was smooth. There were no threads to pull nor buttons to press. Karen stared Tess up and down then leaned towards the girl beside her, whispering something that made her snigger. Tess felt her cheeks flame and she turned away, rummaging purposefully in her bag as if she could be rescued by what was in there.

Their form teacher was called Miss Richards and she was one of the teachers who believed in them, no matter how uncooperative or obnoxious they were. When she'd given them a few minutes to catch up, she clapped her hands and they settled into their places. 'Lovely to see you all, girls.' She smiled round at them. 'Tomorrow morning, we'll share our New Year's Resolutions but for now you need to choose your enrichment class.' She was handing out slips of paper as she spoke. 'You'll need permission from your parents for sailing as there is an added charge for that. All the other options are free.'

On Friday afternoon they were timetabled for 'enrichment', which wasn't so much enriching as confusing or anxiety-inducing or just plain boring depending on the subject and the teacher. There were ten activities on the list. Tess searched for the lesser of the evils. Her mum's boyfriend had recently moved into their house with his daughter Saskia who was in the parallel form. Tess knew she'd choose drama so that was one for her to avoid. Chess was a no-no because the teacher was a young man with a nervous tick and that made her feel sorry for him. French conversation was dire – she'd tried that last term. Karen and her witches always chose it because the teacher was depressed and the class ran rings round her. Hockey might have been worthwhile but the teacher was male, young and fit, and he sent her pulse sky high. She became a giggly, sycophantic mess. She ticked the box for school newspaper. The sixth formers hogged the writing and editing but she knew they'd send her to the library to fact-check for them and that suited her fine.

When they'd handed back their completed slips of paper, Miss Richards said, 'Oh, one other thing before you head off. We have a new girl joining the class today. She'll be arriving first lesson.'

That set off an expectant buzz, the girls' eyes darting and rolling. Where was she from? What was she like? How would she fit in?

The bell rang and they made their way to the language department. The corridors were long and cold, the windows had wooden frames that were warped in places so that the moisture leaked inside and formed thin layers of ice on the panes. The radiators didn't work properly. They made a show of creaking and wailing but never grew warm. Keeping their coats on, the girls clustered together trying on each other's hats and scarves. Some scraped their chairs across the floor to the windows where their breath condensed on the glass and they drew love hearts, twinning their initials with boys from the boys' grammar school.

Mr Salisbury was five minutes late. When he came striding into the room his hair was dishevelled and his expression pained. They knew from the grapevine that he was going through a divorce – he'd caught his wife having sex with the hockey teacher, yes, really – and another reason Tess could never choose hockey for enrichment. She enjoyed languages, and Latin, although technically dead as a dodo, interested her. She liked making connections between the words of old and their current vocabulary. She could lose herself for hours reading random pages in the dictionary – and that was a secret because she'd have had the piss ripped out of her if anyone knew, even more so by her family than the likes of Karen.

The teacher rapped a wooden pointer on his desk. '*Ecce Romani*.' They rummaged in their bags and pulled out textbooks. Every copy was old and tatty. If there were more modern texts then they hadn't reached their school yet. He named the page and then his glance fell to the right. 'Tess Carter. Conjugate the verb. Perfect subjunctive, please.'

She focussed on the page. '*Amaver … im, amaver … is, amaver—*'

The door opened. Twenty-five pairs of eyes swivelled towards it. The winter sun was behind the new girl as she walked in. Her shoes were lace-up with two and a half inch heels and scuffed at the toes. Black tights raced up long legs, skirt smooth from the waist to the top of her thighs where it lapped into pleats that shimmied as she walked. Her grey shirt was pulled tight over breasts that belonged to a woman. Her hair was blonde, short and spiky with Gothic black running through it. Wide green eyes – summer grass, Christmas trees, the silvery sheen of snakeskin – and a smile to knock the lid from a coffin.

Tess stared at her. Everyone stared at her, while she glanced around, drawing conclusions with a slight tilt of her head, a minute raising of her eyebrows.

The teacher banged his book on the desk and glared. 'You must be Lydia Green?'

A surname to match her eyes, Tess thought.

'And you must be Mr Salisbury.' She flicked him a smile up through her lashes, like Princess Diana with attitude.

'Well sit down then, Lydia Green.'

Lydia wafted in Tess's direction and slid into the seat beside her. Tess held her breath.

'Did you study Latin in your last school?' the teacher called out.

'Of course.' She smiled back.

Tess inhaled, discovered that Lydia smelled of vanilla and sugar, peppermint and an underlying whiff of tobacco. Lydia turned towards her. 'Is it always this cold?' she asked.

'They'll have the heating working by the spring,' Tess replied, her voice a whisper.

Lydia rested her chin on her hand, and when Tess met her eyes, she felt a great bobsleigh ride. Greased runners. Hot friction on cold ice that drove into the pit of her stomach.

'I think we're going to be friends,' Lydia said.

Lydia

So far, so … manageable. We'd been living in Ashdown Village for one whole week. I stayed close to home. So close to home that I hadn't gone beyond the garden. I was getting through each day one minute at a time, jumping out of my skin if the doorbell rang and peering through the window from just behind the curtain if I heard a noise outside.

Adam had started at his new school and was loving it. Zack drove him there, and when he returned home he'd make us both a coffee and tell me about the parents he'd met. 'We have a dinner invite,' he told me on the Friday.

'Already? You must be making an impression.'

'They're friendly in the country.'

I raised my eyebrows at this. I was unpacking one of the boxes, transferring hats and scarves, gloves and rain jackets to the hall cupboard. Unpacking was taking me forever but I wouldn't let Zack help me because it was giving me a reason to stay at home.

'The cleaner's coming at ten thirty to give us a quote,' he said, checking the diary on his phone. 'She's called Vanya. She works for a company called Maids of Honour. Nothing to do with weddings. Their cleaning products are environmentally friendly.'

'Great.' I smiled. Or tried to.

A few seconds of silence swelled the air. 'Mum was really hoping to see you today,' Zack said, his tone questioning.

I nodded. 'And I want to see her.'

'She really loves you, Lydia.'

'And I love her too. I just need to be sure that I'm over the stomach bug.' I stared down into the box, wincing at the lie. I didn't have a stomach bug. My stomach was upset because I was anxious. It churned and grumbled constantly as if eating itself.

'Lydia?' His voice was loud and I looked up with a start. He took a pile of scarves from me and put them on the shelf. 'We won't need any of this for at least a month. Please just leave the unpacking for a bit.' Then he held me in his arms, tight but not too tight. It made me want to cry.

'Sorry.' I pulled away before my heart burst and all the anguish spilled out. 'I'm just not sleeping very well.'

'It's like you're permanently in a daze.'

'They do say moving house is one of life's main stressors.' I took a steadying breath. 'You know what? I will go and see your mum today.' I nodded to convince myself. 'If you don't mind staying in for the cleaner?'

He hugged me again. 'I can do that.'

The drive to the hospice was a straight road with a couple of right turns but I went the long way round so that I didn't have to pass through the streets that were familiar to my teenage self. Still, I kept looking over my shoulder, checking for ghosts that I was sure were lurking at the corners of my vision. Just because I didn't see any, that didn't mean they weren't there.

The hospice was bright and welcoming, not hospice-like at all, or not what I had imagined anyway. A lavender scent hung in the air and I could hear laughter at the end of the corridor. I'd been to visit Paula once before when we came down to look at houses so I knew the way to her room. It was large and light with three easy chairs and a door to an en suite. The view through the window showed off the forest in all its glory, every shade of green stretching to the distant horizon. Paula was propped semi-upright in a large hospital bed, medical equipment and Adam's drawings adorning the wall behind her. Her eyes were closed and that gave me the chance to absorb the changes in her. She had lost so much weight since I had last seen her, her shape slight beneath the thin cotton sheet. Her hair was wispy and sparse, a pale imitation of the black curls that had set her apart. Her skin had a translucent quality that reminded me of insects' wings. Adam had gone through a phase of briefly trapping wasps and flies in a magnifying glass jar. We had examined the membranous, glittering wings with fascination before releasing the insects to fly again. It struck me that dying took us back to the natural world. As adults we outsourced, avoided, did everything we could to deny our own mortality. We kept ourselves firmly at the top of the food chain as if we were exempt from death.

She opened her eyes and they lit up at once. 'Lydia!' She reached out her hands to clasp hold of mine. 'How long have you been standing there?'

'Not long.' I bent to kiss her cheek.

'I'm constantly nodding off. I don't know what's wrong with me.' She frowned and pretended to think. 'Oh no, wait a minute, I do!' She laughed. Her sense of humour had always been on the darker side. 'I spent years as an insomniac and now I do nothing but sleep.'

I pulled one of the chairs close to the bed and sat down. 'I'm sorry I haven't been to see you for a few weeks. The move and every—' I shook my head. Paula was someone who saw through bullshit and I was sure a cancer diagnosis hadn't changed that. 'I have no excuse, Paula. I've just been—' I stopped again, lost for words. I couldn't tell her a lie, I couldn't tell her the truth and there were no words that balanced on the tightrope in between.

'Lydia, you have nothing to apologise for.' Her hands sought mine again. 'I know how places like this can be a trigger.' Her voice dropped. 'Losing your dad at sixteen could not have been easy.' I was staring down at our combined hands, too afraid to meet her eyes. Little did Paula know that my dad had died in this very village and was buried in the churchyard. 'And I know how much you loved living in London. Moving here must be tough on you. I tried to get Zack to drop the idea but you know what he's like when he gets a bee in his bonnet.'

I looked up then. 'We all wanted to be closer to you, Paula. Really.'

'Thank you, my dear.' A tear trickled down her cheek. 'Runny eye.' She wiped it with the back of her hand. 'Or is it a rheumy eye now that I'm an old lady?'

'Stop it!' I laughed. 'You'll never be old. You're far too sharp.'

'If only.' She gave me a wistful smile. 'Oh, before I forget, I want to thank you for all your messages. I *so* look forward to them. They're a window on the world. And Adam! What a treasure he is.'

'He's had his best week ever.' I told her about how much he was enjoying his new school, and one subject led to another until almost two hours had gone by and I could see that Paula was beginning to flag. 'I'm going to leave you in peace now,' I told her.

'It's been such a treat seeing you.' She looked at the clock on her bedside table. 'I have time for a little nap before they bring me lunch. It's like the Ritz! We had smoked salmon yesterday.'

'Zack's been telling me about Jenny and how kind she is,' I said, lifting the chair back to its spot by the window. 'And Adam tells me she makes good shortbread.'

'Yes, she is kind. She's a widow like me.' She rested her head back on the pillows. 'She comes in the afternoons.' Her eyes closed.

'I'll be back very soon.' I kissed her cheek and whispered, 'Thank you for being so lovely.'

I walked to my car, feeling both happy and sad. I was going to miss Paula and I was only just realising how much. As I turned the key in the ignition, I wondered whether I should challenge myself. I could, couldn't I? I could drive home the easiest route, pass by her house – if it was still *her* house – see whether she was living there. Would she still be there after thirty years? Would I be tempting fate by even looking?

He who hesitates is lost, as my dad used to say, and thinking of my dad I knew where I needed to go first, before anywhere else. I should never have put it off this long. I drove the couple of miles into Ashdown Village and parked in a side street. It was almost lunchtime and people were drifting towards the cafes and the wine bar. Back in the day, the wine bar had been a bank but now, Paula had told me, there were no banks and a dozen places to buy coffee, from the hairdresser's to the bookshop.

A few weeks after I met Zack, I spoke to him about my dad passing away and how I'd moved in with my aunt. My mum and I had never been close, and I'd lost touch with her. We talked of my dad often because I wanted more than anything to keep him alive in my heart. I walked a thin line in terms of revealing some information but not too much, just enough to keep Zack interested without him asking too many questions. I had never once mentioned where my dad was buried and he had never asked.

I opened the wrought-iron gate and walked into the graveyard next to the church. It was a hotchpotch of resting places, the contours of the graves aligning with the rise and fall of the land. I followed the brick pathway past the weather-beaten headstones, some of them tilting sideways and overgrown with moss, the dedications no longer legible.

There had been an adding of graves through the decades, extra portions of land tacked on, but my dad was buried halfway between the church and the perimeter. I remembered my mother choosing the plot. I stopped in front of his gravestone and read the inscription:

Adam Green
12.12.1950 – 30.07.1994
Beloved husband to Genevieve and father to Lydia
May he rest in peace

My hands began to shake. I gripped my fists tight by my side and concentrated on breathing. It was thirty years since my dad had died and not a day had gone by when I hadn't thought of him. Coming back to the village had one silver lining. It meant that I would be able to visit his resting place. To talk to him. To explain things to him. To ask for forgiveness – all of this too late, of course. My head knew this, but my heart hoped he would hear me.

Tess

'Are you all right?' Vanya asked, nudging her shoulder. They were standing at the edge of the pitch watching their children play in a football match. 'You look sad.'

'I'm sorry.' Tess stifled a yawn. 'I was up late last night writing an advert for the local magazine, so now I'm tired, and when I'm tired it's hard for me to stop thinking about Steve.'

'Oh, Tess.' Vanya's expression was kind. 'I can work an extra few hours this week if that helps.'

'Thanks, Vanya.' She sighed. 'I wish I could just … somehow …' she struggled to find the right words '… fast forward through this grief.'

'It's only been seven months.' Vanya gave her a sideways hug, her front arm resting above Tess's baby bump. 'Don't be so hard on yourself.' She held her for several beats before she pulled back and said, 'Shall I get us a drink?'

'Please.'

'Coffee?'

She pointed to the bump. 'Coffee gives me terrible reflux. A mint tea if they have one.'

Vanya went into the clubhouse, and Tess shielded her eyes with her hand as she searched for Bobby on the football field. He was across the other side, tackling a player in the opposing team. He was concentrating hard, his attention fixed on the ball as he gained possession and ran the length of the pitch. His shot at goal ricocheted off the bar and his shoulders briefly slumped before he ran back into position. 'Nice try, Bobby!' the coach shouted, and Tess clapped along with the other parents before her hand strayed back to her bump, cupping it protectively.

Life wasn't all bad. Her days were punctuated with pockets of joy: Bobby's smile so like his dad's, his optimism a constant, even although he was grieving too. 'The thing is, Mum,' he'd told her, 'I had my dad for more than nine years, so I'll always remember him and that's more than lots of children get.' He'd stared up at her with bright, earnest eyes. 'Some children never have a dad. Not even for a minute.'

If a nine-year-old could count his blessings then why couldn't she?

Tess glanced behind her and saw Vanya close to the clubhouse, holding two take-out cups and chatting to a group of mums. They lived in a village where everyone knew everyone; incomers were quickly spotted and welcomed. She'd clocked the unfamiliar car in the car park when they arrived – it was hard to miss; a gunmetal grey four-by-four, huge and squat like an oversized beetle. There was a new boy in the team, Bobby'd told her. He'd met him at the practice session midweek. 'He's called Adam and he's really nice, Mum. He used to live in London but they moved here to be close to his grandma.'

The woman with her back to her must be his mum. She was wearing a knee-length, white cotton dress and a denim jacket, with strappy sandals tied at the ankles. She stood with one hip slightly forward, her face turned away from Tess, her hands moving through the air in a graceful arc as she spoke. Tess felt the nudge of something familiar but swivelled back to the pitch when she heard Maisie call out, 'Adam! Over here!'

Vanya's daughter Maisie, the team's captain, was several metres away, her arms waving above her head so that Adam could locate her. Tess moved back a step as he thundered down the wing and came to an abrupt stop in front of her, lifting the ball up into the air so that it landed just a short distance from Maisie's right foot.

'Well done!' Tess called out to him, and he glanced up at her, his green eyes wide and clear. At once, the nudge of something familiar became a jolt of recognition so strong that Tess gasped.

Lydia! Lydia Green. Adam was the image of her! If she'd been asked to imagine what Lydia's child would look like, this was exactly the face she would have visualised. Could he be Lydia's son? Because that would change everything, wouldn't it?

She felt a shiver of sweet vertigo that made her eyes swim. If Lydia was back in the village the future would be brighter, less scary, more hopeful. Vanya was her best friend. She had helped her through the last six months and was her birthing partner, on speed dial for when she went into labour – but *Lydia*? Lydia was her first true friend. Lydia knew her inside out and back to front. Lydia was the closest she'd ever felt to any other human being apart from Steve and Bobby.

Her feet moved of their own volition. Her eyes were glued to the back of the woman in the white dress as she walked towards her.

'We fundraise twice a year,' Vanya was telling her. 'Have you been added to the group chat?'

'I have. And I was thinking—'

'Lydia?' Tess interrupted, her voice high with surprise and disbelief.

There was a split second of hesitation before Lydia turned towards her and their eyes met. Like Tess, she was now a woman in her mid-forties. Her hair, once short and spiky, was tied up in a casual knot that looked chic. Her eyes were still a startling green but now there were crow's feet at the edges and the hint of dark shadows beneath. Age had been kind to her. She was still the beautiful, vibrant Lydia that Tess remembered, and thirty years fell away as if they had never been, as if the last time she saw her and now – here – were two points on a compass that lay only a fingertip's length apart. There was no time, no distance between them. She had stepped through a portal and found her best friend waiting on the other side.

Tess smiled and then laughed, as if someone had just given her the most longed for present. 'It is you! Oh my God! Lydia!' She moved forward to hug her but Lydia stepped to one side so that Tess's baby weight, her centre of gravity, propelled her on. Her arms windmilled and she knocked into Vanya sending one of the cups flying backwards over her shoulder. Another mum caught her before she fell, and Vanya immediately held her elbow with her free hand while she steadied herself.

'Oh, my gosh! Are you okay?' Lydia smiled at her. Tess didn't smile back because she could tell that Lydia's smile wasn't genuine. It was one for the audience, a fake, face-saving smile. 'I'm so sorry. I'm hopeless with names and faces. I have such an awful memory!'

A warning bell sounded close to Tess's heart. *How could Lydia not recognise her?* 'But we were best friends,' she said quietly, not getting it, not getting it at all.

'Maybe, I …' Lydia faltered, blinking rapidly, as if she was desperately trying to grasp hold of an elusive memory.

Tess frowned, waiting for her to say that she was joking, that she was winding her up. At any moment she would grab her and hug her, and they'd talk for hours, catch up on all the years they'd missed. They'd be inseparable. They'd meet every day to share their lives. Their boys would become best friends. Adam would come to them for sleepovers and Bobby would be happy going to theirs.

Seconds ticked by. 'Come on Lydia,' Tess said softly. 'Is this for real?'

Lydia's lower lip trembled. She stared right and left as if seeking help before saying, 'I'm so sorry. Perhaps we could catch up some time and you could remind me how we know each other?' Her eyebrows were raised in a generous arch. 'Yeah?'

There was silence all around them. None of the mums had lived in the village back then apart from Vanya, but she had gone to a different school. Tess caught Vanya's eye, saw confusion and pity in her expression. Tess had an abrupt realisation of how this must look. Messy-haired, in-debt-up-to-her-eyeballs, hippo-sized Tess was insisting on a past friendship with an elegant, clearly well-heeled, kind-faced woman who was a magnet for everyone. She would have no problem making friends. She would have diaries full of dates with friends. She would have forgotten more friends than she could ever remember.

'Let's go and get you a tea,' Vanya said, putting her arm through hers.

Tess turned obediently, too numb to resist. She walked alongside Vanya, meek as a lamb, and when she glanced back, Lydia was in the centre of the group, the shining star surrounded by satellite planets basking in her light.

1991

The first week of school went by in a flash. Lydia could have chosen anyone for a friend, from Elizabeth to Karen and all the girls in between, but she'd chosen Tess who woke up every day with a smile on her face. For the first time in her life, she had a best friend! And she was as happy as she'd ever been. Happy beyond rhyme. Happy beyond reason! She was just so incredibly happy.

On the Friday lunchtime they'd eaten bloated, over-cooked pasta in the dining hall and were standing in the shadow of one of the towers moaning about pains in their stomachs. The wind was brisk and wickedly cold so they huddled close together.

'Do you want one of my gloves?' Tess handed Lydia a fingerless, stripy glove. Her dad had appeared out of nowhere and given them to her for Christmas. He'd disappeared just as quickly, and if it hadn't been for the gloves, she would have doubted that he'd been there at all.

Lydia was watching Karen holding forth to her cronies, her eyes narrowing as she pulled on the glove. 'I've met her type before,' she said to Tess, indicating Karen with a slight raising of her chin. 'She's like a starving hyena.' The cold had brought a ruddy glow to her cheeks and her eyes were greener than ever. She leaned into Tess's neck and whispered, 'Let's take her on.'

Tess giggled. She was always giggling now. Lydia brought out the child in her. 'How do you mean?'

'See that girl there?' She pointed to one of the girls in the year below. 'Karen's constantly having a go at her.'

'Yeah, but she's not bothering us.' Tess's ungloved hand was elbow deep in her bag, rummaging past the books, stray pencils and discarded wrappers until she felt the top of a small bottle. 'So that's the main thing.'

'Don't you think we should help her?' Lydia asked.

'She looks okay at the moment,' Tess replied, not even looking. She opened the bottle of clear nail polish and started to paint some at the top of the ladder in her tights.

'I heard a girl left last year because Karen bullied her,' Lydia said.

'She did,' Tess affirmed. She pulled the tights away from her thigh to prevent the blob of nail polish welding the tights to her skin. 'But the girl didn't help herself. She was a natural victim.'

'So that makes it okay, then?' Lydia asked, her gloved hand lifting Tess's chin to force eye contact. 'Did anyone take her side?'

'No.' Tess could see Lydia's anger at the injustice, and her gaze dropped, her cheeks flushing with shame as she remembered how the whole class was questioned but nobody gave Karen up, not even Elizabeth. 'Nobody helped her.'

'Why not?' Lydia asked. She nudged Tess's shoulder with her gloved fist. 'Where were you when this was going on?'

'I thought it was better to stay out of it,' she said lamely, wondering whether this was the moment when Lydia stopped being her friend. Because she lacked courage.

She was happy being one of the masses, neither a mover nor a shaker. Tess would never raise her head above the parapet. She wasn't brave like Lydia.

'For evil to flourish all it takes is for one man to do nothing,' Lydia said, delivering the line with a significant find-your-backbone stare in Tess's direction. Then she walked off towards Karen, calling back over her shoulder, 'I hate bullies.'

Lydia

Why did I pretend not to remember Tess?

Because seeing her was a shock I hadn't bargained for. Never for one moment had I imagined that she would still be living here. She was the cleverest girl in our year. She had an aptitude for languages, and absorbed the principles of science and maths as if it was second nature to her. I thought she'd have gained a first-class degree from Oxford and be flying high in New York or Dubai.

I watched her walk towards the clubhouse with Vanya while the mums filled me in on her life.

'Poor Tess, she's had a really hard time lately.'

'Her husband Steve died seven months ago.'

'He had an aggressive cancer.'

'She's really struggled.'

'He died before they knew she was pregnant.'

'We've all tried to rally round but Vanya's done the most. They've been friends for years.'

'Strange that she thought she was such good friends with you, though,' one of the mums commented, her eye catching mine. 'Did you live around here?'

I ignored her question and said quickly, 'So about the club fundraising. I have a few ideas.' I went on to tell them about a fun day I'd part organised in London and within seconds the mums were brainstorming activities and venues. I tuned out, and stared beyond the playing field to where the land stretched towards the reservoir, sweeping downhill and then up again towards the long ridge of trees on the far horizon. It was a far cry from London, where the playing field was a squashed oblong, bordered on all sides by houses and flats. The nose to tail traffic was often tiresome but I loved the liveliness, the closeness to my neighbours, the diversity on every street. *Just breathe*, I told myself. *In for three, hold for four and out for five.*

We drifted towards the touchline where the children were gathering in a huddle for half-time, gulping water from their bottles as they kicked the ball between them. Adam was already making friends, and I watched him doing keepy-uppies with a couple of the other kids. I tried to work out which of the children belonged to Tess but I couldn't see any resemblance in either the boys or the girls. Tess had faded blue eyes and strawberry blonde hair. I remembered her being teased as a 'ginger' when we were at school. 'Gingers have no soul,' Karen, the class bully had said to Tess, her henchgirls chanting the taunt along with her. Karen was a class A bitch. I remembered having a go at her when she was being cruel to a girl in the year below. She'd crumbled more quickly than I thought she would. I imagined I could take anyone on, back then. Little did I know.

The game restarted and I kept my eyes on the pitch, cheering the team on when they played well, clapping as they high-fived each other when they scored a goal. Tess and Vanya were standing a few metres away. Tess was staring down at the ground while Vanya held her arm and talked to her, her expression caring and sympathetic. I'd met Vanya last week when she came to clean for us. I was full of apologies – I found it embarrassing to have a cleaner when I had the time and physical health to do it myself. I even said as much to Vanya and she had laughed. 'Don't be silly! I need the work. And your house barely looks dirty so it will be an easy couple of hours.'

One of the mums had said Tess's husband's name was Steve. Was it the same Steve? The one who lived next door to her when she was growing up? *She married him?* I'd thought he was just a crush, a teenage longing that wouldn't stand the test of time. I remembered how much she talked about him, how her eyes would be glued to him when we mixed with the boys from the grammar. And I also remembered how disappointed and afraid I'd been when she dropped me so suddenly to spend all her time with him. We were best friends. We shared everything, from the mundane every day stuff like what flavour of crisps to eat or film to watch, to our secret fears and impossible dreams. But when Steve asked her out, I was forgotten. Just when I needed her the most, she ghosted me.

I shivered at the memory, my fists tense. *Not now, not here.* I blinked and then forced a smile onto my face. That usually worked and it did this time too. When Zack came to watch the second half of the match, I made an excuse and went to sit in the car. I told him that I had emails to send, that I'd neglected my work in favour of unpacking boxes. In my twenties, I'd built a company from scratch – who knew there was so much money in yoga pants and accessories? Me, as it turned out. I'd sold the company just after Adam was born and, nowadays, I worked with young entrepreneurs, writing business plans, sharing advice and contacts.

I didn't have any emails to send but I did need to be alone. I needed time to think, to catch up with what had just happened. There was no use pretending that Tess wouldn't be a problem because I knew she would be. Seeing her here had unnerved me. She had a starring role in my nightmares, after all. And she expected to resume our friendship as if nothing had happened? I took a small flask from my bag, swallowed a mouthful of vodka and shuddered. *Was she crazy?*

I buried the flask deep in my bag again and watched Zack and Adam walk towards the car, both of them smiling and chatting. What was a thirty-year-old secret when my husband and son were live in front of me? They were my present day, my every day. My everything.

They were my family.

Tess

She chose one of the shoeboxes scattered across her bedroom floor and opened it, grabbing handfuls of photos of her and Lydia back when they were teenagers. 'I mean, look!' she said to Vanya, pointing to the two of them with their arms around each other on the beach at Camber Sands, outside Buckingham Palace, eating ice creams in the village square. 'How can she pretend she doesn't know me?'

'That's her, right enough,' Vanya said holding the photos up to the light. 'Why would she pretend? I don't get it.'

'Neither do I!' Tess was exasperated. She went to the top of the stairs and called down. 'Dad?'

'Yeah?'

'Would you come here a minute?'

Her dad appeared almost at once, a dishcloth over his shoulder and a wooden spoon in his hand. 'What's up?'

'Do you remember Lydia Green?'

He frowned. 'I do. Not very clearly though because when you were friends with her—'

'You weren't around much. I forgot. Sorry.'

'You know I regret it!' her dad reminded her.

Tess went back to Vanya who was sitting on her bed, the photos spread out either side of her. 'They're renting that big modern house between the osteopath and the road down to the reservoir,' Vanya said. 'They signed up for a weekly clean. I went there on Thursday. They seem like a nice family.'

Tess was on her hands and knees reaching under the bed. 'I wrote about us in my diaries. I used to stick photos in there too.' She hauled out another box and placed it on top of the duvet before struggling to her feet, her hand cupping her bump. 'She came here in 1991 and left in '94.'

Vanya took out an A5-sized book with 1993 written on the front in curly red script. She started flicking through the pages, stopping to read some of the entries. 'You wrote about Steve a lot,' she said. 'Always with red hearts and smiley faces.'

'I was *crazy* about him,' Tess said. 'I don't think anyone would have predicted us lasting but we did.' And he had felt the same. They had often spoken about how lucky they were to find each other so young. She'd imagined they would be together for sixty, seventy, even eighty years. Life had been cruel to them. There was no getting away from it.

'You're right. There are more photos of Lydia in the diary.' Vanya closed the book and hugged Tess's shoulders. 'Maybe she'll come to her senses. Give her time. See what happens.'

A week went by and Tess couldn't drop it. At first Vanya had made sympathetic noises but now Tess could tell that she was growing sick and tired of her going on about it. 'Maybe she's not pretending, Tess! Maybe she had a bang to the head or a brain tumour or something, and years of her life are missing.'

'I suppose so.' Tess hadn't thought of that. 'But then she could tell me that, couldn't she?'

'In front of everyone?' Vanya shrugged. 'Why should she?' They were sitting on a bench with a picnic between them while Bobby and Maisie played in the skatepark. 'And why is it so important to you, anyway?' She stood up to brush some crumbs off her jeans. 'It was thirty years ago!' Her expression was incredulous. 'And you're about to have a baby!'

Rose was born later that week, Vanya holding Tess's hand and championing her through the delivery. The love Tess felt as she held her baby girl in her arms banished all thoughts of Lydia. But without Steve, she was both elated and crushed, energetic and overwound, like a coiled spring about to snap and fly off into the air in a chaotic arc of love and misery.

She lived the first few days in a daze of feeding and changing and very little sleep. She'd been on antidepressants since Steve's death and was worried about breastfeeding. The health visitor reassured her that very little of the drug made it into the milk, but Tess couldn't establish a routine. She had breastfed Bobby so she knew it would take time, but Rose struggled to latch on and Tess's nipples cracked and the pain made her want to cry. Rose was barely a week old when Vanya asked gently, 'Shall I go to the shop and buy some bottles?'

Tess nodded. She felt like a failure. She took to her bed, but she didn't sleep. Her mind began to pop with ideas and images, like a pinball sparking off in different directions. She knew it wasn't normal to have so many thoughts dive-bombing around in her head, but she also knew it was happening for a reason. *Because Steve would never have left her.* They were meant to be together; everyone knew that. They'd been a couple since they were fifteen. It made complete sense that he would find a way to be with her again, if not as her husband, then as her child. The essence of him – his soul – had been reborn in the body of their daughter. It made perfect sense because the odds of her getting pregnant were miniscule. She was forty-six. Steve was having chemotherapy which meant that sperm production was diminished. And he was so exhausted from the treatment that they'd barely even made love in those last few months.

For one whole week she truly believed that Steve had been reincarnated in Rose's body.

There was precedence for this in the Eastern religions. She spent hours on the internet when she should have been resting, learning about karma and multiple lives. She absorbed the essence of what she learned and approached her daughter with awe. Her eyes stayed open for most of that week as she gazed at her newborn.

And then she crashed. She collapsed one morning after multiple sleepless nights. Bobby found her on the floor, her eyes open, mute and still. He went next door to raise the alarm and her neighbour called the ambulance. She was taken into hospital and given enough medication to set her right. Social services only allowed her home because her dad agreed to come and live with her permanently, and she had a back-up support system in Vanya and her neighbour's daughter, Sadie.

And as the days passed, while she knew she should be focussing on her baby, Lydia's pretence started to upset her again. There was so much that was out of her control – Steve was dead, she was worried about making ends meet, she'd given up on breastfeeding – but for some reason, Lydia's betrayal cut the deepest. She couldn't bring Steve back to life, and she couldn't undo the mess she'd made with the loans she'd signed up for, but Lydia? Surely Tess deserved an explanation.

When Rose reached her six-week milestone, Tess went out for the first time. Physically, she felt as if she was fully recovered from the birth but emotionally, she was permanently on the edge of tears. She had an appointment for Rose at the local health centre and stopped at the supermarket en route. Her dad had assured her that he would take care of all the shopping but she felt as if she needed to get back to a semblance of normality. She lifted Rose out of her car seat into a sling and walked into the shop. It felt strange to be mixing with people again; everything was brighter and louder than she could cope with. She had to shield her eyes and her ears from the sensory overload. She kept her head down and gathered up the items she needed into a basket: a litre of milk and a box of cereal for Bobby, fruit for her dad and formula for Rose. When she approached the checkout, she lifted her head and saw Lydia at the next pay point. Immediately, her heartbeat quickened. Within seconds Lydia glanced her way and Tess felt her lips lift in a smile, automatically, because it was Lydia.

Lydia blanked her. There wasn't even a hint of recognition, as if Tess was someone she'd never met, never even seen before. But it was worse than that, because Tess knew that if she was one of the other mums from the football club, Lydia would have come over and asked her how she was feeling, congratulated her on her baby, hugged her even.

It was as if she didn't exist.

Tess's hands shook as she paid for her shopping. She walked out into the car park, tears smarting in her eyes. As she opened the boot, she heard a voice shout, 'Tess!'

She looked up. It was Lydia's mum, Genevieve. Tess hadn't seen her since Steve's funeral. There had been a huge turnout and Genevieve had helped with the gathering in the clubhouse afterwards, preparing sandwiches and pouring drinks. Tess didn't know Genevieve was coming, wasn't sure how she even knew Steve, but her help had been welcome because over two hundred people had come to pay their last respects. Steve had been popular and the turn out reflected that.

'Oh, you've had your baby!' Genevieve walked towards Tess, her face lit up. 'Isn't she beautiful?'

Like mother not like daughter, Tess thought. 'She's called Rose. Would you like to hold her?'

'May I?' Genevieve's eyes shone as Tess passed Rose to her. 'Aren't you a little poppet?' she said softly. 'Babies are such a blessing, aren't they?' She gave a wistful smile. 'Adam and I would have loved to have had more children but it wasn't to be.'

'You must be pleased to have Lydia back in the village.'

'Well, yes.' Her expression was guarded. 'I'm hoping to get to know my grandson. Another Adam! Becoming a grandma, now *that's* something.' Her smile widened. 'And Bobby! What a wonderful boy he is, Tess. He's an absolute credit to you.'

'Thank you.' Tess had never noticed Genevieve at the football with Lydia but that must be where she'd seen Bobby. Apart from at the funeral where he'd spent the whole day glued to her side, wide-eyed and pale as a ghost. She would have done anything to have spared him the grief. 'I'm sorry I didn't have time to speak to you at Steve's funeral.' She couldn't, in fact, remember the last time she'd seen Genevieve before that. Ten years ago, maybe? 'You're looking really well.'

'Am I?' Genevieve let her fingers rest briefly on her hair, which had golden highlights and was blown dry into an elegant bob. 'I do my best.' She had a youthful freshness to her. Her skin and eyes shone with vitality. 'Seventy is the new fifty, apparently.'

'That would make me twenty-six.' Tess rolled her eyes. 'Somehow, I don't think I could get away with that.'

'Now don't you dare put yourself down,' Genevieve said, hugging Rose closer. 'I know you're a wonderful mother to this little one and to Bobby. The tiredness will pass.'

Tess put the shopping in the boot while Genevieve eased Rose into her car seat. 'Goodbye, beautiful Rose. I hope we see each other again soon.' She turned and enveloped Tess in a hug. 'I'm so pleased to have bumped into you.' Then she drew back and said gently, 'Are you doing okay?'

Tess almost laughed. Tears crowded in her eyes and she blinked furiously. What was there to say? *I almost lost my sanity, I need Steve to come back to life, your daughter's a bitch and I'm drowning in debt?* 'I'm getting there. My dad's a great help and so is my friend Vanya.' She took a breath. 'Lydia's pretending she doesn't know me. I'm not sure why.' Her cheeks coloured. 'She was in the store just now. Did you see her?'

'No.' Genevieve frowned and looked over her shoulder as if expecting Lydia to materialise.

'She didn't say hello to me,' Tess continued. 'It's like we were never even friends.'

'Tess.' Genevieve reached for her hand. 'Lydia is …' she bit her lip. '… complicated. She's not the girl she was. I'm so sorry if her behaviour hurts your feelings.'

She hugged Tess again and they both promised they would catch up properly soon. Tess drove towards the exit, noticing Lydia several metres away climbing into her car. Everything about her was annoying. Her fancy car, her waterfall hair, not a split end or frizzy tangle in sight. Her eyebrows were beautifully sculpted; she looked terrific in jeans.

Tess felt a vicious urge to get back at her, to pierce her charmed life with a reality check. On the drive to the health centre she racked her brains. And then a thought occurred to her: there was one thing she could do.

'You're not inviting Adam to Bobby's birthday party?' Vanya asked. They were drawing up a list of names. 'For real?'

'For real. He's not invited. Not while his mother has selective amnesia.'

Vanya raised her eyebrows. 'Tess! Come on. He's a good kid.'

'Well, we all suffer for the sins of our fathers, or in this case, mothers.'

'Tess!'

'What?' she snapped.

'This isn't like you.' Vanya put her hand on her knee. 'You're not mean.'

'I'm not the one who's being mean!' She pulled her knee away and threw out her arms, palms upward. 'Lydia started this, not me.'

When Bobby came in from school, she went through the list of names with him. 'And Adam,' he said. 'He should come, Mum.'

'We have twelve now, love.'

'Because thirteen's an unlucky number?' He lifted a finger into the air. 'We could have fourteen! I could invite—'

'No. That's the number we're limited to.'

'The clubhouse is really big, though.'

'I know. But children's parties are limited to twelve.'

This wasn't even true. Tess watched as Bobby bit his lip, no doubt remembering a party he went to at the clubhouse earlier in the year when there were more than twenty children present. 'But, Mum, I've already told Adam he can come.'

'Well, you'll just have to untell him,' Tess said breezily. 'I'm sure he'll be fine about it.'

Bobby stared at the names on the sheet of paper. 'I would rather Adam came than Sam.'

'You've known Sam longer, love. Let's just stick with the list.'

When the day of the party arrived, Bobby was swept up in the fun of it all. Tess stayed inside the clubhouse preparing the food while her dad and Vanya were outside organising the children into teams. The clubhouse was used by the village cricket, tennis and football clubs, and the walls were covered in team photographs of all three sports dating back to the 1980s. Bobby had thought it was hilarious when he'd spotted his dad in one of the cricket team photos: Steve with a bowl haircut, squashed between two huge boys almost twice his size. The photo was on the wall near to Tess. It wasn't close enough for her to see Steve clearly, but she knew he was there. She could walk a few steps and see the boy who grew up into the teenager she fell in love with.

Steve. Whenever she thought of him, and that was at least every five minutes, the ache in her chest deepened. She was lonely. That was the trouble. Her heart ached constantly. She felt exhausted and afraid for the future. She lifted Rose out of her buggy and held her close while she watched Bobby and his friends playing outside. Perhaps she should have invited Adam. Was Vanya right? Was she being mean?

But it was only a child's party. It didn't really matter, did it?

1991

Lydia made mincemeat of Karen. She told her that if she didn't stop picking on other girls she would destroy her. She said it in such a way that it scared the living daylights out of her. Karen was crying – crying? *Karen?!* Who'd have thought that could ever happen? Certainly not Tess. She'd long ago decided that Karen was to be carefully stepped around like an unexploded bomb.

Lydia was told by Miss Humble that 'it's not the right way to go about things. If you think one girl is bullying another then you should tell an adult, not take matters into your own hands.'

Tess wasn't in the room when this was said but Lydia reported it to her 'verbatim'. 'You are not allowed outside at break times for six weeks,' Lydia said, imitating Miss Humble's upright stance and haughty tones. 'You will stay in the library for extra study.'

The girls agreed that this was hardly a punishment, especially as Tess was allowed to join Lydia. They shared a beanbag, shoes off, feet resting on a low table, surrounded by encyclopedias, pages opened at topics that interested them.

'Fatal flaw,' Lydia said, going on to read the definition, 'is an intrinsic flaw in a character that causes him or her to meet with failure in the end.' She gave Tess a significant look. 'It's not just in stories. It happens in real life too.'

'Does it?' Tess asked, thinking. 'You mean, like politicians with their vaulting ambition?'

'Most normal people's fatal flaw is procrastination. Putting things off til tomorrow and then they die without ever really living their lives.' She closed that book and picked up another, flicking through the pages until her attention was caught again. There was silence for several minutes before she said, 'Sometimes I think I'm a psychopath.'

'You can't be because you care about people.'

'Only you and my dad.'

'Well, that's two more than a psychopath,' Tess replied, her heart lit up with the revelation that Lydia cared about her.

And in the evening, they would call each other and chat for hours. 'What do you even have to talk about?' Tess's mum would shout. 'You see each other every day at school!'

Lydia invited Tess back to her house and she immediately said yes.

Their homes were very different. Tess's was stuffed to the gunnels. When Gary and his daughter Saskia moved in, they ended up with two lots of everything. They had a spare washing machine and tumble drier in the garage, a spare iron and ironing board under the stairs. Tess had to give up her bedroom to Saskia – 'to make her feel welcome,' her mum said. And make me feel unwelcome? Tess thought. She had a tiny box room with a high, miniscule window onto the hall, and a huge pile of unwanted clothes and shoes in the corner covered with a blanket. The stuff wouldn't fit in the garage, the loft or the understairs cupboard and her mum said it had to be stored in her room 'until I have the chance to drop it off at Oxfam'. That was a year ago.

Lydia's house was larger and more organised. It was a neat, symmetrical bungalow with a loft conversion. The rooms were beige throughout. Beige and beautiful, Tess thought. Lydia's mum Genevieve said there should be 'a place for everything and everything in its place' – an expression that had Lydia rolling her eyes but chimed with Tess's very soul.

Lydia's bedroom was one of the rooms in the loft conversion and was thirty feet long. There were dormer windows at one side overlooking the front garden and, on the other side, two huge Velux windows that opened up to the sky. They could stand on chairs and rest their arms on the ledges, staring off into the woods or calling out to the older teenage boy next door, ducking down and giggling when he looked up.

And Lydia had her own bathroom – the height of luxury as far as Tess was concerned. 'I have to share when we have guests,' Lydia said. 'But the rest of the time it's mine.' She pointed to her bedspread. 'By the way, you can laugh at *me* but you must never laugh at my blanket. I crocheted it last summer.'

'It's very ... colourful,' Tess said, stroking the soft woollen squares with her hand. 'Kind of hippyish.'

Lydia pushed her back onto the bed then lay down beside her. 'It's too colourful for Genevieve.'

Lydia called her mum by her first name which to Tess seemed impossibly bold. She did it once, just trying it on for size. 'I'm going to Lydia's after school, Deirdre.'

'I beg your pardon?' Her mother was scandalised. 'What did you call me?'

'Your name,' Tess said weakly, her courage already failing her.

It set her mother off into a frenzy of how-dare-yous, slamming doors and angry tears. 'Your mum works really hard at being a *mum* and she deserves the courtesy of being called Mum!' Gary shouted, pointing at Tess, his expanding belly hanging over the top of his trousers. 'So just bloody well call her Mum!' He stood for a couple of seconds, eyes blinking furiously then marched off to the pub, exasperated, and forever out of his depth.

'Do Gary and Deirdre ever fight?' Lydia asked, as if tuning into the drama replaying in Tess's head.

'Not really. She's always trying to please him. But every so often he goes off on a bender as my granny calls it and then my mum sits at the kitchen table chewing her nails and weeping.'

'Booze is his release valve,' Lydia said. 'Being in a house of women can't be easy when you're a man like Gary.'

'That's one of the things I hate about men. The fact that women have to pander to them.'

'You have to do their bidding and laugh at their jokes.'

'Not your dad though.'

'Not my dad.'

It was plain to see that Lydia's dad was her everything. He was tall and broad-shouldered, and he had a patient, wise manner that made Tess feel instantly safe. 'He never criticises me,' Lydia said. 'It gets on Genevieve's nerves but he says that I should be allowed to be me. It's like he wants the best for me, whereas she wants me to be a certain way to make her look good.'

Lydia had a lot to say but Tess was more than just her audience. Lydia was interested in her. She asked her questions. 'So, what makes Tess tick?'

She hiccupped nervously. 'What do you mean?'

'Who are *you*, Tess Carter?'

Tess had no idea who she was. She spent most of her time trying to either please the people around her or, at the very least, not get into trouble. Who she was and what she wanted had always been questions for the birds. But Lydia pushed her to think about the person she was and could become. It felt thrilling – scary but thrilling – like being on a big dipper climbing towards the sky before plunging towards the earth with a scream and a smile.

Lydia

We'd been living in Ashdown Village for more than two months and my life had fallen into a rhythm. On Tuesdays and Thursdays, I worked all day, visiting start-ups, networking, putting people in touch with each other. Mondays, Wednesdays and Fridays I visited Paula in the morning then drove to the country club and spent time in the gym. Weekends were for family. We always had breakfast together on Saturday mornings. Zack and Adam made pancakes, a huge stack that we munched through, topped with maple syrup and blueberries.

'I really like living here,' Adam said, smiling at me with front teeth that were crooked. He'd need braces before too long, but as far as I was concerned, he had the most beautiful smile in the world. 'It's better than London.' He tipped his head to one side as he ate around the edges of his pancake. 'I like Maisie and Bobby. I don't know why Bobby didn't invite me to his birthday party. At first he said I could go and then he changed his mind.' He pierced me with the same green eyes as my own. 'Maisie said it's because you don't get on with his mum.'

'I don't think that's true,' I said lightly, quietly seething at the fact that Adam had been excluded from the party. Every other child in the football team had been invited. It was a blatant snub on Tess's part. 'We just haven't spent much time together.' *Recently.*

'What's this?' Zack asked, glancing up from his phone.

'Bobby's party,' Adam said. 'Everyone else on the football team went to it.'

'That's a bit unkind, isn't it?' Zack looked across at me.

'Maybe,' I said. 'But I think it's better if we rise above it.'

'What does that mean?' Adam asked.

'We don't let it bother us.' I stood up to get more coffee, kissing the top of his head as I walked past. 'Why don't we all go up to London and see a few of your old friends?'

He agreed that this was a good idea. He would visit his grandma first and then we'd drive into the city. 'I'm going to invite Bobby to *my* birthday party when it comes,' he said. 'I know it's not for a while but I'm not going to leave him out.'

'That sounds like the right thing to do,' I told him.

Whenever I was anxious, I suffered from insomnia. I fell asleep easily enough, usually around eleven, but then I would wake between two and three, my mind switched on. I could lie awake for hours trying to turn off the thoughts, until I gave in and got up, pulled on a dressing gown and checked on Adam. He was always fast asleep, pillow tossed onto the floor, my ancient teddy next to his cheek.

That night, I made myself a drink, a large one with ice and lemon. Then I went back upstairs to sit on one of the comfy chairs on the landing, drawing my legs up underneath me. Zack and I were in the habit of sitting here in the evenings watching the sunset, Adam playing Lego on the floor beside us. I held the glass in my hand and stared out into the night, a full moon my only companion.

Two months had passed and I still hadn't bumped into my mother, but I felt as if she was stalking me, her presence forever at the edges of my vision, like a black dog slinking in the shadows. There was a war going on inside me, voices shouting to be heard. I'd had a long stint of therapy in my late twenties and one of the main takeaways was 'never mistake your internal monologue for the truth'.

I was winding myself up. I was imagining things that weren't true. I was paranoid.

Or was I?

When I'd gone to visit my dad's grave for the third time, I'd parked close by and walked the short distance into the cemetery. It was an early autumn morning and there was nobody about. The only sounds were birdsong and the brisk tap of my own feet on the cobblestone pathway. I'd felt a welcome uplift because I was *doing* something. I couldn't bring my dad back but I could honour his memory. I could tend to his grave, keep it clean and leave fresh flowers every week. The world would know that he was still loved. And if by some spiritual miracle he was looking down on his final earthly resting place, he would see me and he would know that I had never stopped loving him. Not for a moment.

But when I'd arrived at his grave, there was a bouquet of twelve red roses in a glass vase in front of his gravestone. I stared down at the flowers, frowning. When I'd visited two days before there was nothing here. Forty-eight hours later and the grave had been swept, stray weeds pulled out and flowers left in their place. Everything I'd intended to do but someone had beaten me to it.

I'd noticed there was a tag hanging from the bouquet. I bent down to read it:

For Adam, my beloved husband. Never forgotten, love Genevieve

My head had filled with ice. I gripped the edge of the stone to stop myself from falling over. My vision narrowed to a pinprick. My mouth was dry; my heart was racing. Classic signs of a panic attack. I'd been here before. I simply had to breathe my way through it. *Take it slow*. I filled and emptied my lungs several times to steady myself and when I felt my heart rate return to something close to normal, I glanced quickly over my shoulder to check that she wasn't behind me. Watching me. Like a predator watches its prey.

My mother was still living in the village. *My mother was still living in the village*. Did she know I was back? Was that why she'd laid the flowers? To send me a message? She would have guessed that my dad's grave would be one of the regular places I'd visit. It didn't help that I'd had a feeling this would happen, that if she was still living here, returning to the village would open a door that I didn't want to walk through.

I stared out into the garden and presented myself with the two opposing possibilities. On the one hand, my mother had no idea I was living here. She could have been visiting my dad's grave every week for the past thirty years, for all I knew. And even if she had realised I was back, did that have to mean she was scheming against me?

People changed as the years went by, didn't they? They learned from their mistakes. They mellowed. There was nothing to fear from her. The past was the past. And perhaps, in her own way, she had loved her husband. At sixteen what could I have known about marriage? My dad was my dad. To me he was perfect.

On the other hand, I *knew* my mother. Time would never change her. She'd lost none of her guile and manoeuvring. She was playing with me. There were times when I was sure I felt her eyes on me: in the supermarket, the library, collecting Adam from school. But whenever I turned around, she wasn't there. I would scan strangers' faces for her features but it was never her. She was elusive. A trickster.

What if she came up to me in the street when I was with Zack and Adam? What would I say? How could I explain myself when the story I'd always told was that we'd lost touch? Years ago, I'd toyed with the idea of being truthful with Zack but his experience of family life was so different from mine that I knew he wouldn't get it. Not unless I told him the whole truth. And I hadn't told anyone that. Not then. Not in between. And not now.

'She went to live in the Far East when I was eighteen,' I'd told him. And when we were planning our wedding, 'I've tried looking for her, but there's no answer from her last known address, and no one knows where she's living now.' The lies sliding off my tongue with ease.

'But that's so sad!' he'd said. 'She'll miss our wedding.'

So here I was, in the stark, untruthful present day, with a husband who thought Adam's only grandma was *his* mum, when *my* mum could be living a mile away. I had to know one way or the other.

The next morning, I dropped Adam at school and drove to the outskirts of the village. I parked off the main road in one of the forest car parks, pulled on my boots and jogged a few hundred yards along a path that was once a railway line. Apart from the odd dog walker, it wasn't a popular place to stroll because it was heavily shaded by trees either side and usually muddy underfoot. I stopped when I reached a large oak tree at the corner of what had once been my home. The slant of the trunk left a gap before the fence that divided the garden from where the path began. It wasn't quite the gap I remembered. There was a waist-high overgrowth of brambles filling the space and I had to force my way through, thorns hooking into my coat and piercing my jeans.

When I made it onto the grass, I rubbed my legs and waited in the shadows, observing the bungalow. The garden stretched away from me up to the patio area and the long, low extension to the rear. I hadn't been back here since I was sixteen. I stared up at my former bedroom window and immediately felt the sharp end of bad memories increase my heart rate. I turned away, my teeth gritted against a wave of nausea. The summer house was to my left, partly obscured by a weeping willow, the trailing branches covering one whole side. Staying in the shadows of the oak trees, I walked towards it, keeping my eyes on the bungalow to make sure no one was standing at a window watching me. Regardless of whether this was my mother's house or not, I was trespassing. I expected an angry householder to appear at any moment, but the seconds ticked by and no one came outside.

The door to the summer house was hanging on its hinges, the surrounding frames splintered at the edges. I pushed the door open and went inside. Leaves carpeted the floor, spider webs criss-crossing the space, thick and sticky, hanging down from the ceiling and giving it a spooky, Halloween feel. There were benches all the way round and I sat down, the house still in my sights. I rested my back against the wooden panelling and took three deep breaths. I sat there for almost thirty minutes, waiting, just waiting. I wasn't sure how long I'd stay. All I knew was that, after two months of worrying that I'd be spotted in the street, in a shop, in a restaurant, being here felt like the right thing to do.

Suddenly, a woman appeared at the patio door, and I pulled myself back into the shadows, my heart pounding.

I watched her walk out onto the patio to restock the bird-feeder. It was my mother. No doubt about it. She walked with a brisk, efficient step as always, stopping on her way back inside to pick up some stray leaves that had blown onto the paving stones.

The door closed behind her, and gradually I felt my heartbeat settle. A sense of calm washed through me. At aged sixteen and grieving for my dad, all I could do was flee. I'd read a lot since then about the teenage brain, how the wiring was yet to fully connect one area of the cerebral cortex to another. That meant there was an absence of understanding. Teenagers take risks because the fundamental rule of cause and effect is not a reality. They fail to see the significance of their behaviour because they are literally unable to think it through.

Now, almost thirty years later, I had the wisdom of maturity. I was thinking it through, remembering what had happened in this house where there was yet to be any measure of punishment. Dark thoughts crowded my mind reminding me that there were scores to settle. I could begin by turning the tables on her; the watcher becomes the watched. She wouldn't like that. Not one bit.

Tess

By the time she'd lifted the buggy out of the car and strapped Rose into the seat, Bobby had run off into the clubhouse to change. She tucked the blanket around Rose's feet and pushed the buggy towards the front of the clubhouse where the parents congregated. It was already December and the air was chilly, the ground damp with melting frost. Her breath condensed in front of her as she walked. She pulled her gloves and scarf from the storage compartment in the bottom of the buggy and put them on, her eyes scanning the huddles of parents for Vanya. Instead, she saw Lydia, standing at the edge of the playing field, a take-out coffee cup raised to her lips. She quickly looked away before she was caught watching her. Not that she *was* watching, or *ever* watched her. But she didn't want to draw Lydia's gaze because whenever she did, she was left in no doubt that her presence was unwelcome.

She'd made some poor choices after Rose was born. She really had. She couldn't believe quite how much of an idiot she'd been but there was nothing she could do about it now. She'd spent most of the last few weeks hiding at home, worrying. Worrying, worrying, worrying. The anti-depressants helped dampen her anxiety but they didn't sort out her life and they wouldn't bring Steve back either. Nothing would bring Steve back. She just had to live with it. And she had to try harder for Bobby and Rose's sake, if not for her own.

She was putting her best foot forward. Starting tonight. The football mums were getting together for a pre-Christmas meal in the Italian restaurant. She'd seen the sign-up list; Lydia's name was on it. Perhaps there would be the chance for an honest conversation. 'Could we have a chat, Lydia?' she'd say, and Lydia would follow her off to one side. They'd wind back time and Lydia would acknowledge their friendship. Tess would apologise for any hurt she'd caused, especially to Adam. Not inviting him to Bobby's party was petty. But she hoped that Lydia would forgive her.

And then they could move on. The thought of having Lydia as her friend again gave Tess a warm feeling in the pit of her stomach. She knew that she'd recover more quickly with Lydia by her side and maybe they could even recreate some of the happiness they felt as teenagers.

'Morning.' Vanya nudged Tess's elbow. 'Bloody freezing again.'

'You're telling me.' She rubbed her gloved hands together. 'Luckily the kids don't seem to feel it.'

They both looked towards the field where the children were warming up. They were waiting in two lines before dribbling and passing the ball and running to the goal mouth to shoot. Maisie was partnered with Bobby and was shouting instructions to him as they ran.

'She's such a bossyboots,' Vanya said with a sigh. 'I wish she'd relax and let life happen instead of always trying to control everything.'

'I wonder who she gets that from?' Tess said lightly.

'Moi?' Vanya exaggerated an astonished look. 'Controlling? Do you know me at all?' They both laughed. 'I'll make sure never to let you and Erica spend too much time together. Suddenly she'd have evidence for everything she suspects.' Vanya's wife Erica was a sergeant in the police. They'd met when they were both married to men and had a whirlwind love affair. Vanya described their meeting as a revelation. 'It was like my head had been on the wrong way round my whole life and I never knew it.'

Rain started to drizzle and Tess raised the hood on the buggy. 'Shall we sit inside?'

'Good idea. If we can bag a window seat we'll be able to see the game from there.'

Tess swivelled the buggy towards the clubhouse and Vanya fell into step beside her. 'You still coming this evening?'

'Of course.' Before she could stop herself, her eyes flicked towards Lydia and back again. 'I'm looking forward to it.'

'You're a hopeless liar, Tess,' Vanya told her, slipping an arm through hers. 'But one of these days you're going to tell me what happened between you and Lydia so that the spell will be broken.'

'Spell?' She frowned. 'She hasn't cast a *spell* on me, Vanya. We were teenage friends, that's all.' She stopped talking. Maybe Vanya wasn't so far off? She paused to acknowledge the thought. Had Lydia cast some sort of spell on her back then? She remembered her granny's comment when she'd returned from a weekend away with Lydia's family. They'd gone to Oxford because Lydia's dad had high hopes that she would apply for university there. 'You too, Tess,' he'd said. 'You're clever girls, the pair of you. You should be aiming high.' She

67

must have been fifteen because it was the same weekend that her stepsister Saskia had her appendix out and she was glad to have missed all the drama. 'You're completely in Lydia's thrall,' her granny had told her on her return. 'And I'm not sure it's a good thing.'

'If she *is* pretending not to know you,' Vanya said, opening the door wide enough to make space for the buggy to pass through, 'there must be a reason. What did you do? Steal her boyfriend? Throw her under the bus at school?'

'No,' Tess replied. 'Nothing like that. We were best friends. We were loyal to each other.'

'So how come you lost touch?'

A good question, and one that Tess had asked herself many times. 'She left the village around the same time I started going out with Steve. Her dad died and she went to live with her aunt in London.'

'You could have called each other. And visited. London's not that far away.'

'I know! But I didn't have her aunt's details. I asked her mum to pass a message on to her but maybe she didn't. I'm not sure.'

'Why didn't she stay with her mum?'

'They didn't get on.' Tess manoeuvered the buggy around tables and chairs. 'She still lives here. I bumped into her the other day in the supermarket car park. She was really kind to me. Just like always.'

'I don't think I've ever met her,' Vanya said.

'Her name's Genevieve. She helped at Steve's funeral.'

'Ah, yes! I remember her,' Vanya said. 'She made a ton of sandwiches.'

'I told her that Lydia's been blanking me and she said that Lydia's changed.'

'In what way?'

'That she's complicated, not the girl she was.' Tess glanced towards the counter, the mention of sandwiches reminding her that she hadn't had any breakfast. 'I can't remember who's on duty today. If it's Tom's mum, she'll have made her chocolate brownies.'

'I'll check,' Vanya said. 'You grab us a seat.'

Tess found the last free window seat with a view over the pitch. The opposing team had joined their children on the grass and were also warming up, running in zig-zag lines, kicking balls to each other.

The photo of Steve was on the wall next to her. Sadness bubbled up through her chest. If she wasn't careful she'd be in tears in no time, so she hummed to distract herself, removed her coat, then let her attention be caught by a pigeon pecking the ground close to the window, the feathers on its neck puffed up into a collar of soft, grey down. He turned a beady orange eye towards her and she automatically looked down at Rose intending to lift her out of the buggy and show her the bird, but she had fallen asleep, her head relaxing sideways onto the padding. Tess tucked the blanket around her legs again and kept the hood of the buggy raised to shield her from the lights and any unwanted attention.

Vanya was almost at the head of the queue. She pointed to the plates of cakes on the counter and gave Tess a thumbs up. Tess returned the gesture and checked her phone. There was a message from her dad saying the job was running over and he wouldn't make it home for dinner and another from her babysitter Sadie asking what time she should arrive that evening. She replied to both and glanced up just as Vanya was walking towards her with a tray.

'We're in luck with the brownies. I got a couple for Maisie and Bobby too.'

'Thank you.' Tess lifted their drinks and brownies off the tray while Vanya removed her coat.

When she sat down, a couple of the mums stopped to chat to them, and one dipped her head to smile at sleeping Rose in her buggy. 'See you this evening,' they said as they moved on to another table.

'By the way, Maisie and Adam are having a playdate tomorrow,' Vanya said, cutting her brownie into four. 'Maisie has been after me for weeks to organise something.'

Tess swallowed a mouthful of tea before saying, 'That's good for Maisie.' She felt Vanya check her expression: Adam was Lydia's son and she was probably expecting more of a reaction.

'I don't want you thinking that this makes me Lydia's friend because it doesn't.'

'Duly noted,' Tess said. 'But if I hear of you two down the pub together then I won't be happy.' She meant for her words to sound light, half jokey but they didn't. 'I'm only kidding,' she added. 'It's really not a big deal.'

'Tess.' Vanya's expression was serious. 'Whatever happened between you two. I hope you get the chance to work it out.'

'Yeah, well, we're not teenagers any more.' Tess stared through the window as she said this, watching Bobby in the thick of it, charging down the field and taking a shot at goal. 'I'm going to try to chat to her this evening.' She sighed. 'I need to apologise to her for not inviting Adam to Bobby's birthday party.' She took a bite of the brownie and felt sweet, dark chocolate coat her tongue. But the sweetness couldn't counter the bitter taste in her mouth. 'You were right. It was mean of me.'

'It was, but ...' Vanya shook her head. 'With Rose and everything, you haven't exactly been yourself.' Rose and *everything.* Vanya was being kind. The *everything* covered a multitude, from her breakdown to her slide into debt.

'Why not leave it for a bit?' Vanya's expression was concerned. 'We could duck out of this evening and you could come over to mine instead.'

'It'll be fine.' Tess smiled. 'Have some faith in me!'

'It's not that I don't have faith in you,' Vanya said quietly. 'Far from it. But you're tired and if she still doesn't want to know you, it might make you feel worse.'

Tess took another moment to watch Bobby run up the pitch and kick the ball towards the goal, just missing by a couple of feet. 'I get what you're saying,' she acknowledged. 'And I'm sorry I'm such a sad sack. Being in the club doesn't help.' She glanced towards the photo on the wall. 'Steve is here but not here, you know.'

'Oh, love.' Vanya reached across the table for Tess's hand. 'I know it's still really hard for you.' Her dark eyes were flooded with sympathy. She was the physical opposite of Tess, petite, with olive skin and a heart-shaped face. 'And it's not even a year since he died,' she added.

Tess stared up at the ceiling, thinking. 'Bobby's dad, the love of my life, my best mate, the main breadwinner. And he never even got to meet Rose.' She took another bite of brownie. 'All my eggs were in one basket.' She gave a weak smile. 'Not to be recommended.'

Bobby was always slow to change so Tess was one of the last mums waiting outside the clubhouse. Vanya and Maisie had headed home and so had Lydia and Adam, holding hands as they walked towards their four-by-four.

While she waited, her eye was caught by a lone man standing on the opposite side of the road. His right hand went into the pocket of his leather jacket and he pulled out a packet of cigarettes and a lighter. He shook a cigarette into his hand, placed it between his lips and lit it, cupping his hand around the flame. It was then, as he took the first drag, that he lifted his face to stare across at her. He had a cap on his head, casting his face in shadow, and she was unable to fully make out his features, but she felt a shiver pass through her. And suddenly she was fifteen again, playing hockey on the pitches at school, when one of the girls had said to her, 'That man's been watching you and Lydia all match.' And she'd glanced around quickly, seen him standing there and felt her insides turn over.

1991

It was week five of Lydia's punishment and they were in the library at break. They had both signed up for the school newspaper and had been asked by the sixth formers to research women's Grand Slam tennis. They had grabbed over two dozen books from the shelves and had them scattered on the floor beside them. As usual, they were distracted by more interesting facts. 'Munchausen syndrome by proxy,' Lydia announced, reading from the large volume resting on her lap, 'is when the caregiver, often the mother, creates health problems in her child.'

'Weird,' Tess said.

'Video surveillance without the caregiver's knowledge can be a way to catch them.'

'Awful for the kid,' Tess said. She'd started reading about how much money men won playing Grand Slams compared with women. It led her down a rabbit hole of reading that men were paid more for everything they did, from working in local government to driving a bus. 'I think this is an example of misogyny,' she declared, glancing across at Lydia. This was one of their hot topics – feminism was their favourite F-word – but Lydia hadn't heard her. She was staring into the distance, her expression thoughtful as if she was working through a problem. 'Earth to Lydia.' Tess nudged her. Lydia smiled then shook her head as if to dispel intrusive thoughts. (They'd read about intrusive thoughts the week before – mental illness was another of their hot topics.) 'Are you okay?' Tess asked.

'Yeah.' Lydia stood up and did some stretches, lifting her arms up into the air, her face turned away from Tess. A shift in the pit of Tess's stomach warned her that something was wrong. Was Lydia crying? Because Lydia never cried. Or very rarely. She was saving her tears for something serious, she told Tess, as if somewhere deep inside she already knew that there was trouble in the offing. When she sat down again, her face was composed. She was back to her normal self. 'Talking of misogynists,' she said – so she *had* been listening – 'my mum's cousin is one. You'll meet him on Saturday.' She tugged at Tess's hair to pull her face towards her. 'And I'm warning you now that he's weird.'

'So where are we meeting him?'

'At home. My mum's doing afternoon tea. My dad has a big case on so he'll be working the weekend.' Lydia placed a hand over Tess's mouth. 'Never catch his eye,' she whispered. Her own eyes were wide and sincere as she said this. 'He's like a vampire. You must never invite him into your life. Do you hear me?'

Tess nodded. As ever, she was excited by the drama that Lydia introduced into the everyday. Life was never boring with Lydia for a friend.

Tess did her best, but she was only in his company for ten minutes when she caught his eye. By mistake. She was concentrating so hard on not doing it that she did it. Genevieve introduced them to each other as soon as she arrived. 'Tess, meet Oscar, and Oscar, meet Tess.

Oscar is my cousin,' she said, gazing at him indulgently. And grinning. Tess had never seen her grin. She smiled a lot but it was always in response to something external whereas this grin came from within, happiness welling up inside her like a burst water pipe.

Tess said hello to Oscar but managed not to look at him. She stared off to one side where Lydia stood, looking more bored and closed-off than Tess had ever seen her. And she was dressed in clothes that would be welcomed in a religious community. A shapeless, checked dress that hung away from her body and well past her knees, and a pair of furry ankle slippers. She was only missing the headscarf.

'I'm joining a commune,' Lydia mouthed at Tess, who smiled in response. She loved that about them. They always knew what the other one was thinking.

They sat next to each other at the dining table, Oscar and Genevieve opposite them. Lydia held Tess's hand, pulling on it constantly so that she kept her attention. She whispered in Tess's ear: school stuff, comments about people they knew, books she had read, anything to hold her attention, her eyes bright and concentrated. Tess expected Genevieve to tell them off for being rude but she only had eyes for Oscar. Tess was aware of their interaction from the corner of her eye. Genevieve was stroking his arm and laying kisses on his cheek. 'You'd think he'd just returned from the war,' Lydia said into Tess's ear.

It was when Genevieve went into the kitchen to refill the teapot that Tess slipped up. Lydia's legs were constantly moving and she'd kicked off one of her slippers. She disappeared under the table to retrieve it and pulled on Tess's hand for her to follow but, at that moment, Oscar made a strange clicking sound with his tongue.

Tess's attention automatically shifted and suddenly she was looking at him. He had regular features, a receding hairline and pavement-grey eyes that held her gaze. He licked his lips and pushed out his tongue, flicking the tip of it up and down. Tess smiled vaguely and looked away. Lydia's head popped back up and when she saw what he was doing her lip curled. 'Fuck off, Oscar, you filthy git.'

'Ooh, potty mouth.' He widened his eyes. 'What would Daddy say?'

Lydia grabbed Tess's hand and took her out of the room and up the stairs, taking them two at a time so that Tess had to run to keep up. She closed the bedroom door behind them and wedged a chair underneath the handle. 'For fuck's sake, Tess!' she hissed. 'I told you not to catch his eye!'

'I couldn't help it! You were under the table and he was clicking his tongue. I thought maybe he was having a stroke or something.'

Lydia threw herself back onto the bed. 'Fuck! I wish my dad was here. He never tries it on when he's around.'

'Tries what on?'

'You're such an innocent.' She gave a weary sigh. 'But you're my innocent and I won't let him corrupt you.' She pulled Tess down beside her. 'Now listen.'

Lydia

'Am I going to play with Maisie tomorrow?' Adam asked me, his foot banging rhythmically against the chair leg.

'You are.' I placed a glass of water down next to him. 'Her mum will collect you from school.' My eyes drifted towards Zack. He was taking a phone call in the garden, shielding his eyes with his free hand when he triggered the outdoor lights.

'Her mum's called Vanya,' Adam said. 'Maisie told me.'

I walked back across to the sink which was overflowing with dishes. For three people we generated a disproportionate amount of mess. I began organising cutlery and crockery into types, rinsing and then stacking them in the dishwasher.

I was almost finished when Zack came inside, the door closing behind him with a bang. 'I thought we could ask Jenny round for dinner tomorrow evening,' he said. His hair was ruffled and he smoothed it back over his head. 'She's been so helpful with Mum.'

'Sure.' I was yet to meet Jenny because she wasn't there at the times I visited Paula. But the big news was that Paula was doing well. The hospice medical team had put together a drug regime that stabilised her symptoms. 'It turns out death is not for everyone,' she'd told me with a wry laugh. 'Or not for me. Not yet, anyway.' I'd hugged her then, and cried because visiting her was something I looked forward to and I was so happy to know that she wasn't about to pass away.

Zack's sister was flying over from America. She was a doctor and had taken a month off work to be with her mum. She was hiring a camper van and taking Paula to Cornwall. 'We're going on an adventure,' Paula told me. 'Can you believe it?' Her eyes shone. 'Such a wonderful surprise. I don't suppose we'll have the best of weather but that's okay.'

'You'll be cosy in the van with a mug of hot chocolate in your hands and the rolling sea for company,' I said.

'And we'll all be together for Christmas?'

'You bet.' *We needn't have moved back here then,* the voice in my head reminded me but I squashed it down, hugging Paula hard as if to prove this to myself.

'So where are you off to this evening?' Zack asked me.

'Football mums.' I added the cutlery to the basket. 'We're meeting in the Italian restaurant.'

'These earrings match your eyes.' His fingers briefly touched the emerald drops in my ears before his hand slid to the back of my neck and then my shoulder. 'Crofty's got a bad throat so I'm not going out now. We can cancel the babysitter.'

'It's a bit late to cancel.' His hand was cool and strong, and I wanted to lean into him, let him wrap me up and kiss me. Instead, I moved away. 'She'll be on her way.'

'I expect she'll be relieved to have the night off.'

'She uses the money to pay for her drama lessons.'

He shrugged, and then smiled. 'I'll still pay her. How about that?'

'Sounds good.' I tried to smile but failed, and turned away before I was expected to acknowledge the look in his eye asking me what was up.

As usual since living here, I hadn't sleep well last night. I was cold and then hot, worried and then angry. The king-size bed felt like a single, Zack's limbs and torso were everywhere all at once. Several times I'd pushed him onto his side but he rolled back again, landing next to me with a decisive thud. I'd finally got up and sat at the kitchen table nursing a glass of whisky, turning memories over in my mind.

'Any dads brave enough to join in with the football mums?' Zack asked.

'Not even one.' I added a small brick of detergent to the dispenser and closed the dishwasher door, twisting the knob into the start position. 'You fancy coming?' I smiled and then laughed at the look on his face.

'Not on your life,' he said. 'I'm not sure I've got what it takes to cope with you all.'

I didn't go straight to the restaurant. I asked the taxi driver to drop me in front of the church. It was already dark and bitterly cold. I buttoned my coat and wrapped my scarf around my neck and over the back of my head. I usually visited my dad's grave in the daytime but I felt the need to be with him now, even though he wasn't really there. Even though he had been dead for thirty years. This resting place was all I had, and recently I had begun to share my thoughts with him, mostly about how much I wanted her to be punished. Seeing her in the garden had been a shock. Knowing that she was still alive and well had narrowed my focus. She had committed a crime and I hadn't been able to tell the truth. Aged sixteen, I had neither the skills nor the strength to go through with it. But now? Now I was stronger. Now was the time to follow through on what I knew. 'I'll make you proud, Dad,' I told him, my gloved hand resting on his headstone. 'I will.'

Tess

Sadie arrived at the house for seven-thirty. She lived next door and was Tess's go-to babysitter, helping out when she needed to work and her dad was busy.

'Bobby's asleep but Rose is taking time to settle,' Tess told her, balancing the baby on her shoulder as she paced across the floor in her stockinged feet. 'She's a right little minx in the evenings.' Rose wailed and pulled up her knees. 'Bobby was the same when he was this age.'

'I think I can manage if you want to leave her with me,' Sadie replied, her arms outstretched.

'She needs to bring up some wind,' Tess said and, as if on cue, Rose gave a loud burp. 'There you go!' She nuzzled her cheek against soft baby hair. 'Now you'll feel better.' Rose gave her a watery smile. 'You stay with Sadie,' she said, kissing her firm cheeks, 'and I'll be back before you know it.'

She handed Rose across to Sadie who immediately settled her in the crook of her arm. 'I'll keep my mobile on the table so I'll see if you call,' Tess said, slipping on her shoes. 'Let me know if you have any problems.' She moved aside a pile of cushions and a blanket as she searched for her purse, and finally found it lying on the floor beside the coffee table. 'I doubt my dad will be back before me.'

'Eat, drink and make merry!' Sadie said, following her to the front door. 'And don't worry about us.' She smiled down at Rose. 'We'll be fine.'

'I won't be any later than eleven,' Tess called out as she ran to the car. 'Help yourself to anything in the fridge.' Not that there was much to choose from. 'There are some biscuits in the tin!'

Sadie waved her away and she climbed into Steve's car. She was still in two minds about going to the restaurant but, on balance, she felt it was important to join in. This was the first time she'd been out socially since Steve died. It was a necessary milestone, and she'd feel better for doing it because she'd have achieved something, taken one of the first steps in moving on.

And then there was Lydia. She really needed to make this better. She would start by asking Adam for a play-date to show Lydia that she had changed.

She smiled to herself. It was good to feel like she was taking charge of her life.

There were no spaces in the village car park, so she parked in a side street. As she walked away, she glanced back at the car – an Audi RS 5. To most people it was nothing special. But Steve loved it. It was Steve's car. It would never be her car, always his. And that was the way she wanted it to stay.

It was early December, and the village already had a festive feel to it. Christmas lights were strung between lamp posts. A grinning plastic snowman, also bedecked in coloured lights, stood on a patch of ground to the left of the chemist and a wooden nativity scene was in front of the church, the crib still empty. She tried not to think about the presents she couldn't afford to buy – Rose didn't need anything and she'd gathered together some stocking fillers for Bobby – but she wanted to give him a big present, something that would make him jump up and down with joy. She reminded herself that Christmas wasn't about stuff. It was about families sharing happy times and making new memories. But this would be their first Christmas without Steve and she yearned to counteract some of the sadness.

She weaved her way between two groups of people who were clogging up the pavement, pulling her collar in close to her neck. It didn't help; it was below zero and she was wearing the wrong coat. The wind funnelled down her back and her teeth began to chatter. When she saw the restaurant up ahead she ran the last few metres, her numb feet almost tripping her up. The door opened and the restaurant wrapped her in warm air and the buzz of voices. She surrendered her coat to the pony-tailed waiter and followed him to where the football mums were seated at a long table in the window recess and were already tucking into their starters. 'Hi Tess!' they called out, raising their charged glasses in her direction.

'Sorry I'm late.' She smiled around at them, avoiding Lydia's eye as she always did. There were eleven mums in total, five either side and Lydia at the head of the table. 'I couldn't find a parking space.'

Vanya grabbed her hand and pulled her down into the remaining seat at the opposite end to Lydia. 'We ordered some antipasti to share.' She kissed her cheek. 'God, you're freezing!'

'I had to park down by the flower shop.'

'I thought your dad was giving you a lift?'

'He's working in Guildford.' She pulled her chair in closer to the table. 'Earning some extra cash for Christmas.'

Vanya reached for the bottle of red close to her and tipped it towards Tess's glass. Tess immediately covered the top of the glass with her hand. 'Not for me, thanks.'

'I'm not drinking either,' Vanya said. 'Erica and I have promised each other no alcohol until Christmas Eve.' She passed the bottle down the table then looked back at Tess. 'All well at home?'

'Bobby was so tired after the match he was asleep at seven. Rose was grumbling a bit when I left.'

'Maisie was shattered too,' Vanya said. She lifted a finger into the air. 'Oh, remind me to give you the money from Mrs Taylor. She paid for four weeks in cash.'

'Did she ask you to clean her car again?'

'Not this time. She stayed in her bedroom. She was on her mobile most of the time.'

Tess glanced along the table to where Lydia was showing a video on her phone to the women either side of her. The mobile was soon passed from hand to hand and the mums smiled as they watched their children playing to the camera. In the final few seconds, Bobby's arms were around Adam's shoulders. When Tess passed the mobile back, Lydia was watching her, her expression neutral, then she leaned in to Romilly, the mum next to her, and said something that made her laugh. Romilly's eyes briefly met Tess's before she reached for her glass.

Tess felt a hiccup of paranoia cut through her good intentions. She wore an anxiety wristband and she pulled at the band now, several times, felt the small crack of pain as it snapped back onto her skin. Thinking that people were talking about her was one of her insecurities. She had always been like this but it had grown worse after Steve died. 'And so what if they are talking about you?' he used to say to her. 'Those people mean nothing! It's family that counts.'

'Steve was right,' she whispered to herself. 'He was always right.' She took a steadying breath and listened in to the conversation Vanya was having. It was a funny story about someone's husband who pretended to be Santa Claus. He literally got stuck in the chimney and Tess laughed along with the other mums, relaxing into the fun of the evening. More wine was ordered every twenty minutes or so and Vanya gave Tess a look that said – how much booze can these women drink? She and Tess were the only ones not drinking, and while Tess felt like a party pooper, not only was she driving home, but Rose often woke overnight and had her pacing the floor.

She checked her mobile several times to make sure that everything was okay. Sadie had sent her an emoji-filled text showing books, television, dragons and sleeping babies. She replied with champagne glasses and a smiley face.

It was just after ten when Tess felt the pull of family and home. She was about to say as much to Vanya when Lydia got up from the table, cigarettes and a lighter in her hand, and walked out through the rear of the restaurant. Tess knew this was her moment. Lydia would be softened by wine and a relaxed evening with friends. She hesitated for only a second before following her, and found Lydia standing outside under an awning where there was shelter from the rain, a small heater in the corner to keep the cold at bay. She was wearing brown leather trousers with short stiletto-heeled boots. Her white blouse was topped by what, back in the day, they would have called a tank top. The diamond on her finger was huge. She was sleek and well-groomed but still Tess saw the girl in her and it reminded her again of how close they had once been.

Tess breathed in the smoke. 'Can we talk?' she asked.

Lydia flicked ash to one side but didn't lift her eyes.

'I'd really like us to be friends again,' Tess said. 'I don't understand why you pretend not to know me.' She bit her lip. This wasn't what she'd intended to say. She was supposed to be apologising to Lydia, not accusing her. 'I'm sorry if I did or said anything that offended you. And I'm sorry that I excluded Adam from Bobby's birthday party. I don't know what I was think—' She stopped abruptly, biting her lip again as a memory popped, unbidden, into her mind. She wanted to tell Lydia that while she was waiting for Bobby to change after football, she thought she saw him. *Him.* It was on the tip of her tongue to blurt it out. *I saw someone today, outside the clubhouse. He reminded me of Oscar.* The very sight of him had triggered confusing memories. And the unease was yet to leave her, even though she'd told herself that the man just *looked* like Oscar that's all. And so what? It was nothing.

She pulled several times on her wristband. It helped settle her breathing, reminded her that she was safe. She was in control of what she said. She could focus. She could make sense. 'I tried to contact you when you moved away,' she said loudly. 'But your mum wouldn't give me your address in London.'

At the mention of her mum Lydia met Tess's eyes, a frown line forming between her eyes.

'She told you I'd tried, didn't she?' Tess asked.

Lydia's expression returned to impassive. She stared at a point somewhere beyond her own foot. Her fingers trembled slightly as she flicked more ash into the tall metal ashtray. It was then that Tess realised she was drunk. Even when they were teenagers, Lydia could hide it well. Alcohol seemed to have very little effect on her. Unlike Tess who became braver, louder, larger-than-life, and remembered nothing the next day, Lydia remained upright, attentive, coherent. All that gave her away was the faint tremor in her hand. 'I watched Bobby and Adam playing today,' Tess said. 'I think they could be really good friends.'

Seconds ticked by. Instinct told Tess that she should walk away, that this one-sided conversation was going nowhere, and she should quit while she was ahead. She'd apologised, like she'd planned. And she'd let Lydia know that she'd tried to contact her back then. What else was there to say?

Well … nothing. Except that chic, grown-up Lydia was still the same Lydia, wasn't she? Her teenage self was still inside her, somewhere, just waiting to wake up. This realisation made Tess reach out. She took Lydia's hand. And to her surprise, Lydia allowed it. The power of skin on skin … within seconds, Tess felt memory bloom in her chest. She closed her eyes, automatically relaxing into that distant, yet familiar groove where the world was kinder and smiles were wider. She was transported back to days spent laughing, dancing, lying on Lydia's bed and staring up through the skylight to the starry night beyond, swapping hopes and dreams, doing their home-work together, spying on the teenage boy next door.

They stood like this for what felt like minutes, hands held, a profound stillness between them, before Lydia pulled back, gently, unhurried. She exhaled a full breath before she said, 'I'm not interested in being your friend, Tess.' She paused to widen her eyes. 'I'm asking you nicely to please leave me alone.'

'Why? What have I done?' Tess felt suddenly frantic, as if they were finally getting to the crux of Lydia's pre-tence and she was in danger of letting the truth slip away. 'Tell me! Please, just tell me!'

Lydia was unmoved. She gave a low, slow sigh before saying, 'I was friends with you back then because I felt sorry for you.' Her tone was casual as if it was an ancient truth that had been explained to Tess countless times. She moved past her, adding quietly, 'Stay away from me.'

That was it.

Tess blinked and blinked again, stunned. A tide of embarrassment and shame washed through her, bitter as mud. She stayed where she was, pulling on her wristband, talking herself round before her heartbeat settled and she dared return to the table. When she finally did, her legs were jelly and her gait unsteady. 'Are you okay?' Vanya asked.

Tess shook her head. 'I'll tell you later.' She reached for a napkin and squashed it tightly in the palm of her hand. There was movement at the other end of the table. A few of the mums were getting ready to leave. Thank God. Tess was desperate to get home, to kiss her children and dive under the duvet. 'Could you bring the bill, please?' she asked the ponytailed waiter who was hovering close by.

Vanya retrieved her bag from under the table and passed Tess the envelope from the Taylors. Inside there were ten twenty-pound notes – enough money for food shopping and nappies for at least three weeks. Depending on any extra food Tess could salvage from Airbnb cleans, it might even stretch to four. The tension in her shoulders relaxed a millimetre. She slid the envelope into her pocket and watched Lydia make a show of hugging and kissing each of the mums who were leaving. They agreed to pay her later, and when their cab pulled up, they tipped out onto the pavement and climbed inside. As soon as they were gone, Lydia grew restless. She scanned the room, smiling and chatting to a woman at the next table, and when the waiter returned, she reached for the bill. The mums waited while she used the calculator on her mobile to do the maths.

'Six hundred and eighty-five divided by twelve makes fifty-seven pounds each, give or take,' Lydia said at last. 'Service is included.'

'That's not fair,' Vanya whispered to Tess. 'Our share of the food couldn't have been more than fifteen quid each. Plus two diet cokes and a fizzy water.' She rummaged in her bag and pulled out three tens. 'That's all I've got.'

Tess was in no position to pay over the odds either. 'Is there any way the bill could be shared more fairly?' she called out, tightening her grip on the napkin. 'Most of the cost is wine, and Vanya and I weren't drinking.'

Lydia's eyes flicked towards her. 'Would you like me to recalculate?'

'Yes, I would,' she replied sharply.

One of the mums leant in towards Lydia and said something that made Lydia smile, her eyes lifting from her mobile towards Tess again.

Tess felt her stomach shrink. It was obvious that Lydia knew about her money troubles because people talk. *Poor Tess! In so much debt. Steve didn't have life insurance so they took out loans and remortgaged the house.* They'd needed money to travel to Frankfurt where they were trialling a brand-new treatment for Steve's type of cancer. It gave him a few more weeks but it wasn't a cure, and when he passed away, Tess was left with a mountain of debt, to say nothing of a broken heart. But she didn't regret trying. Not one second of the time they'd clawed back was wasted and she would do it all over again to have him at the centre of their family.

'We've got yours down to twenty-five pounds each,' Lydia said. 'Is that okay?'

Vanya had her money in her hand. She stood up but Tess pulled her back down into her seat. 'Don't,' she said quietly. She raised her voice and addressed Lydia again. 'You know what? It's fine!' The envelope of cash rested comfortably against her leg. Two hundred pounds was a small fortune to her. And every penny of it had been earned. But humiliation was seeping through her like water through a sponge and she was heavy with it. Heavy with months of scrimping and saving, with always being the person everyone felt sorry for. Her self-esteem couldn't plummet any lower and she'd had enough. 'How much did you say it was?'

'Tess!' Vanya hissed. 'I can't afford to pay the full amount.'

She waved Vanya aside. 'I'm paying for you.'

'Twenty-five is your share,' Lydia said. 'You were right to query it. It wasn't fair that you and Vanya should pay so much.'

Moments ago, Lydia had treated her with derision. She'd told her that she'd only been friends with her because she felt sorry for her. And here she was, the epitome of reasonableness because there was an audience. Tess felt a surge of heat begin in the pit of her stomach. It travelled to the tips of her fingers and the ends of her toes. She imagined walking to Lydia's end of the table and slapping her. Hard. Hard enough for her to cry out. Hard enough for an injury that took days to heal so that every time she looked in the mirror she was reminded of what she'd said and how much it hurt.

Instead, she stared at the table and practiced calming herself. The surface was piled high with napkins, empty bottles and glasses. There were wine stains and crumbs, stray cutlery and half-eaten desserts. In her mind's eye, Tess visualised clearing the table, neatening the edges of a fresh tablecloth, aligning clean cutlery on individual place settings. She was so caught up in the vision that she started to act it out. Her hand was on the rim of a plate when Vanya took her arm. 'What are you doing, Tess?'

What *was* she doing? 'I have the money!' She pulled the envelope from her pocket. Her voice was loud and carried, not just the length of the table, but right across the restaurant. Multiple pairs of eyes turned in their direction. 'Never let it be said that I can't pay my way.'

Apart from Vanya, the mums who remained were other prep school mums, more Lydia's new friends than her old ones, but still, she felt their discomfort surround her like a cloak. 'I'm happy to share the bill more fairly,' one of them said, glancing from Lydia to Tess and back again.

'It's only money!' Tess said, her grin forced. She took six of the twenty-pound notes out of the envelope and walked to the other end of the table to lay them in front of Lydia. 'This will cover mine and Vanya's.

She was walking away when she heard Lydia say quietly, 'Still playing the victim?'

Quick as a flash she turned back and grabbed a half full glass of red wine off the table. She threw it hard and fast in Lydia's face. She watched her gasp, startled and then shocked. 'What the—'

'You think you know me but you don't,' Tess said through clenched teeth, leaning in close, her hands on the arms of the chair, pinning Lydia to her seat. 'Don't make a fool of me again.' She watched Lydia's green eyes harden. 'Consider yourself warned,' Tess said and then she walked away, her head high, her heart racing like a train.

The pain was physical. She felt as if she'd been stung by a bee in her belly and now it was on fire.

She drove home in a boiling fury, her mind full of questions. How could Lydia treat her like that? What was wrong with her? *Why was she such a bitch?*

And what was she thinking following her outside? Reaching for her hand? *Was she mad?*

She stopped short at exploring that thought because it wasn't a question she liked to ask herself. Her struggles with mental health after Rose's birth made it feel too close to the truth.

Round and round her thoughts turned as she mulled over what had just happened, moving from anger to shame, embarrassment to disbelief until she felt as if there was no end to it. Her heart surged briefly at the sight of her front door before she remembered that Steve wasn't behind it. And he never would be. The reality of his death was a sucker punch that just kept on giving.

When she went inside, Sadie was half-asleep, surrounded by A level textbooks. The wood burner had long since fizzled out and it was almost as cold inside as out. She was wearing a bobble hat and fingerless gloves. 'How was it?' she asked, pulling herself upright. 'Did you have fun?'

'It was okay.' The memory of Lydia's words – *I was friends with you back then because I felt sorry for you* – flooded her mind like shit in a sewer. 'I'm sorry it's so cold in here.'

'No worries. My mum's the same. It's too expensive to keep the heating on.' She gathered her books into a pile. 'Rose settled into her cot by eight so I got loads of work done. I'm writing an essay for my new psychology module. It's called "how the context of memory shapes us".'

'That sounds interesting,' Tess said, and immediately one of her own memories raised its hand: Lydia and her in the library, reading about the workings of the brain, how the hippocampus shrinks after trauma and memories aren't always stored.

'There's loads to say, so I don't think I'll have any problem making the word count,' Sadie said, going on to explain what the topic entailed. Tess watched her become more and more animated. 'My tutor says it's the perfect topic for me because it'll allow me to draw on personal experience, like when my dad left us and I went off the rails.' She flinched at the memory, then immediately changed the subject. 'When do you need me next?'

Tess lifted her diary from the book shelf and they went through timings for the coming week. She sometimes took Rose to work with her but now that she was sleeping less, she could only do it for short stints or when she was cleaning with Vanya. She relied heavily on her dad but he had taken on carpentry work in Guildford to help make ends meet. Sadie recorded the times on her mobile and Tess saw her to the front door.

'Oh, by the way,' she said as she pulled on her boots. 'There was a man came looking for you.'

Tess's scalp prickled. All this talk of memory had her remembering the Oscar lookalike outside the clubhouse. 'What man? When?' she asked. Her breath caught. 'What did he look like?'

'It was around nine-thirty,' Sadie replied. 'At first I thought you'd been swiping right but then he told me you cleaned his place.' She had an expressive face, her eyebrows moving up and down with her thoughts. 'Although he didn't exactly look like he was someone who had a cleaner.'

Swiping right? *Dating?* 'I'm not …' … *over Steve. Not even close.* She gave a false laugh.

'He didn't seem like your type,' Sadie continued. 'He had tattoos on his knuckles but then Steve had a tattoo, didn't he?'

Steve had a Japanese symbol inked on his shoulder. Good fortune. That's what it said. And no, the irony wasn't lost on her. 'I'm not dating anyone,' she said.

Sadie faltered, shaking her head. 'Sorry, that was rude. My mum's always on the hunt. I know it's not the same for you because my parents are divorced and— Sorry!' She hugged Tess. 'I need to say less and listen more! That's what my mum's always telling me.'

'Did he give you his name?' Her tone was sharp. 'Was it Oscar?' It felt dangerous saying his name out loud and her stomach lurched at the sound.

'Who's Oscar?' Sadie waited for an answer. She watched as Tess tried to form a reply, her lips moving but no sounds coming out. 'Sorry, I didn't ask him his name.' She touched Tess's arm. 'Are you okay? You don't need to worry. He says he'll catch up with you tomorrow.'

At the very least Tess should have asked her again what he looked like but her tongue couldn't make the right shapes because her mind was stuck on that one phrase. *A man came looking for you.* She watched as Sadie crossed the grass to her house next door, used her key and went inside. Then Tess immediately locked the door. She pushed the handle up and down several times to make sure that it was actually locked. She couldn't secure the chain just yet because her dad wasn't home but she checked the back door and the locks on the windows downstairs. *In case the man comes back.* Because he would, wouldn't he? And the very thought made her want to retch. She held a hand over her mouth until the feeling receded then she texted her dad to ask him when she should expect him home?

'I'm about fifteen minutes away,' was his reply.

She climbed the stairs slowly, twice looking behind her as if she was expecting to see Oscar standing there. *You're making it worse,* she told herself. *It's what you do. You know that. The man could be anybody! Maybe he is a client.*

She checked on Bobby, pulling his duvet up over his shoulders, then stared down at Rose who was lying on her back, wearing a pink, furry sleepsuit that she'd found in a charity shop. Tess immediately felt her sore heart ease a little. The very sight of her children was a tonic, a beacon of hope, a signifier of better times ahead. Tess touched Rose's forehead to make sure she was warm enough – she was. She seemed to emanate heat from her own internal radiator.

She undressed quickly, cold air freezing her exposed skin before she pulled on her pyjamas and dived under the duvet. She shivered for a minute or more before the bed warmed up.

Steve was her electric blanket. Steve was her fun and her security.

Steve was.

She didn't close her eyes at once. There was too much on her mind, the strands of her worries tangling in her head like ribbons around a maypole. Her lack of money, the need to grow her business, how to raise her children without a dad. And now there was Lydia's meanness towards her and this mystery man. Mystery made it sound like someone exciting. *But what if it was Oscar?* He had never been exciting. He'd often appeared by Lydia and Tess's side when they were walking home from school. He'd be in the shop when they were buying an ice cream. Once, he was in Brighton when they'd gone to lie on the beach for the day. Lydia had never let him get away with following them. She'd challenged him every time and he'd pull his cap low over his face and slither off into the shadows.

Tess climbed out of bed and walked the floor, her hand on her abdomen, using breathing techniques to calm herself. If it *was* him then it made a warped sort of sense that he was back in the village again. He could have returned here because of Lydia. Even though Lydia had hated him, warned Tess away from him, refused to have anything to do with him. Could he be nicer now? It seemed unlikely but then so many unlikely things happened every day.

Her teeth began to chatter and she dived into bed again, burrowing deep under the covers. When she heard her dad's key in the lock and his footsteps on the stairs, she closed her eyes and tried to sleep but found no comfort there.

1993

When they were fifteen, they went through a phase of smoking dope. It didn't last long, neither of them could afford to buy it and it was difficult to do it without their parents finding out. There was no room at Tess's house and as Lydia said, 'My dad has a nose for it.' But one early autumn afternoon when her parents were out, they lay on a blanket on the grass at the bottom of her back garden, and Lydia rolled a joint.

'Miss Richards was going on about uni again and I want to study English but my mum will go nuts.' Tess was staring up at the cloudless sky. The deep blue haze was cut through with vapour trails. It looked as if someone had taken a knife to a plump cushion and soft stuffing was leaking through from the other side. 'She says I have to study something that leads directly to a job.'

'Like what?'

'Medicine or law and I don't fancy either.'

'What does Gary say?'

'Gary can't think for himself.'

'Just go!' Lydia laughed, shaking her head at Tess. 'I mean, what can she do? You'll be eighteen!'

Tess couldn't imagine falling out with her mum. What if she threw her out and then she had nowhere to live?

Ever since she was turfed out of her bedroom to make way for Saskia, she'd worried about being pushed one step further until she had to live under the stairs or in the garage. Another step and she'd be homeless. 'I'm not brave like you, Lydia,' she said.

Lydia gave a short laugh. 'You think I'm brave?'

'Yes!'

'I don't feel it.' She took a huge breath before saying quickly, 'My dad's got cancer and I'm crapping myself.'

'What?' Tess catapulted up into a sitting position. 'Oh my God. Are you sure? What the fuck?'

'I know, it's shit.' She stared down at the joint, her hand shaking as she rolled it. 'He was diagnosed a few months ago but I haven't said anything because …' She visibly deflated, her back rounding as she grew smaller. '… I was hoping it wasn't really true.'

'He'll get cured though!' Tess gave her a sideways hug, her arms tight around her waist. 'I know he will!' Tears trickled onto her cheeks and she wiped them away with the back of her hand. 'He will, Lydia, because he's not the sort of person who dies.'

'He better not die.' She stared at Tess defiantly. 'He's having chemo and it's making him sick but it should be worth it. And my aunt knows about alternative medicine, so he's going to this clinic for herbs and stuff. He only eats biodynamic vegetables.'

'Biodynamic?'

She shrugged her shoulders. 'Planted with the phases of the moon or some such mumbo jumbo.'

'Well, shit, Lydia. If it works.'

'Sure.' The joint was rolled and Lydia lit one end before sucking on the other, drawing smoke deep into her lungs. She passed it to Tess, and they lay side by side holding hands, faces turned upwards, the joint moving between them. Within seconds the drug was coiling through Tess and she felt altered, relaxed, dizzy and sweet. The vapour trails began to swell and shift. She held up her hands to look through her fingers and the sky changed again. The blue was deeper, bolder. She reached out further, sure that she would be able to touch it.

'He's so exhausted. He can barely walk across the room,' Lydia said in a quiet voice. She turned onto her side to face Tess. 'I make the vegetable juices for him. Genevieve won't help.'

'Why not?' Their eyes were level. The green in Lydia's irises was luminous. Tess felt as if she could see into her very soul.

'She doesn't believe in the juices. She's basically a bitch.' Lydia gave a tired sigh. 'If I was my dad, I'd have left her years ago.'

Tess raised herself up onto one arm. 'Compared with Deirdre, Genevieve is perfect. And anyway, your dad loves her.'

'She's emasculated him. She's probably got his balls in a jar under the bed.'

They started to giggle. It was irresistible. Lydia's irreverence was always so refreshing. She gave Tess a shove. 'Hey! It's not funny, you know! My dad's a eunuch!' Tess shoved her back and then they were wrestling until her hair was tangled up in her watch strap and they'd rolled off the blanket.

They fell apart and gazed back at the sky, catching their breath. Tess's hair was spread over Lydia's face and Lydia blew it upwards until it slid down onto her neck. Then she squinted at Tess sideways, one eye shut. 'So how's it going with Steve?'

'It's not.'

'And would you like it to?'

'I suppose. Maybe. I dunno.' She sighed. 'We almost had a kiss and that was …' *Perfect.* She tried to laugh it off like it was nothing, but she felt suddenly melancholy because she had a feeling Steve was going out with the-perfection-that-was-Elizabeth and then there was really no hope for her. 'I like him. That's it really.' That wasn't it. In actual fact, Tess lusted after, longed for, ached for Steve, the boy next door. She was waiting for him to be struck by a thunderbolt of realisation, sweep her off her feet and be in love with her until the end of time.

'You need to aim higher than Steve,' Lydia told her. 'He'll be good to practise on, though.'

Tess pushed a cushion into Lydia's face and they laughed again, like laughing was everything and even later when the night air cooled and Tess headed home, she kept erupting like a mad person. She thought about the way Lydia helped her forget that she didn't fit in at home. She thought about the way that Lydia was afraid of nothing – until now. The fact her dad had cancer was awful, but Tess was sure he wouldn't die, because he couldn't die. He was too important to her. Fate could never be so cruel.

She was still a few streets away from home when an uneasy feeling started to grow in her stomach. She glanced behind her and saw a man about ten metres away. He had a cap pulled down over his eyes and his hands in his pockets. Tess quickened her pace but when she glanced back he was doing the same. *Fuck.* Her heart lurched and she broke into a run. She had long legs and could run like an athlete, arms and legs working together. By the time she turned into her street there was no one behind her, and her focus on the man slipped when she caught sight of Steve. He was standing outside having a smoke. 'All right?'

'Sure. You?' She stopped in front of him, breathing hard, and shook her hair out from under her hat.

'You been running?'

She shrugged. 'I got a bit spooked.'

'Gary's back.'

'Is he?' He'd been on one of his benders. 'That'll keep my mother happy then,' she said. Steve was moving from one foot to the other and she wondered how long he'd been outside.

'Where have you been?' he asked.

She shrugged. 'Nowhere.'

He threw the cigarette butt down into the gutter. 'A whole day in nowhere, huh?'

'Yup.'

'So what's his name?'

'Nice try, Steve.' She walked up the path to her house and looked back at him. 'See ya.'

Maybe she had a chance with him after all.

Lydia

The house was quiet when I arrived home from the restaurant. I went immediately into the downstairs bathroom and stripped off. The underfloor heating was on and it warmed the soles of my feet, a luxury I was really beginning to appreciate. No draughty windows or doors in this house. I held my blouse and tank top out in front of me. Red wine stains were splodged across both, and the tangy aroma of wine permeated the air. Tess had thrown a glass of red at me, in full view of the whole restaurant. I understood that she was pissed off, probably hurt, because I'd refused to be her friend, but her reaction was way over the top. I filled the sink with lukewarm water and attempted to shift the stains with a bar of soap but they wouldn't budge. The blouse was silk and the tank top cashmere, delicate materials that wouldn't withstand scrubbing by hand or a high temperature wash. I decided to leave the job for the morning.

I removed the clip from my hair. There were sticky, wine-soaked clumps on one side of my head. I stood under the shower for several minutes washing myself clean, enjoying the rush of hot, steaming water rinsing every part of me. I finished with thirty seconds of ice-cold water that made my skin sing and my heart race.

I climbed the stairs, towel-drying my hair as I walked. The bedroom carpet was a deep pile that absorbed all sound. I crept quietly towards the bed and peered down at Zack. He was fast asleep. I stood over him for a minute or two, hoping he might sense that he was being watched. My head was pleasantly fuzzy from booze. My body was awake. Sex right now would be perfect. I kissed his cheek and nudged his shoulder but short of me shouting in his ear he wasn't about to wake up. He always slept well but even more so now that his mum's cancer was taking a backseat. His sister was due to arrive the following week and then she would take Paula to Cornwall for a month. Zack had arranged for us to join them in St Ives for Christmas. We were all keeping our fingers crossed that Paula would be well enough to enjoy herself.

I went back downstairs and poured myself a drink, then sat in the shadows with the heavy tumbler in my hand, whisky and ice swirling in the glass. I stared out into the garden, which was almost pitch-black, a cloud-covered moon casting a meagre light across the frosty grass. I could hear the proverbial pin drop here and it made me ache for my London life: the vibrancy of a busy street, friends popping in, shopping for each other, impromptu get togethers. Even in the middle of the night there was always a light on, whether it was a young mum up for a 3 a.m. feed or an elderly neighbour with insomnia. We were a community, and I missed the freedom to be relaxed, to be completely myself.

Tess. What should I do about her? She wasn't even drinking and yet she was angry enough to throw wine in my face. I had never seen her behave that way before but then I'd never known her as a woman. So far, I had successfully kept her at arm's length, but it had been obvious well before tonight that she wanted to talk to me.

I'd caught her watching me on multiple occasions. Her doe eyes and needy body language irritated me. As well as Bobby, she had a baby girl to care for – I tried not to be jealous about that; I would have loved to have had more children – and there was significant debt, so I heard.

Bottom line, Tess was part of the 'before' and I wouldn't allow her to be part of the 'after'. There was too much at stake. For her as well as me. And, after tonight, she would surely drop this insistence that we had to be friends.

There had been a moment a few weeks ago when I had almost relented. I was sitting on a bench close to my dad's grave. It was one of my favourite spots to sit and think. I couldn't be seen from the church, nor from the path that led to the front door, but I could hear the hymns and prayers. I was humming along to 'The Lord is my Shepherd' when I noticed Tess approach a grave to the far left of the churchyard. Her expression was completely hollow, as if all of life's vitality had been scooped out of her and she was now simply a shell. She stood in front of the grave, which I later checked belonged to *Steven Jeffries. Beloved husband to Tess, and devoted father to Bobby. Sorely missed.* My heart softened as I watched her rearrange a vase of flowers, quietly weeping into the blooms. And for the briefest moment I wanted to run across and hug her, tell her that all was well between us. We could be friends again! And everything could be like it was before.

Except that was impossible.

Because we weren't children any more. And what was done could never be undone.

Tess

Next morning, Tess was woken just before six by Rose's hungry cries. When she sat up, she winced in pain. She had the mother of all headaches. Tension enveloped her skull like a too-tight swim cap. Her sleep had consisted of one nightmare after another: vampires, axe murderers, wolves, Lydia's sneering face, a man with tattooed knuckles – they'd all visited her in her dreams. She managed to swallow a couple of painkillers before lifting Rose from her cot and taking her downstairs. She gave her the first bottle of the day and her daughter sucked on the teat with a gusto that made Tess smile. Ten weeks old, she had added four pounds to her birth weight. 'Chunky monkey,' she whispered to her and Rose blinked her contentment, her lashes long and luxurious.

After Tess had winded her, she settled her into her bouncy chair – her favourite spot – to watch the apple tree's bare-branch silhouette against the sky. And then, before Tess had the chance to dwell on what had happened the previous evening, her dad joined them. He was showered and dressed and smelled of aftershave. 'Coffee?' he asked.

'Yes, please.'

'How's my little Rose this morning?' While the kettle boiled, he came across to smile down at his granddaughter. And Rose smiled back, her eyes lighting up, legs kicking as if she was ready to get up and dance. 'And how was your evening?' he asked Tess, his hand resting briefly on her shoulder.

'It was okay.' She smiled quickly. 'How's the build going?'

'It's going well. I hung all the doors yesterday.' He reached into the cupboard for two mugs. 'Next stop, the built-in shelves around the fireplace.'

Her dad had retired several years ago from his job as a carpenter but when Steve became ill, he started picking up work whenever he could. He'd drawn down most of his pension pot to help Tess with Steve's medical bills when they went to Frankfurt for what they hoped was a cure. And he paid all the household bills. She couldn't be more grateful. When she was growing up, she hadn't seen a lot of him. She'd thought that he didn't contribute financially but in fact he paid a substantial amount of child support to Tess's mother. She hadn't known that at the time. She'd thought her dad just didn't love her any more, had moved on and forgotten about her.

He sat down opposite her with their coffees and a bowl of muesli. 'Is Sadie helping you out this morning?'

Tess's heart sank. She knew at once that she'd got her days mixed up. She leant in close to read the entry on the calendar – 'Dad working. Arrange for Sadie.' – scrawled in writing that was practically illegible. 'I've screwed up.' She heard the tightness in her tone. 'I'm supposed to be visiting a new client to give her a quote.'

'Could you go tomorrow instead?' her dad asked, chewing on a mouthful of muesli. 'I shouldn't be needed at the site tomorrow. I can look after Rose.'

'I'll do that. Thank you.' One day she'd be organised. She'd stop forgetting things and have a clear head. She moved to the bottom of the stairs and called up, 'Bobby! Breakfast.'

He appeared within minutes, fully dressed and ready for school. He had his dad's hair – thick and curly – and she wet combed it into submission while he ate his cereal and told them about a goal-scoring moment that he'd missed the day before. 'I'll know the next time to pass to Adam and then if he passes back to me, I'll have my right foot ready.'

'It's all a learning experience,' Tess's dad said. 'The important thing is to keep improving.'

When breakfast was eaten and teeth cleaned, her dad walked Bobby to school. That had become their routine since he came to live with them because he enjoyed a morning walk and it saved Tess bundling Rose into her buggy.

She changed Rose's nappy and dressed her in several layers: a long-sleeved bodysuit, a designer woollen tracksuit gifted by one of her clients and a pale green cashmere waistcoat with matching hat and bootees that Vanya had knitted. The hat had pointed ears, like a woodland elf. The bootees were decorated with a trio of red and white toadstools embroidered on the toes. Rose was the definition of cute. She took a photo and texted it to Vanya.

She'd blocked the draught around the window with some strong tape but she checked it again, climbing onto a chair to reach the top. She couldn't feel any air coming in, and took the opportunity to reattach one of the curtain hooks before her attention was caught by a squirrel running along the fence at the bottom of the garden. The garden was several metres long, laid mostly to grass with Bobby's mini goalpost in front of the fence. Behind the fence there was an alleyway, a cut-through between the rows of houses. The fence was higher than head height apart from one small section where the previous owner's children used to scramble over when they couldn't be bothered going round to the front of the house. A chunk of wood had broken off the top. It was a perfect spot for someone to stand in the alleyway and spy on them. *So that's where he'll stand,* Tess thought. *He'll scope out his surroundings exactly like he did before. He'll be bold about it. And he won't stop until he gets what he wants.*

'Stop it!' she told herself. The man who was watching her when she was outside the clubhouse and the one who came to the door when Sadie was babysitting were *not* necessarily the same person. She was putting two and two together and making twenty-two. The man from last night could have knocked on the wrong door. It happened occasionally. They lived in Church Close but sometimes had deliveries or visitors for Church Lane, and vice versa. The streets ran parallel and were easy to mix up. It was a common mistake. And anyway, Oscar didn't have tattoos on his knuckles. Not when Tess knew him. *But that was more thirty years ago, plenty of time for him to visit a tattoo parlour.*

She squinted as she tried to remember whether the man outside the clubhouse had tattoos. She remembered him lifting the cigarette to his lips but he was too far away for her to see his hands clearly. It was the look on his face that sparked a long-ago memory – that determined, con-centrated stare. *I want you.* A creepy, knowing look that, as a teenager, she found disgusting. Although strangely, back then, she wasn't afraid of him. He was an irritant, a misfit, a joke, and when he was out of sight he was out of mind. It was only as a woman that she looked back and felt afraid for her teenage self.

Tess rearranged her meeting with the new client then collected the house keys for her next clean from the cupboard under the stairs. There were forty hooks on a board that Steve had made when she'd started the company. At that point she had five clients and no one else working for her. 'You'll be up to forty clients in no time,' he'd said to her. By the time of his death, she'd reached thirty-six, most of them weekly cleans, a few of them twice weekly. Lydia's keys were on the board, reminding Tess that at some point she was going to have to think about what happened in the restaurant, but not yet.

She fixed Rose into her car seat and climbed into the driver's seat. So many of Steve's possessions were still inside the car. In the glove compartment was the last novel he'd been reading, a packet of chewing gum and his sunglasses. His jacket was still in the boot, his water bottle in the holder, and having these reminders strengthened rather than weakened her. They kept Steve present in her life. No doubt that was something else that would make Lydia sneer but she didn't care.

Before she drove off, she checked her emails. Several had attention-grabbing titles, capital letters and a red font – two dodgy companies with sky-high interest rates she owed money to. There was no point in reading them but she had to do something so she moved a few pounds from her bank account – a pittance, but it might placate them. Robbing Peter to pay Paul; nothing was solved. But nothing was ever going to be solved. She was waiting to hear from a friend of Steve's who had promised to help her but she didn't hold out much hope. She'd either win the lottery or have her house repossessed and she knew which one was more likely. Her legs went weak at the thought of what they would do. She broke out into a cold sweat just thinking about how she'd cover the mortgage and loan payments that month. And how could she tell her dad that despite all the help he'd given her she'd still managed to deepen the debt?

The work was out there for the taking but she needed to find reliable staff, which as any small business owner would tell you, was easier said than done. Most people didn't see cleaning as a career. It was considered to be low-skilled, poorly paid and non-aspirational. Tess didn't see it that way. Cleaning was therapeutic for her. She could listen to audiobooks, practice another language, catch up with podcasts that informed her or made her laugh. She could lose herself in the repetitive nature of the task and get her daily exercise without anyone breathing down her neck.

Her first job was about fifteen minutes away and took her past the private school Adam attended. It was already well after nine o'clock and she was surprised to see Lydia's four-by-four stopped on the yellow zigzag lines outside the school gates. Traffic was coming towards her and there was no room to pass so she waited. At first Lydia didn't notice her. She was busy making sure Adam had everything he needed. The guitar case came out of the boot then went back in again when he shook his head. Tess glanced in her rear-view mirror. Traffic was building up. The driver directly behind her was tapping his steering wheel impatiently but Lydia and Adam weren't finished. Next it was the games kit. Lydia rummaged through Adam's sports bag to make sure everything was in there. Adam took some of the clothes from his mum's hand, holding them up against himself. More conversation … the games kit looked like it might have shrunk. Either that, or Adam had had a growth spurt.

Finally, he ran off into the school grounds and Lydia glanced up. She mouthed 'sorry', then recognised Tess and her expression flattened. Tess watched her stumble as she climbed back into the car and drove off.

Tess met Vanya at one of the seven-bedroomed houses on the edge of the forest. For the last year it had been let out as an Airbnb, which hadn't pleased the neighbours. Some tenants were as quiet as mice. They came and went with the minimum of fuss. They left the house spotless. They stripped the beds and filled the dishwasher. They tidied up the garden furniture and admitted to any broken crockery. Others took the opportunity to forget their manners. They rampaged. They moved furniture and stole towels. They had noisy parties that spilled into the garden and wrecked the ambience.

Tess never quite knew what they would find.

'I expect it will be a mess inside,' Vanya said when she pulled up beside her. She was standing on the gravel driveway taking her cleaning products out of her car. 'Look over there.'

She pointed to two of the stone flowerpots which normally stood on plinths, but had been knocked over, probably by a reversing car. Earth and flowers spread across the gravel. 'The gardener will sort that out,' Tess said. She lifted Rose out of the car, still in her seat, and Vanya immediately reached for her.

'So who's the cutest baby?' she cooed. Rose's eyes opened wide and her gummy grin was heartfelt. 'Who looks like a forest princess in her smart little outfit?' Vanya continued, and Rose cooed a response.

Tess left them to their mutual love and unlocked the front door. She spent the first ten minutes walking from room to room taking photographs of breakages, discarded pizza boxes, their contents spilling onto a beige carpet, and damage to the fixtures and fittings. In one of the bedrooms, the wardrobe door had been punched in. In another, the window blind had been pulled from the wall. Tess immediately forwarded the photos to the management company so that they could withhold the deposit.

When she was finished, she found Vanya and Rose in the master bedroom. Rose had a rattle grasped in her tiny fist, but already her eyelids were growing heavy. Vanya was wearing compostable, disposable gloves, elbows pulled in, hands pointing upwards as if she was a surgeon who was about to operate. 'The demon drink,' she said, indicating three champagne bottles lying in the corner of the room.

'They've certainly had their fun,' Tess said.

'How are you doing?' Vanya asked, taking a moment to really look at her friend. 'After last night?'

'Fine.' Tess thought about telling her about the tattooed man but she knew what Vanya would say. *I see weird guys on street corners all the time! And you know your address gets mixed up with the Lane.* And she'd be right but Tess still couldn't shift the nagging feeling that Oscar was back. 'Bit of a headache …' She shrugged.

'Have you been in touch with Lydia?'

'Why would I be?'

'Well … the wine?'

'No, but I saw her just now.' Tess hadn't forgotten about throwing wine in Lydia's face but she had yet to properly turn it over in her mind. 'She was dropping Adam off at school.'

'A bit late, isn't it?' Vanya started stripping the bed. It was a superking with a deep, heavy mattress. 'They must have overslept.'

'Or maybe she took Adam to an appointment first thing.' Tess went to the other side of the bed and lifted up the mattress to pull off the sheet. Now that Vanya had mentioned last night, unease was creeping in at the edges of her mind. 'I do feel guilty about throwing the wine at her,' she said. But Lydia had provoked her – *'still playing the victim'*, that's what she'd said, and it was what finally made Tess snap. 'Should I call her, do you think?'

'Might be a good idea.' Vanya was rolling the dirty sheets into a huge ball. 'She'll never get the wine out of her clothes. The blouse looked like silk and I bet the sleeveless jumper was cashmere.'

Tess gathered the towels from the en suite bathroom and dumped them in a pile in the hallway. 'I should offer to pay to replace them.' *With what? Beans?* Her only currency was elbow grease. 'I know what I could do,' she felt momentarily hopeful, 'I could offer her a week's free clean.'

'And the rest,' Vanya said. 'Those two items must have cost a couple of hundred quid, minimum.'

Tess found another towel halfway under the bed and added it to the pile, pausing for a second to blink against the smarting in her eyes.

'So what did you talk about when you were outside with her?' Vanya asked.

'Nothing really.' She couldn't tell Vanya what Lydia said to her because it was hurtful. Saying it out loud would likely make her blub for a good half hour. She had neither the time nor the energy.

'I think she's an alcoholic,' Vanya said bluntly. 'She drank an absolute bucketload. Did you notice? And it's not the first time she's done that on a night out.'

Tess didn't reply. Lydia had said she had only been friends with her because she felt sorry for her. *How was that possible?* It upended all of her memories from that time. Upended them and scattered them to the four winds.

'I want you to take the money you paid for my meal off my next wage,' Vanya said.

'I'm not—'

'I *mean* it,' she said, vigorously shaking the duvet cover. 'I'll stop working for you if you don't.'

'Well, there's a threat!' Tess gave her a weak smile. 'Will you stop being my friend too?'

'Deduct the money from my wages or I won't be happy.' She gave Tess a look that brooked no further argument then went into the en suite. 'Leave all the bathrooms for me. I'm in the mood for shining up tiles.'

'Sure.' Tess lifted up the huge armful of laundry and headed back downstairs. When she'd filled both the American-style washing machines, she went to her car to fetch her cleaning kit. She mixed the products herself using everyday ingredients: vinegar, sodium bicarbonate and lemon juice. It was eco-friendly science that had been understood for centuries and she felt the wisdom of generations of women give power to her elbow.

The next set of tenants were due to check in early afternoon so they had four hours to bring the house back to pristine. Tess was a great believer in doing the worst jobs first. She started on the oven. She was lucky; they obviously hadn't spent time cooking. Apart from some baked-on pizza spillages, there wasn't much scrubbing to do. She worked methodically around the kitchen and then the dining room. The time flew by. They continued through lunch, only stopping to feed and change Rose.

The final job was always emptying and cleaning the fridge. Usually they threw most of the leftovers into the bin. They had a rule not to keep anything that was already open unless they were sure it hadn't been handled or spat on. Tess lined up the spoils at the back door: unopened packets of snacks and breakfast cereal, coffee and tea-bags, fresh berries and a large pot of yoghurt. Before they left, they shared it between them and said their goodbyes. A quick return home before pick-up time.

Bobby's class was waiting in the playground. The last year had been tough on them but Bobby had fared as well as Tess could have hoped. He was a straightforward little boy who had been able to accept his dad's absence. Every now and then he cried, especially when other children had their dads cheering them on at football matches, but mostly he was philosophical. 'It wasn't Dad's fault he died and wherever he is he still loves me.'

When he spotted his mum, he ran towards her kicking a football ahead of him. 'Can we go to McDonald's on the way home?'

'Not today.' She managed to catch him in a hug for all of two seconds. 'But I've got packets of nuts and cereal bars, and some of those crisps you and Grandad like.'

'The posh crisps with the funny flavours?'

'That's right.'

He told her about school and the project they'd just started with Mrs Frost – frost by name but not by nature. She was a warm and imaginative teacher who had got Bobby hooked on reading and interested in all sorts of subjects that were broadening his mind.

They were almost home when Vanya called. 'Tess, I'm really sorry. I'm sure this is the last thing you need but Mum's been admitted to hospital and I was supposed to pick up Adam for a playdate. I can keep Maisie with me, but I won't make it to collect Adam. I've tried Lydia's phone but she's not answering. And neither is anyone else I've tried and – yes, I'm just coming, thank you.' The last few words said to someone else, in a high-pitched tone which Tess knew meant that Vanya was stressed. 'Would you mind?'

'Of course not. I'll collect Adam,' Tess said, making it sound perfectly normal. Lydia would most likely be angry. But meeting again today might be just what they needed. Tess could apologise in person for throwing the wine at her and ruining her clothes. She wouldn't mention their past friendship. She would be strictly unemotional. She would make amends by offering free cleaning services.

'Thank you so much,' Vanya said. 'I'll call the school to let them know you're coming instead.'

They stopped at Adam's school and waited forty minutes until his pick-up time. Rose had nodded off again and Bobby climbed into the front seat where Tess read out the questions for his maths homework. He'd lost his way with his lessons soon after Steve died but had quickly caught up again and was going through an easy phase. 'It's nice here, isn't it?' he said, staring across the stretch of playing fields that adjoined the prep school buildings. 'They have a climbing wall in their gym. Adam told me. And *four* football pitches.' He turned to her, bright-eyed. 'Could I go to school here?'

Tess hesitated, knowing the truth could hurt, before saying, 'I'm sorry, darling, but we can't afford it.'

'You have to pay?'

'You do, and it's very expensive. It costs more money for one child than I earn in a year.'

'Adam's parents must earn a lot!' He looked wistful for a few seconds then immediately rallied. 'Well, I like Mrs Frost so it's actually fine and I wouldn't want to stay here until *five* every day. Even though it's got all the facilities and stuff.'

'That's my boy.' Tess kissed the top of his head, and when they saw Adam coming out of his classroom, Bobby climbed into the back again.

Adam was pleased to see them. 'Thank you for coming for me,' he said, sitting next to Bobby. 'My teacher said that Vanya couldn't make it and I was worried.'

'No need to worry,' Tess told him, watching both boys through the rear-view mirror.

'We can practice our shots in the garden,' Bobby said. He looked slightly in awe of Adam who was wearing a formal blazer and striped tie. 'You could borrow some of my clothes, if you like.'

'It's okay. I've got home clothes, and I've remembered my boots.' He held up his sports bag and smiled. He had Lydia's eyes and for some reason that made Tess feel sad. 'Were you out with my mum last night?' he asked her.

'I was! We went to the Italian restaurant next to the bookshop.'

'She had a really sore head this morning. She had to have two tablets and then she was almost sick.'

Tess didn't comment. She started the engine and drove them home, letting the boys chat without interruption. They talked about football and more football, listened and laughed with one another and then entertained Rose when she woke up.

When they arrived home, Adam helped carry Rose's car seat inside and Bobby showed him her favourite game. He tied a red ribbon that was attached to balloons round each of her ankles. Every time she kicked her feet, the balloons flew up into the air. She was transfixed by the colours, and the more she kicked, the more the balloons bounced in front of her.

'Look how much she loves it!' Adam said, his expression animated. 'That's really clever!'

'She's a really cool sister,' Bobby said, smiling at Tess.

After a quick snack, the boys went outside to play and Tess stood at the window watching them, her eye continually drawn to the gap in the fence where she imagined being spied on by Oscar. It would happen. She felt it in her gut. When Lydia came to collect Adam, she could ask her whether she had seen him, whether he was back in the village. Lydia would know.

1994

'One of us had to get a boyfriend first,' Lydia said to Tess. 'And now that you're going out with Steve …?'

She left the rest of the sentence hanging in the air for Tess to catch hold of. Tess wasn't going out with Steve but she wasn't *not* going out with Steve. They were on the cusp. She had been alone with him the week before when they drank beer together behind the function room his parents had hired for their twentieth wedding anniversary. It turned out he wasn't interested in Elizabeth. It turned out it was Tess he liked. 'I think we should go out,' he'd said, and she made a silly comment along the lines of 'you'll need to ask me first', and then his brother Josh appeared on his skateboard triggering the outside lights and ruining the moment.

A week later and she was trying again. She rang the doorbell and held herself firmly on the step. She wanted to run. She wanted to stay. She wanted to be a lot more confident than she was.

'Come in, Tess!' Angie, Steve's mum, called out. She was on the phone, in the downstairs loo by the sound of it. Either she had ESP or that was Tess's mother she was talking to. One day she'd actually have her own life. 'He's in the kitchen.'

She walked past Josh who was on his Sega MegaDrive, clutching the controller and swerving from side to side in time with the car on the screen. Steve was looking in the fridge, whistling along to a tune on the radio. He turned when she came in. No 'hello', just kept on whistling.

'Steve?'

The fridge was interesting. First the cottage cheese, then the ham, then a jar of pickles, then he put that down too and grabbed a can of Coke.

'I was wondering if you could help me with some algebra.'

He glanced across at her in a challenging way like they were about to draw guns.

'Steve?' He kept whistling and she considered thrusting out her hips a little or dropping her book so that she could bend down at his feet and he could look down her top.

Christ.

'Tess needs your help, Steve,' his mum called. She popped her head around the door. 'With some maths, isn't that right, Tess?' She was in the middle of highlighting her hair. She had a cap on with bits of hair poking through the holes. She looked like an extra from *Star Trek*. Her head slid away out of view and Steve kept on whistling.

Tess opened the book and pointed to the algebra. 'So maybe if you could just help me with this equation?'

He carried on whistling.

She'd reached her humiliation limit. A huge lump blocked her throat. She wished she could flounce from the room but she didn't do flouncing. She did do huffing and puffing though. 'Never let it be said that I didn't try.' She pointed an angry finger his way. 'And never let it be said that I held a grudge.' She stared at him meaningfully although there was no meaning to be had because there was no reason to hold a grudge. And then she moved one of the kitchen chairs to give her a straight way out. 'And never let it be said—'

'For fuck's sake!' He threw a playful punch into her shoulder. 'Give it here, then.' She passed him the book. 'Can't have you struggling now, can we?' he said in mock teacherly tones. He looked at the page. 'I did this last week. Got the answers in my room. Coming?'

She hesitated. It was what she wanted but maybe …

'We won't sit on the bed,' he said, reading her mind.

She blushed and followed him, sidestepping his mum who was hovering at the bottom of the stairs. 'Maths only, now!' she called after them. 'No hanky-panky!'

If there was such a thing as death by embarrassment she would have died by now. She thought about how she would describe all of this to Lydia. 'He completely ignored me! I had to practically beg! And then his mum said no hanky-panky!'

She was already looking forward to making Lydia laugh.

Steve's bedroom was a mess. In this respect their mothers differed – she'd be lynched for less. There was a huge mound of books and folders in one corner. He handed her his Coke then pulled at the pile so that it spilled over his feet. He scrabbled about, pushing papers aside until he found his maths book. 'I hear your friend's making waves again,' he said.

Lydia had been insisting for months that the school should encourage them to have a wider range of influences. Miss Humble had finally agreed to hold a forum on the topic and Lydia planned to talk about the value of inviting in speakers for the day. There was a tendency for the school to revere women who were already dead: Marie Curie, Florence Nightingale, Amelia Earhart. Lydia was pushing for women who were alive. There was a woman in Brighton who ran a hostel for the homeless, another one in Croydon who raised funds for creative projects.

Tess frowned at Steve. 'Where did you hear about it?'

'Elizabeth told me.'

'Elizabeth?'

'I saw her yesterday.'

She pulled back. Her skin was bumping up as if she'd just fallen in a patch of stinging nettles. 'Elizabeth?' She didn't want to believe it. 'How come?'

'How come what?' he said, Mr Nonchalant.

'How come you met Elizabeth?' She enunciated each word like he was learning to lip-read.

'We went to the cinema.'

Her eyes smarted. She put the can down on his desk and turned to leave.

'Hang on!' He beat her to the door and stood in front of it. 'Not just me and her! A whole group of us were there. Like I said the other night, she's nice and everything, but you're much more my type than she is.' He leant back against the door and stared down into her face. 'Tess Carter, will you please go out with me?'

'Yes, Steve Jeffries,' she answered immediately, her smile wide. 'Of course I will.'

His smile was even wider. 'You don't really need help with algebra, do you?'

'No, I don't. I get higher grades than you.' She looked up through her eyelashes. 'Just saying.'

He pulled her in for a kiss. It was the best moment of her life.

She was walking on air. Lydia had called her earlier to say they should meet at the hardware shop and she floated there, smiling inside and out. She felt as if she might explode with happiness. She had arranged to meet Steve the next day. They'd spend their Sunday in Brighton. They could walk along the pier. They could eat fish and chips on the sea wall. It was going to be amazing.

Tess spotted Lydia first. She was standing outside the shop, a white carrier bag held low and banging against her leg. 'Lydia!' She waved like a five-year-old, and when she was close enough for Lydia to hear, she blurted out, 'Steve and I kissed!' She twirled round on one foot. 'We're going to Brighton tomorrow.'

'Wow!' Lydia gave her a hug. 'Go, girl!'

'Is it okay?' Occasionally Tess remembered that everything wasn't about her. 'I know we were going to hang out?'

'Of course!' Lydia grabbed her hand and pulled her into the mini supermarket. 'Let's get an ice cream.'

'Steve has loads of friends, and I could—'

'No, fuck no! I need to focus on my dad. There will be plenty of time for boys.' She made a face. 'I sound like Miss Humble.'

They chose their ice creams and went to the till where Lydia insisted on paying for them. When they were leaving the shop, she stopped suddenly, her arm shooting out across Tess's middle to hold her back. 'Wait here,' she said, her tone low and flat.

'What? Why?' Tess began, and then she saw him. *Him*. He was outside the community centre, leaning against the wall. Lydia was across the road in seconds, right up in his face. Tess couldn't hear what she was saying but she could guess from her body language that she was leaving him in no doubt that she was fed up with being followed.

'Creep.' Her cheeks were flushed, her eyes wild with anger when she came back to Tess. 'How many times do I have to tell him to fuck off?'

'He's like a bad smell.' Tess hugged Lydia's shoulders but they were tense and unyielding. 'Have you told Genevieve?'

'I've tried.' Lydia sighed. 'She thinks the sun shines out of his arse.'

'I could try,' Tess said. She'd always found Genevieve approachable. She was far nicer to her than her own mum was. 'She might be more likely to listen if it comes from both of us.'

'Maybe,' Lydia said. 'But I doubt it.'

'Your dad then.'

'No!' She gave Tess a serious look. 'He needs all his strength to get better. I can't expect him to help me.' She drew in a slow, deep breath. 'I can manage Oscar. I've been doing it for months. Let's forget him.' She nudged Tess's arm and asked for a blow-by-blow account of what happened with Steve.

Tess spared her none of the details and had Lydia wide-eyed, laughing and gasping for breath as she told the story of her evening, exaggerating for comic effect when the need arose. They were halfway back to her house when Tess pointed to the carrier bag. 'So what did you buy?'

'A lock and some fixings.'

'What for?'

She paused for a second before saying breezily, 'Just some DIY.'

Before Tess had the chance to ask anything else, Lydia changed the subject back to Steve, and Tess was more than happy to carry on talking about him. Any passers-by would have thought they were just two carefree teenagers chatting about boys.

Lydia

Ten minutes after I dropped Adam at school I was stopped by the police. I was driving within the speed limit. I hadn't jumped a light or shown any signs of erratic driving, so when the blue light flashed behind me, I was surprised. I pulled in at the kerb and waited, watching in my side mirror as a young officer with a neat haircut approached the car. He tapped on the window and asked me to climb out. 'Good morning. I'm PC Sam Chalmers.' His tone was brisk. 'Could you tell me your name?'

'Why have you stopped me?' I concentrated on relaxing my facial muscles into the shape of a polite smile. 'Have I done something wrong?'

'I have reason to believe that you are driving under the influence.' He held a breathalyser out towards me. 'I'd like you to blow into this device.'

Reason to believe? How? Why? I knew I was within my rights to refuse but I also knew that failure to provide was in itself an offence. I quickly decided that cooperating was the lesser of the evils. I blew into the mouthpiece and within seconds I was told, 'You're close to three times over the limit.'

Fuck. My heart dropped. I wasn't surprised I was over the limit, but three times?

'Your name, please?'

'Lydia Green.'

'Lydia Green, I am arresting you on suspicion of driving while over the prescribed limit. You do not have to say anything, but it may harm your defence if you do not mention when questioned something which you later rely on in court. Anything you do say may be given in evidence.'

I wasn't handcuffed. There was no drama, and no one was watching. I quietly gathered up my belongings, locked my car and climbed into the back of the police car. I'd been in a police car before, albeit thirty years ago. My dad was a policeman, and for the very first time in my life I was glad he wasn't alive to see me. I had driven my precious son to school when I was three times over the limit. *Three times.* No matter that I was a good drunk. I could operate machinery and my reaction times were exceptional, but I wasn't stupid enough to think that made it okay. I had two jobs as Adam's mother: to love him and to keep him safe. All the rest was gravy. The private education and the trips to Disneyworld. The music lessons and the latest computer tech. It was all gravy.

I'd let my son down and that filled me with shame.

I was legally obliged to repeat the test in the station which, unsurprisingly, gave the same result. I was led to one of the rooms in the custody suite to 'sober up'. The room was small and bare. There was a hard bed with a pillow and blanket, and nothing more. I took off my shoes and lay down.

Six hours in the custody suite gave me plenty of time to think.

My name is Lydia Green and I'm an alcoholic.

I hadn't spoken those words since before I met Zack. I was twenty-seven, living in London, and had a work-hard-play-hard mantra that landed me in hospital with a serious kidney infection. On day two, when I was hooked up to dialysis, every fibre of my being craving a drink, the consultant, who reminded me of my departed dad, sat on the corner of the bed and went through my blood results with me. He told me how my life would pan out. He said the words with kindness, but he left me in no doubt that he'd witnessed this trajectory many times and that I was on a path of self-destruction. I'd had well-meaning advice before and taken no notice but, this time, I listened. I could never say whether it was the drugs or the infection or the alcohol withdrawal that made me more open – or perhaps it was his skill and sincerity – but the words touched me with an integrity that propelled me from the hospital bed to AA meetings. After that, I never touched a drop, not even a glass of champagne at my own wedding.

I had my first drink almost five months ago when I knew that, barring an act of God, we were moving to Ashdown Village. And I'd drunk every day since.

I drank with other people; I drank on my own.

I drank.

My name is Lydia Green and I'm an alcoholic.

Zack was the most straightforward person I had ever met. What you saw was what you got with him. And his family were the same. He was blessed with lovely parents and a trouble-free sibling. He said his upbringing had been ordinary but as soon as I met his mum and dad, I knew that wasn't true. I believed that one good parent was enough for a child to grow up healthy and well adjusted. Two good parents and the children hit the jackpot. Zack and his sister had hit the jackpot. His parents were a smiley, easy-going, hard-working couple who gave their children everything they needed to grow into confident adults.

Zack had no idea how lucky he was. And that made him naive, and trusting, especially of me. He was unconcerned when his previously teetotal wife became a drinker. He'd joked that I'd finally joined the human race and realised that a glass of wine was a fast track from work to leisure, when in fact it was the very mention of moving back to Ashdown Village that had led me back to the bottle. He didn't seem to notice that it wasn't just one glass and it wasn't only wine. He had never checked up on me, never even passed comment until just before we left London when I caught him counting the bottles in the recycling bin, a bemused look on his face. 'We get through a lot of booze!' he laughed. 'I don't suppose next door is using our bin, are they?'

'Geez!' I stared down into the bin, seeing not only wine bottles but vodka and whisky too. 'We'll need to keep an eye on them,' I joked, tipping my head towards the neighbours. 'We might have to stage an intervention.'

I expected that to be the end of it but I noticed him giving me the side-eye when I went back to the fridge for more wine. So I curtailed my drinking in front of him and stored empty bottles in the boot of my car, dropping them in the recycling bins when I shopped at the supermarket.

My name is Lydia Green and I'm an alcoholic.

I remembered my dad with a ferocity that kept him alive in my heart. I didn't want to forget any of the details that made him who he was. Where to start? He took two sugars in his tea and his favourite biscuits were custard creams. He polished our shoes every Sunday evening while he listened to Sinatra. He sang show tunes in the shower. He wore an apron when he cooked, and that was most Sunday afternoons because a roast dinner was his speciality. He couldn't read music but he played the piano by ear, his light-fingered touch accompanying mine as we practiced duets together.

I knew I was lucky to have a dad like him and sometimes that made me anxious. I worried that there was a catch – maybe I wasn't his child? He laughed when I told him this and reminded me that he had green eyes identical to mine, just like his own mother had had. She'd died before I was born but I knew he felt about her the way I felt about him. There was a lot that was unspoken between us, not because we didn't say the words, but because the words didn't need to be said. He got me. I was his only child and he loved me unconditionally.

My name is Lydia Green and I'm an alcoholic.

I hadn't expected to make a best friend. It was the third time I'd moved school in as many years because my dad kept being promoted. 'This is the last time now, Lydia,' he'd told me. 'No more moving.'

I wasn't nervous on my first day at the girls' grammar. School was something you got through until real life started. It wasn't worth stressing about. As soon as I walked into any classroom, I sensed who was who. There was always the bright, pretty one, the slouchy bored one, the bully and the sheep. But then, this time, I spotted Tess. She was willowy and delicate, the freckles on her cheeks dormant from lack of sunshine. I felt an unexpected jolt of recognition and in that moment, I knew that we would get along. That we were destined to be friends. That her hopes and dreams mirrored mine.

Where we were different was that she was fearful and I was not. She was someone who cared about what others thought of her. I didn't. She was innocent, bordering on gullible. I saw the dangers around us. She didn't.

I did my best to keep us safe.

I sat up and swung my feet round onto the floor. A thought had occurred to me. Someone must have reported me to the police. Otherwise, why would they have pulled me over?

Tess's car was behind mine when I dropped Adam at school. She saw me stumble before I climbed back into the car. It wasn't a drunken stumble – more the combination of a chunky heel and a weak ankle. I remembered the look on her face when she threw the wine at me. She was mad as hell, furious that I was denying our friendship. Furious, and now by the looks of it, vindictive too. She'd already excluded Adam from Bobby's party and now she was upping the ante.

I visualised her watching me drive off and then very deliberately taking out her phone, pressing the keypad and calling the police on me. I knew I'd pissed her off – hurt her even – but why didn't she get that we couldn't be friends again? What planet was she living on that she thought we could take up where we left off, when where we left off would have had us both sent to prison? Our friendship couldn't hold up in the present, not after what had happened in the past. But to call the police on me?

These thoughts revolved in my mind on a permanent spin cycle until I was back at the front desk being prepped for release. 'Could you please tell me who reported me?' I asked the custody sergeant.

He stared at the paper in front of him, his expression studiously blank. 'I expect it was a concerned member of the public,' he replied slowly.

'You're not allowed to give me a name?'

He pursed his lips and regarded me with a weary eye. 'Here are your summons papers, Ms Green. Please note where and when you are required to appear in court.'

The date was in mid-January – more than a month away. 'Am I allowed to drive my car in the meantime?'

He gave me a look that said, Really? You want to carry on being a danger to the public? 'Yes, you can drive your car until then,' he conceded. 'But I strongly advise you not to drive under the influence of alcohol or drugs.'

'I don't take drugs,' I told him.

His right eyebrow raised in languid disbelief. It almost made me smile. I liked him. Day in and day out, human nature in all its complexity was laid out before him but somehow, he still managed to show up for work. He had to be one of life's optimists.

'My dad was a policeman,' I told him, my voice catching. 'Thank you for doing the job that you do.'

'Don't be coming back,' he said. 'That's all the thanks I need.'

I called a taxi, waiting on the steps of the police station until it arrived.

And now I was going to have to tell Zack.

The house was still when I went inside. Zack was working from home; I could hear him on the phone, his tone upbeat as always. I went into the open plan kitchen and considered what I would say to him. I wasn't averse to lying but I could only justify my lies if they related to my past, not my present.

My fingers itched to reach for the vodka bottle. I could do with a drink to get me through the next hour. I visualised a glass of neat vodka with boulders of ice and a wedge of lemon, and felt the dizzy rush of anticipation, my mouth filling with saliva, my shoulders relaxing away from my ears. I was in two minds whether to pour one and was erring on the side of why not when Zack came into the kitchen.

'Lyds!' He was pleased to see me. I fell against him and he laughed, kissed me in an absentminded way. I wanted the kiss to last forever but he pulled away. 'I didn't hear you come in.'

I followed him across the room and hugged his back. 'We should get a pet. A dog or a cat to welcome us home. Adam would love that.' I linked my hands around his waist. 'What would you prefer?'

'I grew up with both.' *Of course, he did.* He switched on the kettle then turned around within the circle of my arms. I wasn't letting go. I needed this moment to last. 'What's brought this on?'

'Just … family,' I said into his chest, not sure whether he meant getting a pet or clinging to him like a limpet.

'You've always been against pets. Too much of a tie, you said.'

Why had I said that? Surely that was my mother talking, not me.

'A dog would be great,' he added. I sensed him thinking through the details. 'There are all the trendy poodle crosses, dachshunds and now corgis, but I'd like to go pure Lab.' He started to reminisce about a dog he had when he was growing up until the kettle finished boiling and I had to let him go.

He made us both a coffee. 'Are you okay?' he asked as he passed me mine. 'You look pale.'

'I spent today at the police station,' I stated, my tone devoid of emotion.

His eyes met mine over the rim of the mug. 'What?' Startled, he bumped the mug down on the counter. 'What happened?'

131

'I was over the limit.'

He frowned. 'You were drinking at lunchtime?'

'No.' I swallowed a mouthful of coffee. 'I was taken into custody after I dropped Adam at school.'

Silence. He frowned as he tried to process that. I waited, apologies tumbling through my mind like confetti along a windy street. I had to speak. 'I'm so sorry, Zack. I feel sick with shame. I really do.'

'You drove Adam to school when you were drunk?' His tone was disbelieving, surprised rather than shocked or angry. But I was afraid those emotions wouldn't be far behind.

'I wouldn't describe myself as drunk,' I said slowly. 'But I know that what I did was wrong. It was reckless and it was potentially dangerous.' I clasped my hands together. 'I feel so awful about it.'

He took my hands and walked me across the room where we sat down opposite each other. He leant forward, his elbows on his thighs, staring at me with an intensity that I found unnerving. 'Talk me through it,' he said.

'Well, I drank a fair bit last night when I was out with the football mums and then I knew I wouldn't sleep immediately, and I stayed up ...' I took a breath. 'Drank some more.' *At least three large ones.*

He frowned, thinking. 'But that's unusual for you, right?'

'No ...' I hesitated. 'I don't always sleep very well.'

'You drink during the night?'

'Three a.m. is a difficult time for me.'

'Why don't I know this?' His cheeks reddened as if he was embarrassed.

'You're asleep!'

'Then wake me up!'

132

'Zack,' I gave him a quick hug before drawing back so that I could see his face, 'this is not your fault. It's a reality check for me because I've let things get away from me. But it's fixable! It's going to be okay. I'll get help.'

'Hang on!' He raised a hand. 'So the bottles that were in the bin back in London ...' his eyebrows raised '... and there were a lot of them, Lydia. They were yours?'

'Yes.'

He was shocked by this. 'But I never notice you drinking any more than I do.'

'I know, but it's only been going on for a few months.'

'Since when?'

'Since there was talk of us moving house,' I admitted.

'Why?'

Usually I didn't mind being put on the spot but this was different. This was about opening myself up and laying bare the truth. And that was never going to happen. 'I guess moving here made me think about my life. And about death.' That wasn't a lie.

'My mum was worried about that,' he said nodding, 'with your own dad dying of cancer.'

'It's brought it all back.' *And some.*

'Driving over the limit, though? Lydia.' He stared down at his hands. 'That's serious.'

'I know.'

'And with Adam in the car.'

I bit my lip.

'Why not speak to me?'

'I should have.' My head dropped. 'It was wrong not to.'

'But you've been stressed before and never turned to drink.' Doubt flashed across his face. 'Have you?'

'No.' I held his eyes. 'Never. Not since I met you.'

'So, before we met?' He was frowning again. 'You had a problem with alcohol before we met?'

I heard a message ping on my phone. It shouldn't have distracted me, but it did because I was looking for a reason to escape. The message was from one of the mums but I noticed there were several unread texts from Vanya, the most recent one informing me that Adam was at Tess's house. My temper flared. 'I need to collect Adam,' I said, making for the door.

'Wait!' He stood over me as I pulled on my shoes. 'Can't he stay a bit longer? We need to talk.'

'And we will.' I kissed his cheek. 'Let's save it for this evening when Adam is in bed.'

'I arranged for Jenny from the hospice to come for dinner this evening,' Zack reminded me. He pulled his mobile from his pocket. 'I'll call her to cancel.'

'No,' I said, grabbing his hand to stop him making the call. 'Let her come.'

'Lydia …' He shook his head, at a loss for words.

'I know, but she's been kind to your mum and I expect she's been looking forward to it.' I kissed his cheek. 'Let's not disappoint her.'

Tess

It was after six o'clock, and the boys were playing in the back garden, when Tess noticed a taxi pull up outside. Her thoughts jumped to Oscar and her heart began to race. But Oscar wouldn't arrive by taxi, would he? His style was to lurk, wait, watch from the shadows – and then Lydia climbed out and Tess immediately felt relieved. She shouldn't have. She opened the front door, smiling with relief that it was Lydia and not Oscar. Her guard was down and she was completely unprepared for what came next.

'You reported me!' Lydia said. She slammed into Tess, hard enough for her head to snap back and rebound off the wall behind her.

'What the—' Tess pushed her away. 'That really hurt.'

'Do you know what you've done?' Lydia said quietly. 'I'm going to lose my licence.'

'I *literally* have no idea what you're talking about,' Tess replied. She took hold of Lydia's arm and pulled her into the kitchen, closing the door behind them. 'What's going on?'

'Like you don't know?'

Her aggressive stare made Tess flinch. 'I don't! I don't know.'

'I was pulled over by the police and breathalysed at the side of the road.' Her voice was loud and sharp. 'Is this your way of getting back at me?'

'Please, Lydia!' Tess pointed through the window to where Bobby was in goal and Adam was practising his shots. Rose was in her buggy watching them both, her legs in her winter all-in-one kicking along with them. 'They'll hear you.' Her head hurt and she cupped the base of her skull in her hand. 'When did this happen?'

'This morning.' Her eyes bored through Tess's. 'Ten minutes after you drove past me.'

'Then?' Tess was genuinely confused. 'You were over the limit this *morning*?'

'You *saw* me when I dropped Adam off at school.'

'I'm not denying that.'

'So, it's no coincidence that the police turned up, is it?' Lydia was standing so close that Tess could see the flecks of gold in the green of her eyes. '*Is it?*'

Tess drew back. 'You think that someone reported you after you dropped Adam off?'

'The police don't just appear out of nowhere.'

'Well, it wasn't me. I didn't tell them.' Tess shook her head. The sound of the boys' voices filtered into the kitchen. 'They're having fun,' she said, hoping to diffuse the tension and give herself time to think. This morning? Lydia was over the limit *this morning*?

'Don't you dare bring the boys into this.'

Tess took a breath, her hands out in front of her, a barrier keeping Lydia at bay. 'But why would you think that I'd call the police?'

'You threw wine in my face. Remember?'

'Of course I remember. I was reacting to what you *said*.' The throbbing in her head increased. 'You were mean, Lydia.' Her lips trembled and she tightened her jaw.

'I get it! I'm not friendship material. I'm a widow. I have a new baby. I'm skint!' She felt the rush of tears and blinked furiously. She shouldn't be playing the pity card; she should be apologising. Why, in the heat of the moment, did she always forget what she'd planned to say? 'But I'm sorry. I should never have thrown the wine. And we won't—'

'And this morning you saw another opportunity to get back at me.'

'No!' Lydia was drilling so deep into Tess's eyes that she took another step back, closing her eyes for a blessed second, just so that she didn't have to bear Lydia's scrutiny.

'You've never been a good liar, Tess.'

The kitchen door was thrown wide open. Adam and Bobby came running in. 'We've invented new words!' Bobby said. They looked at each other, grinning wildly. Neither of them had sensed the mood in the room. 'They could go in the dictionary. The first one—'

'Gruncle!' Adam butted in.

'It means great uncle,' Bobby added helpfully.

'And muncle is an uncle who's a monk!' Adam shouted and they fell together giggling helplessly.

'And buncle—'

'Get in the taxi, Adam!' Lydia shouted. 'NOW!'

They both jumped at her tone which was more animal than human. Bobby's mouth fell open, and then he was completely still. Adam's limbs were trembling and tears wet his lower lashes falling onto his cheeks as soon as he blinked.

'Wait in the hall, boys,' Tess said, holding their shoulders and leading them through the door. 'We'll be out soon.' Neither of them spoke. 'Don't worry,' she whispered, closing the door on their wide-eyed and scared faces. She knew how they felt. She took a deep breath and turned back to Lydia who was staring through the window, her arms folded, her foot tapping, anger radiating off her in waves. Tess didn't know what to say to make it better. Not that it was even up to her. She hadn't called the police. This wasn't her fault. 'I'm sorry you're losing your licence, Lydia. I reall—'

'No, you're not.' Lydia faced her again. 'This is you being spiteful.' She held her eyes, and behind the anger Tess sensed sadness and something else, something deeper that Lydia wasn't about to share. 'You of all people,' Lydia said softly. 'After everything I did for you.'

A cold-water stillness settled inside Tess's ribcage. 'What does that mean?'

Lydia didn't reply, not with words anyway. They shared several seconds where Tess felt as if she crossed into Lydia's mind and Lydia crossed into hers. The tentacles of their thoughts wrapped around each other, entwined, inseparable, like a mesh of octopus limbs. When Tess blinked and drew away, memory flickered at the corners of her mind, too elusive for her to grasp hold of.

Lydia left the kitchen, snatching Adam's hand on the way out. As they drove off, Lydia stared through the window, and Tess felt fear trickle down her back, as if traced by a witch's finger.

1994

Lydia drilled more holes in her bedroom door frame than she needed to because she couldn't get the two lock pieces to align. She would have loved Tess's help but she knew she couldn't ask her because Tess would be horrified – *Oscar comes into your bedroom? What the fuck, Lydia?* – and she would insist they tell someone and that would mean her dad would get to know and it would stress him out. He was in and out of hospital a lot these days, and whenever he was home, she liked everything to be happy and calm. He would never recover if he had her dramas to deal with.

She repositioned the drill and tried again. She had covered the carpet with a dustsheet but she knew Genevieve would go nuts if she saw the mess she'd made of the doorframe. She'd have to touch it up with the white paint from the garage before she came up the stairs.

She'd tried speaking to her mother about Oscar – twice she'd tried – and got nowhere. When her dad had been in hospital last month, her mother had let him stay the night and he had come into her room. She hadn't heard him until he was hovering beside her bed. He must have stood on something sharp because she woke up to the sound of him cursing, one bare foot lifted off the floor.

The moon shone down through the skylight. She saw the glint in his eye and the shape of his torso, naked from the waist up. Before she had the wherewithal to react, he used one hand to pull the duvet off her while his other hand was down the front of his trousers.

She screamed and grabbed for the duvet, tugging it out of his hands and up to her neck.

'I'm just looking,' he'd said, grinning at her.

When he left the room, she lay completely still, her heart beating like a drum, tears soaking her pillow. *How many times had he been in her room and she had slept through it? What did he want from her? What was she going to do to stop him?*

Next day, when they were coming back from the hospital, she'd plucked up the courage to say to her mother, 'Could Oscar please not stay with us while Dad's in hospital?'

Her mother had stopped the car by the side of the road, widened her eyes and laughed. 'Really, Lydia? Who said Oscar was staying?'

'He was here last night.' She took a breath. 'He's … ' She tried to find the right words but couldn't. 'I'm afraid of him,' she managed at last. 'He's …' *I'm scared he's going to rape me.* 'He's just … scary.'

'Afraid of him how?' Genevieve said, her tone surprised. 'Afraid of him why?'

'He came into my room when I was asleep,' Lydia said flatly. 'His hand was down the front of his trousers when he pulled the covers off me.'

Her mother reached across and yanked at her hair, hard enough for Lydia to scream. 'How dare you!' Her tone had accelerated, lightning quick, from understanding to threatening. 'Oscar is my *cousin* and you will speak of him with respect.'

That evening, Lydia put a chair under the door handle, but it was precariously balanced, wobbling on two legs. It wouldn't stop him. Or not for long, at any rate. She dressed in underwear, pyjamas and socks, a tracksuit over the top. She lay awake thinking of ways to keep him away from her: she could arrange a trail of broken glass on the floor, she could steal a starting gun from the school PE department and fire it when he came in, best of all she could put a lock on the door.

And so here she was, trying and trying again until finally both fixings were screwed into the wood and lined up perfectly. She burst into tears of relief, let herself cry for less than ten seconds before she rushed to tidy up the mess. She used filler on the misaligned holes and painted over the top, opened windows and sprayed air freshener to get rid of the paint smell. Job done. Thank God she'd managed it!

That night she stayed awake until well after midnight, lying in bed fully clothed, a five-inch knife in her hand. If the lock didn't hold then she wasn't afraid to stab him. She could do it. She had practised in front of the mirror, lunging upward with the knife. Under the ribcage. Quick as a flash.

When she heard his tread on the stairs, she tightened her grip on the knife, her breath held. There was a pause before he tried the handle, twisting it all the way round and pushing. The lock held. He pushed again and again.

The lock held.

Lydia could breathe now. But just in case, she remained fully clothed, the knife under her pillow, before she turned onto her side and fell asleep.

Lydia

As soon as I climbed into the taxi, I knew that I'd handled the situation badly. I should have kept my cool. I *meant* to keep my cool, but seeing Tess in that moment, the picture of innocence, smiling – *smiling?* – as if she had no idea who had called the police, triggered me in a way that I hadn't predicted. I'd told her she wasn't a good liar but actually she was. I'd seen her do it when we were teenagers. She was one of those liars who was so convincing that she even convinced herself, rewrote the story in her mind as she spoke. It made her performance come across as authentic.

Adam sat stiffly beside me, his cheeks red, his mouth pinched. I tried out opening gambits in my head – I'm sorry for embarrassing you, I'm sorry to have shouted, I'm sorry that I've upset you. But before I got a sentence out, he asked, 'Why are we going this way?'

'I left the car on one of the roads close to your school.'

'Why?'

He was the one person in the world I didn't bullshit or lie to but still I baulked at being completely truthful. 'I wasn't able to drive it after I dropped you off.'

'Does it need to go to the garage?'

'No.' I reached for his hand. 'Unfortunately, I was over the limit for alcohol.'

He frowned. 'That's a really bad thing to do.'

'I know.' I was grateful that he let me keep hold of his hand. 'And I'm very sorry to have done it.'

He sighed. I sensed the wisdom of a well-adjusted nine-year-old, fed up with stupid behaviour. 'I like it best when everything goes well and everyone's happy.'

I gave a short laugh. 'I think that's true for all of us, bud.'

'Will Daddy be annoyed?'

'I've already explained everything to Daddy, and he's been very understanding because he knows that I didn't mean it and I'm really very sorry.'

He smiled then, and his head settled against my shoulder. It was at times like this that I was grateful he had his dad's forgiving nature.

When we came through the front door, I could hear voices in the kitchen. Zack and a woman. My heart slammed to a halt when I recognised the voice.

'Jenny's here!' Adam said. 'You'll get to meet her, Mum.'

Jenny. My mouth was open as I followed Adam into the kitchen. She was sitting on a high stool at the breakfast bar, her feet crossed at the ankles. Her hair was short, bobbed, sleek. Exactly the way she wore it when I was young. She turned towards me and I was so blindsided by the sensation of her eyes meeting mine that my legs went to jelly and I fell over, landing heavily on my back, my skull bumping against the floor tiles with a dull thwack. Immediately, my head swam with black water and then lights flashed painfully bright, dazzled and dizzied me as if I was on fairground ride. My hand shook as I shielded my eyes but that didn't help because the lights were inside not out.

'Jesus, Lydia!' Zack rushed to help me. 'Are you okay?' He lifted me up onto a low chair, then crouched down in front of me, his expression concerned. I tried to stand up but he gently held me in place. 'Give it a minute, love. That was quite a bang. Did you lose your footing?'

I looked at him through half-closed, watering eyes. I'd bitten my tongue as I fell and the metallic taste of blood coated the inside of my mouth. I tried to swallow but found that the blood was too thick and sticky.

'Lydia!' Her voice. *Her voice.* 'Lydia, it's you! This is wonderful! This is so incredible!' She tried to hug me; I shrank away from her. 'The shock, my dear. Of course. Let me get you some water.' I watched her walk across to the sink, take a glass from the shelf above and fill it with water.

She gave the glass to Zack. He handed it to me and I took cool sips, my mind trying to catch up with what was playing out in front of me. Zack knelt at my feet and removed my shoes. He laid them to one side then held both my feet in his hands, tenderly, staring down at them as if looking for clues as to why I'd fallen over.

'I can't believe this!' Jenny was saying. 'What a wonderful moment of serendipity!'

Zack looked from her to me, his expression uncertain. 'Do you two know each other?'

'Why, Lydia's my daughter!'

She gave a merry laugh. It sounded like cut glass falling onto a stone floor.

'What?' Zack started back. It was his moment to be blindsided. 'Lydia?'

I stared at him. I still couldn't speak but I hoped that he was reading my mind. This was one hell of a coincidence. Serendipity? Fuck no! This was planned. I would have staked my life on it. I was already beginning to work out how she might have engineered this, clues aligning in my mind. I'd always kept my maiden name. I wasn't on Facebook or any of the other socials but when I sold my company, I became googleable. There were several interviews for business magazines where she could have gleaned information. In one of them, I was sitting in our house in London with Zack standing behind me and underneath: Lydia Green married Zack Purdew, a fellow entrepreneur, in 2009.

'That means you're my granny!' Adam said. He hugged her around the waist. I wanted to scream. My mind revved up a gear. I hadn't even imagined that the Jenny Zack talked about would be her. Jenny? *Jenny?* Since when had she called herself Jenny? She was always very particular about being called by her full name, never shortening it. Genevieve. Always Genevieve. Jenny was way too common. Not nearly special enough. And the hospice work. When had she ever done volunteering? When had she ever baked shortbread?

'Well.' Zack gave a short laugh. I could see that he didn't know what to say next. 'Quite a turn-up for the books.'

My mother wasn't wasting any time. She was busy making plans for her and Adam to spend time together. 'I can collect you from school!' she told him. 'You can come to me for sleepovers.'

I stood up then. 'Over my dead body,' I said loudly.

'Lydia!' Zack's tone was an admonishment.

'Mum?' From Adam it was more of a question.

'Oh my goodness me! No, no, no! Lydia is absolutely right!' my mother said, taking the opportunity to leap to my defence. She stood in front of me, her hands in the prayer position, as if to protect me from them. 'I've just

145

appeared out of the blue. I'm sure you have your routines, and I will happily wait my turn.'

'I'd like you to leave now, please,' I said, taking her by the elbow and leading her to the door.

'Well, I—' She faked an old-lady semi-stagger. 'Of course. We all need time.'

Adam and Zack had both followed me. 'Lydia?'

'What?' I snapped.

'Jenny, I'm sorry about this,' Zack said, his lips drawn into a flat, tense line.

'Not a bit of it, Zack.' She hugged him quickly. 'As I said, we all need time.' She reached for my hand and managed her most sincere fake smile. 'I love you, Lydia.'

It was all I could do not to spit in her face. I closed the door behind her and looked at the two people I loved most in the whole world standing in front of me, waiting for an explanation. Adam's expression was uncertain. He wasn't sure where this was going or why.

'Adam, would you like to watch a film?' I asked brightly.

'I'd rather go on the PlayStation.'

'Knock yourself out,' I said.

'Okay!' He grinned and ran off. What a treat for a Monday!

Zack's expression was a mix of disbelief and anger. 'Explain to me what's just happened, Lydia. Before I start joining the dots for myself.'

'Oh?' I folded my arms and glared at him. 'What dots are those, Zack?'

'We've talked a lot, Jenny and I—'

'Genevieve,' I cut in. 'Her name's Genevieve.'

'Would you let me speak?' He was curt now.

'Go ahead.' I waved my arm magnanimously.

'She's told me all about her estranged daughter.'

She must have enjoyed that.

'She told me—' He frowned. 'A problem with alcohol runs in the family. Her cousin Oscar—'

I held up my hand. 'Do. Not. Go. There.' I steeled myself against the wave of revulsion that passed through me, my teeth chattering against the force of it. 'I mean it, Zack.'

He leaned in towards me again. 'Talk to me, Lydia.' His facial muscles worked as he tried to control his anger. 'What the fuck is going on here? Did you know your mother lived in the village? Have you known all along?' He paused, incredulous, as more dots connected in his mind. 'Did *you* live here?'

She'd laid the groundwork. She'd been working on Zack for months, drip-feeding him information about her wayward daughter, and that was me. And here was I playing catch-up. So much for me thinking I could get ahead of her. Sneaking about in her garden. Why did I ever believe I could take her on?

'Please, Zack.' I placed my hand on his arm. 'I've made a horrible mistake with the drinking.' My voice was quiet and calm. 'But that doesn't mean my mother is right about me. She'll have said a lot about her daughter over the past couple of months. But that doesn't make it the truth.'

I could hear the upbeat, repetitive jingle of a PlayStation game in the other room but between me and Zack the silence was taut as stretched wire.

'So you don't have a problem with alcohol?' he asked sharply.

'Sometimes I do,' I acknowledged. 'And I'm going to do something about it. I've sorted myself out before and I can do so again.'

'So that part was true?

'Some of what she says will be factually correct,' I agreed.

'And you lived here? In Ashdown Village.' His tone was disbelieving. 'For three years. Your dad is buried in the churchyard.' He waved his arm. 'Any of that true?'

I nodded.

'And you chose not to tell me?' He was hurt by this. 'Why?'

'Because I was … damaged.' I thought for a moment, remembering, and not remembering. Because to recall all of it would break me in two. 'I was traumatised by what happened when I lived here.'

'In what way?' he asked. 'What happened?'

What a fool I'd been. I had played right into her hands. She'd been sowing seeds, poison ivy, to choke me with. What did she want? To humiliate me? To ruin my marriage? 'To take my son,' I said quietly to myself.

'Lydia.' Zack took hold of my shoulders and gently shook me. 'Please help me understand why you would keep such huge secrets from me.'

He didn't know the half of it.

'Why do you think she wasn't shocked when she saw me?' I asked him. I gave him a few seconds to think about this. 'I was *so* horrified to see her in my home that I fell over. You were startled. Weren't you?' I raised my eyebrows. 'But her?' I shrugged. 'She was fine. Why do you think that was?'

He shook his head. 'I guess she's just better with surprises than we are.'

'Or maybe she already knew that I was married to you.'

'How?' His face twisted. 'How could she have known that?'

Zack was a good man. He was non-confrontational, annoyingly fair at times, and always willing to see everyone's side. He'd just caught his wife out in a massive lie.

Turned out I was a drunk *and* a liar. Credit to him that he was still giving me the time of day.

I pulled him towards me for a hug, collapsing against his shoulder, desperate to hide my face in his shirt. I didn't want to say any more. There were secrets that I had never spoken of, not to any living soul and I needed to be sure that when I revealed the truth, I could cope with the consequences.

But there was a silver lining in this thunderous cloud. I realised that I was no longer afraid of her. I despised her, but I didn't fear her, and this realisation spread through my chest like black ink on a tablecloth, leaving a stain right next to my heart.

Tess

'I can't say I miss the meat,' her dad said, forking through the tomato sauce. 'Lentils are a great substitute.'

'And we've got nuts.' Bobby's expression was bright. 'People left loads of stuff where Mum was cleaning today. And nuts are protein.'

'It always amazes me the way people leave food,' her dad said. 'You'd think they'd take it home with them. More money than sense.'

'But it's good for us,' Bobby enthused, 'cos we save money and get some nice food to eat.' He smiled at Tess. 'Isn't it, Mum?'

'It is.' Tess moved the penne around on her plate, preoccupied with her looping thoughts that constantly returned to what had just happened with Lydia. She was over the alcohol limit at nine in the morning and somehow that was Tess's fault? Why was Lydia so sure that she was the person who had reported her to the police? There was the coincidence of them seeing each other outside Adam's school but that was hardly solid evidence.

'Could I have more cheese, Mum?' Bobby asked.

'Of course.' She grated some Cheddar over his pasta as he smiled up at her, a tomato sauce smear on his chin. She'd said to Lydia that she was a mess.

She remembered her exact words – *I get it! I'm not friendship material. I'm a widow. I have a new baby. I'm skint!* – and maybe that was all true, but she had to start appreciating what she had. Her life hadn't turned out as she'd hoped it would, but she had a beautiful baby, a wonderful little boy and her dad. Her life wasn't half bad. She had to remember that.

'You're not eating,' her dad said to her, pointing his fork at her plate. 'You know it's important to stay nourished.'

Yes, she knew that. The doctors had made it clear to her that in order to be mentally healthy she had to take care of her body too. 'I've got a bit of a headache.' She went across to the cupboard where she kept the medicines. 'I'll take some painkillers.'

'Are you remembering to drink water?' he reminded her. 'I read somewhere that at least fifty per cent of headaches are caused by dehydration.'

'It's because Lydia was shouting,' Bobby said between mouthfuls. '*Really* loud. It made Adam cry.'

'Lydia was here? With Adam?' her dad asked, his back straightening. Tess had already told him that Lydia pretended not to know her. 'And why the shouting?'

Bobby explained about Vanya's mum falling ill and how Adam ended up coming round to theirs. 'It was really good fun, but I think maybe Adam's mum had a car crash because they had to go home in a taxi,' Bobby said.

'Is that what happened, Tess?' her dad asked.

'No.' She swallowed the pills with some water. 'She was over the limit.'

There was a short silence before her dad whistled through his teeth. 'She was caught driving under the influence?'

'What does under the influence mean?' Bobby asked as he speared multiple penne on his fork.

'It means—'

'Wait, Dad, please.' Tess held up her hand and gave him a look that she hoped communicated *kids tell each other everything. Best to be very careful what you say.* 'Lydia made a mistake,' she said to Bobby. 'And unfortunately—'

Rose let out her first fed-up cry and Tess excused herself from the table.

'Can I finish your pasta, Mum?' Bobby asked, his attention returning to food.

'Of course, love.'

She lifted Rose from her chair and the baby immediately raised a hand to Tess's mouth. She pretended to nibble on her fingers and Rose giggled at her. 'Come on, then,' she said, rubbing her cheeks. 'Let's get you in the bath.'

Her heart was racing. In her dreams she was in the woods, running, running, running, sure that someone was behind her. She heard the crack of twigs beneath her feet. She smelled the stench of foul breath on her neck. She felt the heavy weight of a hand as it grabbed for her arm. And then she woke up, clutching at her chest, unable to catch her breath.

Her eyes filled with tears. She took short, stilted breaths. Her ribcage was tight with dread. She climbed out of bed and stared down into Rose's cot. The sight of her sleeping baby was a sure way to help her calm down. It took a while but finally she was able to breathe more easily. And as for what the dream meant? She would think about that later.

The following morning, she left Rose with her dad and headed out the door just as Sadie was doing the same. They closed their doors within seconds of each other, their eyes catching across the grass between them. 'Morning, Sadie,' Tess said.

'Morning, Tess.'

Sadie was wearing a short denim skirt, multicoloured striped tights and ankle boots. Her velvet jacket was apple green and her woollen hat a lipstick red. Her style reminded Tess of the way Lydia dressed back then, before it was even fashionable to wear biker boots and thick tights. She was always a trailblazer.

'Did that man catch up with you?' Sadie asked.

Tess's heart jumped. 'What man?'

'The one who came to the door the other night.'

She kept her tone light when she said, 'I think he must have come to the wrong house. You know how people or parcels often end up here when it's the Lane they want not the Close.'

'But he mentioned you by name,' Sadie said.

'Are you sure?'

'Yes. He said, "is Tess Jeffries at home this evening?"'

'Oh.' Her knees began to shake and she held onto the door handle to steady herself. 'Well …' She gave Sadie an uneasy smile. 'For now it's a mystery.'

Tess was anxious after her conversation with Sadie but she tried not to let it show when she visited the prospective client and they discussed her requirements. When they'd agreed on a plan, Tess added the client to the weekly spreadsheet and drove to her first job of the day. She always cleaned the same house on a Tuesday. It was a Gothic, red-brick building with turrets, hidden rooms, and a huge 1920s orangery full of rare orchids. The decor was shabby chic. There was barely anything in the whole house that had been bought within the last fifty years. She used the key and went inside. 'It's Tess!' she called out and at once a trio of dachshunds set up a cacophony of barking, hurtling the length of the long corridor to greet her.

Lady P appeared moments later. She was one of Tess's favourite clients: kind, direct and eccentric. 'Tess!' She kissed her cheek. 'Mungo has been shitting everywhere again.' She glanced down at the floor, locating Mungo, a huge tabby cat who was circling between the dogs, eyeing them up with a lazy dominance. 'I swear to God he'll have to go if he keeps it up. Peter won't put up with it.' Her husband, Sir Peter, an illustrious career in the navy behind him, spent all his spare time with the orchids. Tess had rarely met him and whenever she did, he kept his eyes down and scuttled past her as if he was an interloper who should remain below stairs.

'I've scooped the poop so you don't need to concern yourself with that,' Lady P said. Her accent was cut glass, her diction perfect, each syllable as clearly enunciated as a 1950s television presenter. She once told Tess that she was second cousin to King Charles. 'Or maybe third cousin. I can't be sure. So much interbreeding in the royals.'

Mungo jumped up onto the vintage love seat that was positioned next to the rows of shoes and boots. There must have been over a hundred pairs, piled on top of each other in a huge recess that was once an inglenook fireplace. 'Do get down, Mungo.' Lady P waved a dishtowel at him. He completely ignored her. He was much too interested in watching the dogs whose noses were buried in the footwear as they snuffled and searched. 'We have mice again.' She sighed. 'Well, when do we not?'

They watched Mungo tread gingerly across the back of the seat, the furniture lurching to one side as he did so. 'Someone really heavy has sat on this recently, hence the wobbly leg,' Lady P said. Then, more briskly, 'Let's ignore it. There's more than enough that requires fixing around here.' Tess followed her to the foot of the spectacular sweeping staircase that rose up three floors and had a full-length stained-glass window behind it. The window featured a battle. A border of heraldic shields surrounded dozens of men who were wielding swords, the sky blue and grass green background interrupted by the flash of scarlet blood. 'Would you mind awfully giving the oak a polish?' she asked Tess. 'It's long overdue.'

'Of course.' The banister was as old as the house but the wood was solid, well-seasoned and primed to last another couple of hundred years. 'I have my own mix of vegetable and lavender oils to feed the wood and bring out a shine.'

'Lavender was what my grandmother used,' Lady P said, stroking the banister. 'And if it was good enough for Gama then it's good enough for me.'

Tess began at the top. She rarely cleaned on the two upper floors. Most of the rooms were closed off until the family arrived for the summer, when the doors were thrown wide and there was an echo of laughter, squabbling and good-natured teasing throughout the house. It took Tess two hours to work from top to bottom. She had hoped to lose herself in the rhythm of the work and a podcast about Welsh myths and legends. But that didn't happen. There was too much about the manor that reminded her of school: the stained-glass window, the wooden staircase and the sense of history.

When she started to remember one detail, more followed, memories tumbling to the forefront of her mind. Lydia's dad. He was Lydia's lifeline and when he became ill, it was heartbreaking. The worst thing that could ever have happened to Lydia. Tess stopped polishing the staircase to think about that. Had she supported Lydia? Had she been there for her? She wracked her brains but she couldn't remember going to Lydia's dad's funeral.

Could it be that she wasn't as good a friend as she'd thought?

1994

Tess spent most of her time with Steve now. Lydia missed her, acutely. She desperately wanted to talk to someone who knew her, who understood her. But then her dad came back from the hospital, and she rushed home every day to be with him. If she was lucky her mum was out, and they could enjoy themselves without her spoiling everything. Genevieve didn't like to hear them laughing. She would call Lydia into the kitchen and find jobs for her to do. 'You're a selfish little bitch, always tiring your dad out. Think about him for once.'

If Genevieve wasn't there, they would play the piano together, have gin rummy tournaments, tackle impossible jigsaws. And all the time at the back of her mind was the worry about Oscar. When her dad was going through the treatment, she couldn't tell him about Oscar, of course, because he was fighting his own battle and she wanted to support him, not make things worse. He needed her to be okay. 'Seeing your smile, Lydia Jane, makes me know that my life is worth all these drugs.'

After she put the lock on the door, she convinced herself that next time he was home, she would tell him what happened in the house when his back was turned. He would want to know. She was sure of that. But when she had him home, she couldn't bring herself to ruin the mood. She wanted their dad-daughter relationship to be about love and fun. Hearing about Oscar would spoil that and, as her dad wasn't strong enough to climb the stairs, he never saw the lock.

Lydia

When I woke up the next morning my mother had sent me a text:

I expect to hear from you today.

Was there any point in wondering how she'd got my number?

I went downstairs and found Zack chewing noisily on a piece of toast. I'd managed to avoid talking to him the previous evening. We ate the pasta and salad he had prepared for 'Jenny's' visit in the family room while *Star Wars* played on-screen. Zack read to Adam at bedtime and when he came through to our room, I pretended to be asleep.

'Are you working today?' he asked me.

'Why?'

'Why?' He sighed and stared up at the ceiling. 'Because I can't assume anything about you any more. Do you even go to work?' He gave a tight laugh. 'Who knows? Perhaps you have a second family that you visit.'

I frowned at this, both hurt and irritated. My mouth was parched. My hand twitched, desperate to reach out for a glass of something ice-cold and heady. I would happily have smashed every dish and glass in that bespoke kitchen-diner with its doors leading out to the idyllic wild garden. I would have given it all up for a tall glass of vodka tonic or a sunshine-orange Aperol Spritz.

'You drove our son to school when you were over the limit,' Zack continued. 'This revelation closely followed by the fact that your mother lives in the village, has done for more than thirty years. Indeed, you—' he pointed the butterknife at me, 'have lived in this village. Something else you failed to mention.'

Adam's footsteps sounded on the stairs, and I walked to the coffee machine, counting to ten as I stepped. I made myself the strongest coffee known to woman. Alcohol withdrawal was torture. It was only day two and my nerve endings vibrated on a painful frequency. The first week would be the worst. I would be irritable, mean, sad, angry, shaky, anxious, a doom-monger, a naysayer, a troll. I would take every opportunity to slap, kick and bite.

But the sight of my son gave me a sudden moment of hope. I remembered Zack acknowledging yesterday, before my mother took centre stage, that the very thought of moving back here had reignited my drink problem. Maybe we could return to London or seek out somewhere new. I didn't mind which. What was important was the fact that we could change our lives. We didn't have to live here, especially now that Zack's sister was coming. We could join them both in Cornwall for the whole four weeks. If Paula was enjoying herself, we could stay down there indefinitely. We both mostly worked from home and Adam was only nine. He could miss school, catch up next year or the year after. It would all work out.

I took a steadying breath and brought a pile of toast, some butter and jam to the table. Adam followed behind me, carrying the milk and juice. Zack brought the bowls and glasses.

I didn't eat; I couldn't eat. There was a ringing in my ears and when I stretched my arms out in front of me my hands shook as if there was an earthquake happening inside me. I half-listened to Adam and Zack talk about what team was going to win the Premiership and held my coffee mug as tightly as I could between my two sweaty palms. Finally, I interrupted them, my voice loud and bright. 'So, what do you think of this place, Adam?'

He glanced left and right. 'I like this house. There's so much space and—'

'Not the house, love,' I cut in. 'The village. Your school. The football club.' There were ants beneath my skin. I scratched my forearm hard and fast until it burned. 'Do you like it here?'

'Lydia?' Zack had a warning expression on his face. Warning me against what? I wasn't allowed to speak now? He was still munching. He was an irritatingly noisy eater. His mouth was open, and his jaw clicked with every chew. How had I never noticed that before?

I stopped scratching and gave him a false smile. 'Adam?' I drummed my fingers on the table and he looked up from spreading jam on his toast.

'I like it here,' he said nodding. 'I like the school and—'

'But what if we needed to move?' I cut in again. 'We could spend time with your grandma and Auntie Stephanie in Cornwall. How would you feel about that?' I laughed. 'We could live almost anywhere! Dad and I work mostly from home and—'

'Hang on a minute, Lydia,' Zack said, surprise in his tone.

'There's Canada!' I raised my voice. 'We could live deep in the countryside, next to a lake! How would you like that? You could learn to sail. It would be—'

'Woah there!' Zack's voice was louder this time. 'I think you and I should talk about this first.' He pointed to me and then back to himself. 'Don't you?'

'But you understood yesterday,' I said softly. 'When we were talking.' His expression was blank. My fist tightened. 'I explained why moving back here was difficult for me. Why I wasn't coping as well as I might.' I tried to smile at Adam to reassure him that there wasn't anything to worry about but my lips wouldn't stretch.

'Let's chat when I get back from dropping Adam off,' Zack said, his tone firm. His hand encircled my tight fist.

I narrowed my eyes and tightened my fist another notch.

He withdrew his hand and stood up. 'Eat up, Adam, and I'll take you to school.' He walked towards the front door. 'Chop-chop.'

I was getting ready to go out to the gym when Zack returned from drop-off. I picked up my gym bag but he stood between me and the front door. 'I didn't mean to undermine you in front of Adam,' he said. He was twirling the car key through his fingers. I concentrated on that: how warm and strong his hands were, how much pleasure they had given me over the years. 'I just think we need to discuss things as a couple before we involve Adam.'

'Right.' I sighed, shifted my gaze further down and focussed on the knots on the oak floorboards. 'Whatever.'

'Are you saying that you would stop drinking if we moved away from the village?'

'Yup.' I nodded at the floor. 'That's what I'm saying.'

'But, Lydia.' His tone was kind. 'Surely there are better ways to get through this? Think long-term solutions.'

'Meaning?'

'We can do better than that.' His hands rested on either side of my upper arms, a light, supportive touch. 'I think we can get through this together. I'll meet your mum with you. We can talk about your childhood, whatever caused you two to fall out. Get all of your feelings out into the open ...'

He kept talking. It was all very sensible and considered. I kept my face angled downwards. I really didn't want to fight with him. He was a good man. He loved me. And that was surely gold dust especially with what he was finding out about me.

'... we could go to a therapist together if that would help. I want to understand what you're going through ...'

He wanted to be involved in my recovery. Of course he did. I wanted him to agree to move away from here or let me find a way though this myself. He needed to understand that if we continued to live here, there was no amount of talking to my mother that would make this better. We were well past that stage.

'... I can take some time off work and we can de-stress together ...'

Next, he would be suggesting herbal teas and back rubs. I didn't have the energy to educate him. 'Two things, Zack,' I said with a sigh. 'Firstly, I will never be able to reconcile with my mother. Secondly, you should google alcohol withdrawal.' I dared to stare up into his face. I'd barely opened my mouth and he was already looking wounded. 'I can't manage your feelings as well as mine.'

'Lydia, we can do this!' He tried to hug me but I tensed every muscle in my body and he had to let me go. 'Please, don't shut me out.'

'Then you have to *listen*,' I said urgently.

'I *am* listening.'

How to tell him that the Lydia he'd known for fifteen years wasn't the Lydia he was talking to now? That the me, in this moment, was a stranger to him. 'Coming back here has opened up a wound.'

'I get that.' He nodded, keenly.

His hip was leaning into mine and the weight of him made my muscles ignite. I imagined how it would feel to slam my hand into his face, to say every cruel word I could think of, to thoroughly shock him. Thoroughly and irrevocably, so that he would never look at me the same way again. He would divorce me and I could happily, blissfully slide into a life of booze and more booze. Perhaps I'd even buy shares in a whisky or gin distillery. Or vodka. I wasn't picky.

It was tempting. Fuck, was it tempting.

But there was Adam. My sweet boy who had grown inside me and, when he was born, had given me back a piece of my dad. Two Adams who would never meet, bookending my life with love.

I grabbed my bag and coat and ran for the door.

'Lydia!' Zack followed me to the front step. 'Lydia!'

I drove off quickly to stop myself from ruining all of our lives.

Tess

She met up with Vanya at the next clean – a modern, five-bedroomed house belonging to solicitor parents and three teenagers. They made more mess in a week than most families made in a month. While they worked their way from room to room, Vanya told Tess about her mum and how long she was staying in hospital. And then Tess told her about what had happened with Lydia. 'She was raging,' Tess said. 'She's so sure that someone called the police. And she's decided that someone has to be me.' She threw out her arms. 'I mean, why me?'

'She accused you outright?'

'Yes! And she wouldn't listen when I said I hadn't done it.' Tess picked up a dozen books off the floor and put them onto a shelf. 'Why does it even have to be someone? She could have been weaving all over the road just as the police were passing by!'

'There aren't enough police on the streets,' Vanya said decisively. She passed Tess a duvet for her to remove the cover. 'Erica says tip-offs from members of the public is the way it works nowadays unless they're cracking down, but we're not close enough to Christmas and New Year for that.'

Tess stopped to think. 'Well, it could have been anyone then, couldn't it?'

'Yeah, it could.' Vanya moved onto the next bedroom and Tess followed her. 'But was it you?' she asked lightly.

'What do you mean?'

'You were on the phone when you arrived at the Airbnb clean.'

'Was I?'

Vanya laughed. 'Honestly Tess, your face!'

Tess tried to arrange her expression to neutral but her facial muscles wouldn't cooperate. Not because she was guilty but because she was shocked that Vanya had asked the question. She was right, though, she *had* just finished a phone call when she drove into the driveway. But it wasn't anything to do with Lydia.

'*Mrs Jeffries?*'

'*Yes.*'

'*I'm ringing on behalf of Mr Wilkinson. He's very sorry but he's unable to extend your loan at this time. He suggested that you contact the Citizens Advice Bureau who will be able to help you manage your debt.*' She told Tess this in a sing-song, upbeat tone as if she was imparting good news. '*Would you like me to give you their number?*'

'*No. I'd like to speak to Jono directly, please.*' He had been a close friend of Steve's and had promised to help the family. It was an enormous comfort to Steve, who'd known the extent of the debt Tess was going to be left with. And at the funeral, Jono had reiterated his promise to help her reorganise her finances.

'*He's in a meeting at the moment, Mrs Jeffries. You're welcome to email him and he'll reply to your message as soon as he can.*'

'*He made a promise to my dying husband who, incidentally, was best man at his wedding,*' Tess told her.

'I think you'll find no promise was made.'

'I think you'll find it was,' Tess fired back.

'Mr Wilkinson is extremely busy,' she said, puffed up with her own self-importance. 'He is dealing with all sorts of crucial issues.'

'As am I,' Tess said. Who was this woman? 'Please put me through to him at once.'

The phone went dead.

'Everything okay?' Vanya was staring at Tess as if she'd just grown another head. 'I mean, I wouldn't blame you if you had reported her!'

'But I didn't!' Tess laughed too, unwilling to tell Vanya about the phone call she had actually made. She'd pushed it from her mind because the memory made her feel humiliated and hopeless. She knew that Vanya would offer to lend her a couple of hundred quid – she'd done that before – but it wouldn't even touch the sides. 'I mean, why would I?'

'Because Lydia hurt your feelings by pretending not to know you?' Vanya held up a crusty sock that had been stuffed down the side of the teenage boy's bed. 'I don't want to think about what's been going on inside this sock.' She threw it onto the pile of laundry collecting in the hallway. 'And you were really annoyed in the restaurant.'

'Only at the very end when I threw the wine in her face.'

'Yeah.' Vanya stood still and bit her lip. 'About that. Have you seen the …?' She trailed off, her eyes questioning.

Tess's heartbeat increased. She had no idea what was coming next but she knew that whatever it was, it wouldn't be good. 'The what?'

Vanya chewed on her lip before saying, 'I didn't want to be the one to tell you this, but someone videoed you throwing the wine, and they've put it online.'

Tess started back. 'Was it one of the mums?'

'No, it was someone who was outside.' She sighed. 'I didn't notice them doing it or I would have knocked on the window and asked them to stop.'

'Can you show it to me?' Tess asked, not panicked, not yet, because – how bad could it be?

Vanya pulled her mobile out of her back pocket. 'It's had a lot of views but it's not trending so that's something.'

'How many views?'

'Just over a thousand.' She tapped her index finger on the screen several times and then, 'Well, almost two thousand now.'

She passed her mobile across to Tess who pressed play and was immediately transported back to that evening. The video had been filmed from outside the restaurant so there was some reflection in the glass and the sound of cars driving past. She watched herself approach Lydia with the money and lay it on the table in front of her. She was walking away when Lydia made another comment, a parting shot. From memory Tess thought she'd said, 'Still playing the victim?' and that was what made her snap, but now she wasn't so sure that Lydia had said that. While she couldn't exactly lipread, it looked more like, 'Are you okay with it?' *How could she have so spectacularly misheard her?*

She watched herself whirl round and grab for the glass of wine next to her. She was shocked at the look on her face. It was vicious, intense, unforgiving and it was obvious that Lydia was completely taken aback. She watched Lydia gasp in shock as the wine covered her face and upper body, some drops splattered into her eyes and onto her hair, something Tess hadn't noticed at the time. And in the ambient restaurant light it looked like

168

blood, as if Tess had just cut her with a knife. Then she watched herself lean in, trapping Lydia in the seat. Her teeth were bared. She looked like a woman possessed as she spoke into Lydia's blood-spattered face, her head pulled right back to get away from the onslaught. When she was finished, her eyes were ablaze and there was an almost-smile on her lips. She walked toward the exit with the confidence of a seasoned aggressor.

The video ended. There were multiple comments underneath but Tess didn't read any of them. She held the mobile out towards Vanya, her hand shaking so much that it fell onto the bed between them.

'It's erm … I think that …' Vanya was uncharacteristically lost for words. She ran her hands through her hair, her mouth open. 'It'll all blow over,' she said at last, waving her arm. 'I thought it was better you saw it though just in case the kids come across it or—'

'The kids?' This was another level of horror. 'You think Bobby will see it?'

'Well, you know what kids are like, they're always online. Not our two because they don't have laptops and mobiles but some in their class do. And definitely the Year 6s.'

Tess slumped down onto the bed and cradled her head in her hands.

'She wound you up, Tess! Don't beat yourself up about it.'

'I raised the stakes when I attacked her.' A shudder passed through her. 'I brought a gun to a wrestling match.'

Vanya sat down and put her arm around her. 'I mean, honestly. There should be a law against people getting their mobiles out. The recording is completely out of context without seeing what went before.'

Vanya continued to reassure her but Tess had seen the video and she knew how it looked. The worst thing was that it wasn't how she remembered it. In her mind, Lydia had been cold and bitchy towards her and she had held off until she could take it no more. She had thrown the wine, but … *was that really her? Had she really looked like that? Had Lydia wound her up or had she wound herself up?*

She would never have believed that she could be so aggressive unless she had seen it with her own eyes.

In complete contrast with his usual mood, Bobby was waiting at the gate, close to tears. Without a word, he followed Tess to the car and when he climbed inside the words poured out of him. 'A boy in the year above showed me a video of you and you were being really mean to Adam's mum and now everyone says you're a b—' He took a ragged breath. 'I won't be able to go to Harry's house after football and I'm not invited to his sleepover.' Another breath and the tears started. 'Everyone hates me. Maisie says she doesn't hate me but she has to pretend not to like me otherwise the others will get mad.'

'Oh, love.' Tess pulled him in for a hug. There was no resistance. His arms were around her waist and holding on tight as if his life depended on it. Tess wanted to cry too. She wanted to tell him that the video was made-up, that it wasn't really her, that she would never behave like that.

But it was her and she had behaved like that. 'Okay, listen. I know it looked bad on the video. I was completely wrong to lose my temper but I'm going to apologise to Lydia and make it better.'

'And you told the police on her,' Bobby said quietly.

'Who said that?' Tess asked, her lip trembling.

'Maisie. She heard her mums talking and Vanya said you were on the phone and it must have been you.'

Vanya? Jesus.

'I didn't phone the police, Bobby.' His eyes were downcast. 'Look at me.' He stared up, his expression hopeful, his blue eyes wet with tears. 'I promise you. That wasn't me.'

'But why do people think you did it?'

'Because I saw her outside Adam's school and it was after that the police arrived.'

He thought for a moment. 'And she was shouting in our house, but if she was driving when she was drunk then that's wrong. And Mrs Frost says two wrongs don't make a right.' He frowned some more. 'But I don't know what that means.'

Tess started the engine and they headed for home, chatting all the while about right and wrong. He had the unequivocal clarity of a ten-year-old. There were no grey areas. It was wrong to throw wine in someone's face, it was wrong to drink-drive and it was wrong to come to someone's house and shout at them. It was right to apologise. It was right to tell the truth.

When they arrived home, Tess settled him in the living room with snacks and his favourite DVD. Rose was in her bouncy chair next to him, listening with wide eyes as he explained the plot. 'I'll have a word with Lydia and make it better,' she told him, kissing his cheek.

She stood in the kitchen for several minutes, her back against the door and her eyes closed. She'd let Bobby down. She'd let herself down. And she had to try to make it right. If Lydia hadn't seen the video yet then she was bound to at some point very soon. Was it better to speak to her before she saw it? Because she surely would. One of the football mums would send it to her.

Tess couldn't predict the future but what she could do was reiterate the fact that she hadn't called the police. She took a deep breath and called Lydia's number, her heart thudding double time along with the ringtone. Six rings and then voicemail kicked in. She took another breath. 'Lydia, I'm truly sorry you're going to lose your licence and that I threw the wine in your face but I promise I didn't report you to the police.' Her mobile shook in her hand and she held it more tightly. 'I've been thinking a lot about our friendship back then and I don't think I supported you enough. Please give me a call.'

She ended the voicemail, a heavy feeling in her heart. She hoped that Lydia would reply. She stared at her phone, willing it to ring.

But there was nothing.

Lydia

I drove to the country club and spent hours in the gym, on the treadmill, lifting weights, swimming and lying in the sauna. By lunchtime, my limbs were loose to the point of floating, but no amount of exercise could chase out the craving for a drink. I wasn't ready to go home. The day was long when you were uncomfortable in your own skin and there was nowhere to hide.

I had woken up that morning wondering what my dad would think of all of this. He was often at the forefront of my mind but never more so than after having seen my mother again. I kept reliving the moment when I walked into my kitchen and saw her sitting on a stool, for all the world as if she belonged there. The shock was beginning to wear off now and in its place was a hardening resolve. I left the club and drove to the outdoor supplies store, where I stood in the queue with binoculars and a pair of waterproof trousers in my basket. My dad had once told me that action was the enemy of thought, and I was taking action to give myself something to focus on. I knew this wouldn't have been what my dad had in mind, but what if he was across all of the facts? He'd reached the rank of chief superintendent, investigating serious crimes, murders mostly. It was a gruelling job that took an emotional toll on him. When I'd asked him why he'd chosen a career in the police, he'd said, 'There are some bad people out there, Lydia. The public need to be protected. And victims deserve justice.'

Hey, Dad! I was a victim. And so were you. Shouldn't the woman responsible be brought to justice?

I'd been passive for thirty years. I'd put everything she'd done to the back of my mind and stayed out of her way. But living so close to her made that impossible now unless I either drank or fought back. Alcohol made living with the status quo just about bearable, but now I'd been caught I was a drunk driver; there was no putting that cat back in the bag. In January, I would lose my driving licence, for at least a year, and I knew what my dad would have said, 'Lydia, you broke the law and endangered other people's lives. You need to take your punishment.'

When my nerves weren't so ragged and the cravings had died down, I would have a heart to heart with Zack. I would make him understand that my mother was dangerous. Somehow, she was still several steps ahead of me, the way she had always been. But if I said all of this to Zack, would I sound paranoid? He would find it hard to believe me because surely I would have told him at some point over the last fifteen years. Why would I keep something like this to myself?

I parked in the same forest car park and returned to my mother's back garden. Action had the effect of elbowing out the withdrawal symptoms. My nerves were still shot, and my hands shook inside my gloves, but to not feel the craving for alcohol was something, at least. Fear did not sit well with me; I much preferred anger, and it began to burn in my chest, warming me, energising me from the inside. I had returned to the scene of the crime.

Or, to be exact, one of the crimes. And I wasn't going to run – not this time.

The patch of grass in front of the summer house was bathed in the full winter sun. It took me back to when Tess and I used to lie there on those warm evenings. I had never felt as close to any human being as I had to her. When Zack and I met, I had already crossed lines, closed off parts of myself, like the attic or basement that must never be visited because that was where the secrets were kept. He told me that one of the things he liked about me was that I was emotionally self-sufficient. His previous girlfriend had cried a lot and been more needy than he could handle. I wanted to tell him that being emotionally self-sufficient wasn't necessarily a good thing. It meant that I often didn't share what I was thinking, and that's not healthy in a marriage.

Tess had left me a voicemail trying to elicit sympathy. Hearing her voice made me shiver as the sting of her betrayal struck me afresh. It had taken her thirty years to realise that she hadn't supported me. And the more I thought about the time we'd spent together, the more I remembered how self-absorbed she was. She placed herself at the centre of everything. The automatic expectation that I should fall back into a friendship with her just went to prove how selfish she was.

There was no way I was going to make things easy for her. It was an opportunity to be mean and I took it. **BACK THE FUCK OFF** I texted back in bold, upper case. I was a malevolent force, and she would do well to be wary of me.

When I was a child, 'bad things happen' was a phrase my mother was fond of using, as if there was no rhyme or reason for anything that occurred. I would ask her why people lived on the streets, why children went hungry or

175

animals were beaten by their owners. And she would tell me bad things happened. 'Get over it!' She would say this gleefully as if she was delighted that I was learning this harsh lesson.

I was twelve when I started to question her thinking because some bad things didn't need to happen. There were enough homes for everyone and enough food to go round. And why on earth could human beings own other animals anyway? What gave human beings the rights of ownership over another sentient being? I began to work out that there was rhyme and there was reason. People made things happen. Sometimes good and sometimes bad.

If we stayed in this village, I knew that I'd be forced to confront the bad. And I'd have no option but to make something happen that I could live to regret. I'd always had a dark side. Doesn't everyone? I'd kept it hidden behind the mask of smiles and yeses and pleases and thank yous and politically correct everythings. And when times were tough, my dark side was tempered by the hazy, fuzzy, idyllic comfort of alcohol – whisky and ginger beer flooding through shards of ice, in a tumbler that weighed heavy on the palm. But underneath the facade, I knew I was capable of extreme action.

I was my mother's daughter after all.

Lydia, summer 1994

'You go to Wales, Lydia,' my dad told me. His skin was grey today. No matter how many healthy juices I made for him, he never looked any better. And he had lost so much weight; his pyjama top was hanging off him. 'You need a break from all of this.'

'I don't want to go without you, Dad.' I was smiling, for his sake. In reality, I felt wretched and terrified because it was beginning to sink in that he wasn't going to make it.

'Aunty Flo likes to help.' He took hold of my hand. 'And you can't let Tess down.'

Now that Tess was going out with Steve, I was sure she would be happy to get out of a long weekend with me and my mother. Even though she'd come to the same caravan park with us twice before and loved it. We'd been going there since I was young. My dad was a great believer in the power of the sea air to 'blow all the cobwebs away'. But I was afraid that something would happen to him while I was gone. I cornered my Aunty Flo. 'You have to ring *immediately* if you think he's worsening.' I talked her through all his medicines and gave her the phone number of the caravan park. 'Promise me.'

'I promise you.' She gave the best hugs, and as she held me I thought I was going to cry. But then my mother appeared, and I would never cry in front of her if I could help it.

I was ten before I realised that my mother wasn't the way most mothers were. As a child, I assumed that every family was the same as mine, that mothers had bad tempers and would lash out, pull your hair or lock you in a room when you misbehaved. Dads were kind and happy, and when you heard their key in the lock and their tread on the floor, you could relax because you knew you wouldn't be hit in front of them.

I said goodbye to my dad with a heavy heart because it felt like the worst thing in the world to be leaving him. 'I really want to stay, Dad,' I whispered. 'Please.'

'You take a walk along the beach for me,' he said, patting my hand. 'Swim in the sea, catch some waves.' His smile was so tired. 'It'll make me happy thinking of you there.'

And so I climbed in the car with my mother, praying that the time would fly by and that my dad would look better when we got back. We drove to collect Tess and found her waiting for us at the front door wearing a miniskirt and sandals, and with a holdall at her feet. 'Showing off her legs,' her mum said when she followed her to the car.

'Because it's hot!' Tess said, glaring at her. Deirdre tried to kiss her cheek but she ducked to avoid it.

'She's as giddy as a kipper!' Gary was there too. 'It's the Steve effect!'

Genevieve wound down the window to make small talk and Tess threw herself into the back of the car beside me. I knew she found her parents loud and embarrassing but I didn't think they were that bad. She often complained about her mum and Gary but they were dependable. What you saw was what you got with Gary and Deirdre whereas my sands were constantly shifting. Today my mother was unusually happy. She was smiling and whistling as if my dad wasn't dying and being with her daughter and her best friend was all she could ever want.

I should have known she was up to something. She stopped at the first motorway service station so that we could 'stretch our legs'. Tess and I went into the shop to buy some sweets and when we came back, Oscar was sitting in the front seat.

'What the fuck?' I clocked him from several metres away. 'There's no way he's coming.' I ran towards the car and pulled the door open. 'Get out,' I said, grabbing his shirt at the shoulder and pulling hard. His hands reached out and held onto the dashboard while he sat there grinning round at me. I could feel Tess's anxious breathing beside me. 'Get your bag,' I told her, letting go of Oscar. 'We're going back home.'

Tess started scrabbling around in the back seat to gather up her stuff and my mother jumped out of the driver's seat and was at my elbow in a flash. 'If you do not get back into that car, not only will you suffer but your dad will too.' Her voice was low and her fingernails dug into the soft skin on the inside of my upper arm. 'Is that clear?'

This was her latest repeated threat – my dad would suffer. And it wasn't an idle threat. On Monday last week, I'd refused to tell my Aunty Flo how well my mother looked after him, and to punish me she only gave him half his prescribed dose of morphine. When I got home from school, he was tense and sweating with pain. She watched how distressed I was before taking me aside to say, 'You can give your dad some more now. And afterwards you'll call Flo. Do you understand?'

I did as she asked. I gave my dad his dose of morphine, through the pump like the nurse had shown me in the hospital. And then I called my Aunty Flo and sang my mother's praises.

I stood beside the car and quickly thought through my options. It would take Tess and I longer to get back home than it would my mother. She would make something up and upset my dad. By the time I walked through the door my dad would be anxious and my mother would be plotting her revenge.

'The thing is,' Tess was saying to Genevieve, her voice low. 'Oscar has been following us and he's a bit scary.'

'Tess.' Genevieve hugged her. 'Oscar worries about you both.' Her tone was silky smooth. 'He's just been looking out for you.'

'Well, I'm ...' Tess trailed off and stared across at me, her eyes asking the question *what now*?

I got back in the car. Tess immediately climbed in the other side and took my hand. 'Are you okay?' she whispered.

'Don't you worry, girls,' my mother said, staring at us through the rear-view mirror. 'We're going to have a wonderful time.' She glanced across at Oscar. 'Aren't we, Oscar?'

'We sure are,' he said, his hand reaching across to pat Genevieve's leg.

'Are they having an affair?' Tess mouthed at me, wide-eyed.

I shook my head. It was something I'd thought of but never voiced because she wouldn't betray my dad like that. Would she? Surely there was a limit to her cruelty?

And now, for ninety-six hours, I would need to be on my guard. When Oscar was around, I needed eyes in the back of my head. I usually knew what he was about to do next because he'd been trying it on with me since I was fourteen. The lock on my bedroom door had kept him at

180

bay while I was at home but camping was a whole other matter.

He had one eye on me and the other on Tess. I'd need to protect both of us.

It would be a long four days.

Tess

Bobby lived so completely in the moment that a film and some popcorn had wiped what Maisie said to him at school from his mind. Tess was relieved that he had stopped crying about the video of her behaving badly, and she began to almost relax when a text arrived from Lydia – **BACK THE FUCK OFF.** The sight of it made her shiver inside. Was Lydia gunning for her now? Because Lydia wasn't someone she would ever want as an enemy. She knew that Lydia could be ruthless when she didn't like someone. She was fearless in a way that Tess had never been and could never be.

She sat next to Bobby on the sofa and pretended to watch the film. The room was freezing cold and she wore an all-in-one knitted jumpsuit that one of her clients had been throwing out. She always got first dibs on anything the client didn't want and this was a godsend. The hood covered her head and the sleeves were long enough to come halfway down onto her hands. The wool was a bit itchy, hence the reason her client was getting rid of it, but that was a minor inconvenience for Tess. She just wanted to be warm. It was December and winter was just getting started – January and February would surely be colder – and already she felt weary with the reality of seeing her breath condense in her own front room. She presented the whole thing to Bobby as if it was some sort of an adventure – let's see how many layers we can wear and still be able to walk! – but it wasn't. It was mentally exhausting to not be able to afford to heat her home. She felt ashamed. These were her two precious children and she didn't have the means to heat the air around them.

'This is the funny bit, Mum,' Bobby said, nudging her with his furry elbow. He was wrapped up in four layers of wool and soft cotton. A teddy-bear jumper she'd found in a charity shop was his top layer. Luckily, he had yet to show any sign of being fashion conscious.

She laughed along with him, pretending to enjoy the joke as much as he did, and then she returned to her thoughts. The video from the restaurant. Who filmed it? And how had it ended up on the community website? The moderator was slow to take down posts that didn't meet the standards, and by the time it was removed, it had been shared multiple times.

She wanted to watch it again but she was too afraid. It had been such a shock to see herself behaving that way and she didn't want to relive the experience. It would only make her more depressed. As with most of the problems in her life, she could think of no easy way to solve it.

It was just as she was going to bed that she saw the man again. Her dad had gone out just before eight for a game of snooker, and she'd started the bedtime routine soon after that. Bobby lay in bed reading while she bathed and fed Rose, who fell asleep just as her bottle finished, milk dribbling from the side of her mouth to gather in the folds of her neck. Tess soaked up the milk with a muslin cloth before transferring the sleeping baby very slowly from her arms to her cot, barely breathing in case she woke up.

The streetlight cast an orange glow across the carpet and the walls, and when she went to close the curtains, she saw him standing opposite the house. He was wearing the same cap, eyes staring up at her from beneath the brim, and the twist of his mouth, cigarette in one corner, was just as she remembered. She jerked the curtains closed, her knuckles white against the dark blue fabric, her heart in her throat as she waited to see what would happen next.

There was a loud bang on the front door. She stifled a scream, let go of the curtains and glanced quickly into the cot. Rose hadn't stirred so she closed the door behind her and moved into Bobby's room where he had fallen asleep with the book in his hand. Another bang and she froze, but Bobby slept on. She placed the book on his bedside table and turned off the light. Then she stood at the top of the stairs and waited. There was a rattling of the letterbox and then he must have bent down to shout through the gap. 'I know you're in there!'

It was *his* voice – Oscar's voice – she was sure of it. Hearing it again made her teeth chatter and her legs shake. She clapped her hands over her ears and screwed her eyes tightly shut, sliding down the wall to curl up into a ball on the floor. She had never been afraid like this when she was a teenager because Lydia always dealt with him. *She protected me,* Tess realised. This was the first time it had ever occurred to her that Lydia took the brunt of it. Lydia stepped up. Always.

The banging continued for another couple of minutes and Tess stayed where she was, still and small, until just gone eleven when she heard her dad's key in the lock. Then she crawled along the floor into her bed, frozen and stiff from so long on the floor.

Lydia

When I walked through the front door, I was freezing cold and hungry. My stomach grumbled and my teeth were chattering. Next time I went to the summer house, I would be sure to wear more layers. I'd spent two consecutive days sitting there for hours at a time, my binoculars trained on the back of the house. I wasn't even sure what this was meant to achieve only that it gave me strength and satisfaction to watch her moving about the rooms, oblivious to me, the watcher.

I was hoping Zack would be in his home office and I would be able to sneak past him, but he was in the kitchen prepping vegetables for dinner. My heart dropped. I needed to be on my own. The craving for alcohol seeped through every cell in my body like a killer virus. My nerve endings were screeching, I had tinnitus in one of my ears and a shake in both my arms.

As soon as Zack spotted me, he wiped his hands on a cloth and reached for his mobile. 'Have you seen this?'

He tapped the screen a couple of times then held his phone out in front of my face. I was warming my hands above the radiator, too far away to see it clearly. 'What is it?' I asked.

'It's a video of you. It's online,' he added, his tone disbelieving, as if it was too preposterous to be true.

I moved closer. I thought it might be a video of me being arrested, slyly recorded by a curtain twitcher then uploaded onto a website that named and shamed drink drivers. There were armies of neighbourhood-watchers who would condemn me to hell and beyond for driving under the influence of alcohol. And, frankly, I wouldn't blame them. What I'd done was wrong and I deserved to be punished for it.

But it wasn't that. The video was of Tess, throwing wine in my face, looking even more fierce than I remembered. When it ended, Zack said quietly, 'Why on earth didn't you tell me this had happened?'

'I thought I had told you.' That wasn't true. I hadn't told him because it didn't seem important. And he hadn't noticed my stained clothes because he never went into the downstairs bathroom. I didn't much either, for that matter. The blouse and tank top were still in the sink.

'It looks worse than it was,' I said at last.

'Lydia?' His jaw was slack. 'Someone at work sent me the link! It's been viewed thousands of times.'

'Well, people need to find better things to do with themselves.' Could it really only be Wednesday? Not even forty-eight hours since I'd found my mother in my kitchen. I massaged my scalp with my fingertips hard and fast to try to release some of the tension. It didn't work.

'Why aren't you shocked by this?'

I glanced across at him and then quickly away again. I wanted to punch his handsome, stupid, kind and idiotic face. *Be still my fists*. 'I'm sorry if I've embarrassed you at work,' I managed.

'This isn't about being embarrassed. This is assault!'

He wanted me to mirror his shock. I didn't have the energy for that but I threw him a bone. 'I think she was the person who reported me to the police.'

He checked behind him as if he expected Tess to be standing there. 'Why?'

'She's annoyed with me,' I said. By now my nerve endings were screeching so loudly that I could barely hear my own voice. 'I was friends with her back in the day, and she wants to be friends again.'

'Isn't she Bobby's mum? The woman who runs Maids of Honour?' I nodded. 'Why on earth didn't you tell me that she was behaving like this? She excluded Adam from the birthday party, didn't she?' I nodded. 'Lydia, we employ her, for heaven's sake!'

'It's irrelevant.' I sighed. 'She's irrelevant.' I forced my feet to move. 'I'm going for a shower.'

I ran upstairs unable to hear what Zack called out to me because the ringing in my ears was so loud. I locked the door and tore at my clothes. The shower was hot enough to burn my skin, but I relished the feeling. It was a distraction from what was going on inside me.

The video. I could do something with that. I could take it to a solicitor, to the police even. Zack was right – her actions would surely be classed as an assault. The thought of punishing Tess, not for throwing the wine in my face – I didn't care about that – but for calling the police and increasing my mother's power over me, gave me a swell of satisfaction. I felt uplifted. I imagined knocking the smile off her face. It would be no more than she deserved.

Because hadn't I already sacrificed enough for her?

I came downstairs to an empty house. There a chicken casserole simmering on the hob. I grabbed a hunk of bread and covered it with two tablespoons of the casserole gravy. Then I sat at the table with my food. I hadn't looked at my mobile all day and I did so now. There was nothing further from my mother, multiple work-related emails and two messages from friends sending me the video link. **Did you see this??** Romilly wrote. **What are you going to do??**

I didn't reply to any of the messages. I ate the bread and gravy slowly, careful not to upset my stomach. Every few seconds it crossed my mind to have a drink. *No one would know.* We had an off-licence three minutes' drive from the house. I could be there and back in under ten minutes. I could guzzle it directly from the bottle then hide what was left in the garage. Four or five mouthfuls and everything would change. My muscles would relax. I'd be able to smile at Zack when he came through the door and I'd be more relaxed when I had my first meeting with the therapist I'd arranged to see. I mean honestly, what was the point in stopping drinking?

I was on my feet when I heard Zack's car on the drive. I swivelled round quickly and was back, seated at the table, when he came in. He was carrying a huge bouquet of red roses and two bottles of wine. He presented the flowers to me with a flourish and a kiss on my lips. 'The wine is alcohol free. The assistant told me you would never know.' *I'll know. Of course, I'll bloody know.* 'It's made in a particular way.' He went on to explain the process while I arranged the roses in a vase.

When he drew breath, I said quietly, 'I'm seeing the therapist today.'

'Lydia, that's great.' He gave me his full attention. 'Do you want me to drop you there?'

'No. It's okay. She has parking outside her house.'
I leaned my head against his shoulder. 'Thank you,
though.'

Grace Linford had been recommended to me by a
friend in London. She specialised in clients who were
troubled by addiction. I was lucky that she was able
to make space for me so quickly and I made sure to
arrive on time. She answered the door within seconds
of me pressing the bell. 'Come in, Lydia.' She held the
door wide. She was small and slim with wide grey eyes
that were unblinking. 'The room we'll be using is first
on the right.'

She saw her clients in her home, in a south-facing
room flooded with light. The room was exactly the right
temperature and smelled of honeysuckle. She showed
me in and sat down opposite me, her hands settled on
her lap. I sensed she was someone who had never once
raised her voice, and I knew that as soon as the physical
effects of alcohol withdrawal subsided, being in her presence would help me to feel at peace.

I'd been to therapy before so I knew what to expect.
The sessions would go at my pace. I might be gently
nudged towards a thought or a realisation, but most of
the nudging I would do myself. I would listen to my
own voice as I spoke, one word following another. I
would know when I was being truthful and when I had
to dig deeper. I would never lie. Sometimes I might
avoid telling the truth but I wouldn't make anything
up. At times I would resist the process and feel sorry
for myself. Then I would be brave and push through. I
would learn to trust Grace and trust the talking cure.
It was a cliché, but I knew that what happened next

would be a journey, one that I had to travel on whether I liked it or not.

'So what brings you here today, Lydia?' she asked.

'Where to start?' I almost laughed. I felt nervous. I had a sudden image of myself aged sixteen, stricken with grief and anxiety, trying to tell the police what had happened but failing dismally, my mouth incapable of speech. I'd lasted thirty years without telling that story and I didn't want to revisit it now. I had never voiced the details of what happened, and after all this time, I wasn't sure I could find the language. It was better to begin with recent events – being caught drink driving and my mother appearing in my kitchen – than to talk about the bones of me, what made me tick, what lived inside me still. My life existed in two distinct parts, the before and the after, and I couldn't wind all the way back to the before.

I just need to make it through this hour and then I can get a drink. That was the promise I made myself because the urge to flee felt overwhelming, and promising an end to the misery was the only way to keep myself in the chair.

'Begin wherever you feel the most comfortable,' she said softly.

I took a breath and told her about my drinking habit and that I'd driven my son to school while I was over the limit. I was fidgeting as I spoke but my tone was monotonous. I heard my own voice drone on and on and I wanted to squirm, to shed my skin, to shrink from the truth.

'How did being caught by the police make you feel?' she asked.

'Guilty.' I scratched my arm, felt the skin I'd already broken break again. Blood wet my fingertips. 'Adam is my

190

only child and I love him more than I love myself.' I paused for a moment to check that this was true. It was. 'It's my love for Adam that will help me through this,' I added.

Grace nodded. 'Tell me about the people you love,' she said.

I told her about my dad and about Zack, nothing too personal, just the bullet points: two good men who knew how to love me back, and after twenty minutes I came to a natural stop.

Grace allowed some breathing space before gently probing me on my alcohol use. Nothing as direct as 'so tell me why you drink'. Less of the 'why' and more of the 'what'. 'What do you feel when you reach for the glass?'

'Relief,' I replied at once. She waited for me to say more. There wasn't a clock in the room but I felt the passing of time through my own internal clock. I was paying for these minutes – with money and, eventually, I knew I would pay with truths that she would need to tease out of me.

'Drinking saves me having to think,' I admitted, as much to myself as to her, my cooperation moving forward in inches. 'Thinking is the enemy.' I paused again. 'Someone once told me that action is the enemy of thought and I think that's true. I mean we all have things we'd rather not think about, don't we?' I glanced at her face. Her expression was interested but flat as if nothing I could say would ruffle her composure. 'But modern life isn't urgent! Not for most of us. There's no hunting and gathering, no immediate threat to life so a lot of living happens in our heads. And our heads, our thoughts—' *our memories* '—can torment and destroy us.' I nodded to myself as if I'd said something wise. Then I stood up. 'Time's up I think.'

'We still have a couple of minutes,' Grace said.

191

I stared through the window. Since I'd arrived the sun had set and the night was pitch black and starless. 'I'd rather arrive home before the temperature drops below zero. I don't like driving when it's icy.'

'Of course.' Grace led me to the front door. 'You worked hard this session, Lydia.' She smiled at me for the first time. A gentle, non-obtrusive smile that made me feel as if I was in the presence of a saint. 'Perhaps next time we can talk some more about those thoughts.'

'Perhaps,' I said.

Tess

After hearing Oscar banging on her door, Tess had barely slept. She drifted off to sleep for what felt like seconds before awakening with a start, rushing out of bed to check on her children. This went on for two nights and then, on the second morning, she felt slightly calmer. She could go to the police. She knew from a podcast she'd listened to that she needed to gather some evidence – photographs, timings, anything that would help to build a case. Because by now she knew it was definitely Oscar. The voice from last night was the same as she remembered – *I know you're in there* – the words reverberating inside her skull, neon lit, warning her that her life was in danger. He was on to her. He knew where she lived. He had seen Bobby at the football and Rose in her buggy.

She thought back to the first time they'd met, when Lydia had warned her not to look at him. And then, when she had stupidly caught his eye, how Lydia had dragged her upstairs to her bedroom and told her what sort of man he was – a perv, a paedo, a wanker. She didn't spare her descriptions. 'You must have noticed how besotted my mum is with him,' Lydia had said. 'It's seriously weird.'

A mental picture of the campsite in Wales flashed before Tess's eyes but faded just as quickly when she lifted

Rose from her cot. Her baby was in her arms, plump and healthy, smiling up at her. The past was behind her; she needed to live in the present.

When Bobby and her dad set off for school, Vanya called her to say she couldn't work that day. 'Maisie's come down with the sick bug. Has Bobby got it?'

'Not yet,' Tess said. There was no one else to cover Vanya's clients apart from her. And Lydia's was one of the houses on the list. 'I can't go there,' Tess said to Vanya. 'Not with everything that's going on.'

'They're never home on Thursdays,' Vanya told her. 'There's no way you'll bump into her.'

'I don't want to risk it,' Tess said. And then she remembered Bobby's tears when Maisie told him that her mums thought it was Tess who called the police. 'I didn't call the cops on her,' Tess said. 'It wasn't me.' She wanted to ask Vanya whether she knew Maisie had been listening to her conversation with Erica, but she kept quiet because Vanya might be defensive, and Tess might be too. She didn't want to risk falling out with her. Vanya had helped her and Bobby through all their hard times.

She ended the call, wincing as she remembered the look on Lydia's face when she'd come to the house to collect Adam. *'You of all people,'* Lydia had said to her. *'After everything I did for you.'*

What did that even mean? What had Lydia done for her? Tess felt as if the answer to that question hovered at the edges of her vision but somehow, she just couldn't bring it into focus.

She collected the keys for the day and, leaving Rose with her dad, headed off to Lydia's. The house was a showstopper. It was situated at the end of a sweeping driveway, mellow concrete blocks merged perfectly with gigantic panes of glass. She steadied her nerves and rang the doorbell, counting slowly to twenty as she waited. No reply so she used the key. 'Hello! It's the cleaner!' she called out as she went inside. The alarm beeped a warning, and she typed in the four-digit code written on the label attached to the keyring. Then she stood for a few seconds, listening. The house was completely quiet. No one home. Thank heavens. She breathed a sigh of relief and starting upstairs, cleaned and dusted faster than she ever had. She focussed completely on the task. She changed the sheets on the beds and the towels in the bathrooms. She was tempted to look in Lydia's wardrobe, to open drawers and find photo albums or diaries but she didn't. She wasn't that person. She wasn't a sneak or a telltale.

When she went into the downstairs bathroom, she found the clothes Lydia had been wearing in the restaurant still soaking in the sink. She lifted them up and saw that these were stains that were never coming out. 'Fuck,' she said, under her breath. '*Why?* Why did I throw the wine in her face? Why do I always make everything worse?'

There was no answer to that. She sat down on the floor, her head in her hands. Lydia was rich, what did it matter? *That's not the point*, she argued with herself. *The point is* me. *The point is that I'm unable to see things clearly until it's too late.*

She took the clothes through to the utility room and was using stain remover with little effect when the doorbell rang. She jumped guiltily, looking left and right as if choosing in which direction to run. *Run?* 'Calm down,' she said out loud. 'Probably just a package. Lydia wouldn't ring her own doorbell.'

'Tess!' It was Genevieve. 'Fancy meeting you here!' She was holding a bouquet of flowers. 'I'm popping round to leave these for Lydia.' She had a heavy-looking bag over her shoulder. 'And some snacks for Adam.'

'I'm just finishing up,' Tess said, moving to one side so that Genevieve could come into the house.

She gave Tess a quick kiss on the cheek. 'Don't let me disturb you, love.'

Tess went back into the utility room and folded the wet clothes neatly on the draining board. The stains hadn't budged. She would let Lydia know that there would be no cleaning charges for a month. She hoped the gesture would help heal the rift between them. While she cleaned the downstairs bathroom, she could hear Genevieve quietly humming in the hallway and it made her smile. She had always found Genevieve's presence comforting. From ages thirteen to almost sixteen, she had spent more time at Lydia's house than her own. Genevieve had always been friendly and generous towards her. She seemed to enjoy having her there. 'You make Lydia much kinder, Tess,' she'd said to her once. 'You soften her edges.'

Lydia didn't often complain about her mum back then, not like Tess did. Tess was constantly moaning about how much her mum seemed to care more about Saskia than she did about her own daughter. Lydia would nod and remind her that it could always be worse. Her dad had told her about the case he was working on where a child was murdered by her stepfather. 'It's important to keep a sense of perspective,' Lydia had said. 'Most parents are just about good enough.'

Tess remembered one occasion when Lydia *had* vented her frustrations. Her dad was on a course in Manchester and her mum had grounded her for being rude. Tess wasn't allowed to visit for the whole weekend and when she saw her at school on the Monday her expression was dark. 'It's like she owns me. Be this way, not that way. Say this, not that. Go here. Go there. She's a liar and a control freak. I hate her guts. And I hate Oscar. He's a creep and a moron.'

Tess gathered her cleaning equipment by the front door and took her water bottle with her when she went to say goodbye to Genevieve. She was standing in the kitchen close to the sink, deep in thought. At the sound of Tess's footsteps, she looked up, her brow furrowed. 'You may have heard that Lydia's been having a hard time lately. She was caught drink-driving.'

Tess nodded. 'Actually, I'm glad you brought that up.' Her mouth was dry and she gulped some water from her bottle. 'Lydia is convinced that I told the police, and I really didn't.' Her lip began to tremble and she bit it to make it stop. 'It would never have occurred to me that she was over the limit at that time of the morning, and even if it had occurred to me—' She stopped. She didn't want to say any more. She still had a residual loyalty towards Lydia. It was ridiculous but she couldn't help herself.

'Tess, you're a good person. I know that, and I'm sure somewhere deep inside Lydia knows that too. It's absurd that she's blaming you. As you and I well know, she's always been willful. And ...' she trailed off, '... what's troubling me more is—' She wrung her hands together and lowered her voice. 'I had no idea she was drinking so much. Did you?'

'No. I mean we don't talk. I tried to be friends with her when she moved back here but she was busy.' Tess gripped the water bottle more tightly. 'It's been thirty years. It's only normal that she'd want to make new friends.' She heard her voice saying this and knew that she should have felt this all along. Why had she been so insistent? So hurt and offended when Lydia hadn't wanted to take up where they left off? For that matter, where had they left off? Tess had no clear picture of the last time she saw or spoke to Lydia when they were teen-agers. Was it when they returned from Wales?

These last few months she had behaved like the teen she no longer was. If Steve was still alive, she would have been okay about it. His death had made her more needy, more paranoid, more of everything that was negative. 'I've been pathetic.'

'Stop that,' Genevieve replied at once. 'Lydia's not the person you knew back then. She changed when her dad died.' A small tic started up in her cheek and she rubbed at it with her fingers. 'She was … unlike herself. It was a frightening time for both of us.'

'I've been thinking about that a lot lately,' Tess said. 'I don't think I was there for her.'

'Of course you were!' Genevieve said. 'You were always there for her.'

'You know when I gave you letters to pass on?' Tess asked.

Genevieve frowned. 'What letters were those?'

'The letters I wrote to her.' Genevieve's expression was blank. 'When Lydia went to live in London and I wanted to stay in touch. But I didn't have her address.'

Genevieve sighed. 'Ah, yes. I gave her your letters but she forbade me to pass on her aunt's address. As I said, she was troubled.' Her eyes were kind. 'This really isn't your fault, love.' She lifted her bag off the floor and walked to the door. 'Lovely to see you again. Let's stay in touch!' She blew Tess a kiss and went out to her car. As she walked towards it, Tess saw the head of a rose sticking up out of the top of her bag. So she'd decided not to leave the flowers after all? How strange.

Tess reset the alarm before leaving herself and realised that she should have asked Genevieve about Oscar. Why didn't she ask about him? It was a missed opportunity.

Next time she wouldn't be so stupid.

Lydia

Thursday of that week and I still wasn't working. I wasn't ready to visit Paula either. I had been messaging her but hadn't been to see her since before my day in the police station. When I arrived back home to change my clothes after a long session in the gym, I could tell that Vanya had been in to clean. There was a lemony scent in the air. But ... intermingled with the citrus scent, there was something else. I stood still in the hallway and breathed in through my nose. I could smell my mother's presence in the air – she had been wearing *Je Reviens* since I was a child. How could her perfume still linger when she hadn't been here since Monday?

I moved through the house, checking that there was nothing out of place, sniffing the air as I walked. The rooms were a tidier, cleaner version of the ones I'd left that morning. Toys, books, clothes, dishes were all back in the cupboards and on the shelves. My clothes from the night out were neatly placed beside the sink in the utility room. I could see that Vanya had made an attempt to remove the stains.

I wouldn't have put it past Zack to invite my mother round but he was at a business meeting in the city. My imagination, then. Had to be. I was imagining my mother's presence in my house, and no wonder when she was so successfully preoccupying my thoughts.

I changed my clothes and drove to her house. I parked in the same spot as before, several metres from the road and under a tree. I pulled on the waterproof trousers, a hat and gloves. I stashed the binoculars in the buttoned-down trouser pocket and jogged along the path, pushing my way through the brambles into the back garden. I opened the door to the summer house and settled myself on the wooden bench in the corner. A small flask of whisky in my trouser pocket would have been a comfort, each mouthful would have warmed my throat and brought fire to my belly, but I hadn't succumbed to the temptation to bring a flask with me. 'That's something,' I whispered out loud. 'Credit where it's due, Lydia.'

I trained the binoculars on the windows at the back of the house, up to where the brick met the roof and then underneath the gutters, right to the edge of the property. There weren't any cameras that I could see, and it struck me how easy it was, even in this day and age, to spy on someone without them realising they were being watched. I saw her move from room to room, vacuuming and dusting, and then settle in a chair with a cup of coffee. She talked on her mobile for ten minutes and then she disappeared from view. I opened the door to the summer house and listened hard but I was too far away to be able to hear her car's engine start up. I sat back down and waited. I wasn't sure what I was waiting for or what I expected to see. All I knew was that I was bringing the fight to her. 'What fight?' I imagined Zack asking. 'She isn't fighting with you!'

I waited for another half an hour, regularly stretching out my arms and legs to keep myself warm, but she didn't reappear so I came out of my hiding place and hugged the hedge down one side of the garden. The neighbours on either side were some distance away, tall beech trees blocking the sightlines. My footprints were visible on the thin layer of frost that covered the grass so I moved even closer to the tall hedge, walking on the dirt border where bulbs would poke up in the springtime. When I reached the edge of the patio, I stood still and waited for any warning sounds. There were none, and so I crept round to observe the front of the house. She had a ring doorbell attached to the door. It would record an image of anyone approaching from the gravel driveway. I stayed to the side out of its range and observed a burglar alarm box high above the door. Breaking in was out of the question, then. I had no doubt that she would switch on the alarm every time she left the house.

I looked at my watch. It was already three thirty. I'd promised to meet Zack at home late afternoon. 'Why don't we make time for each other today?' he'd asked me. He'd run the flat of his hand down my spine as he spoke. It made me shiver, and not in a good way. 'I'll be back from London by four. We have a lot to talk about, Lydia.'

I'd rather not have to go over everything again but that was asking too much. He'd been more patient than I had the right to expect and I knew that I would have to justify my lies and my drinking. There was so much about me that was suddenly new to him from my drinking, my mother, the fact I had lived in Ashdown Village, to the lack of concern I showed over the video. While the video was clearly more damaging to Tess than it was to me, Zack had been shocked by it and confused by my reaction. It was a big deal, and I wasn't surprised enough;

201

I wasn't shocked enough. He expected more from me. He didn't understand my reaction, and not understanding me fed into my mother's narrative. Because if I could keep my drinking a secret then what else could I be hiding? Nobody gets wine thrown in their face without provocation. Ironically, I hadn't provoked Tess but Zack would never believe that. More to the point, how was I ever going to explain the truth about my mother without it sounding as if I was making it up?

I was going to have to tone it down. Be truthful, but not too truthful. Somehow.

When I arrived home, I could hear Zack on the phone in his office. I spent a few minutes busying myself with my gym bag. I was still acutely irritated. I didn't want to be touched. I needed a drink to calm my nerves. I would have crawled to the village and back again for a thimbleful of vodka. 'I'll get through this,' I said as much to myself as Zack. 'I just need to take it minute by minute.'

'You will get through it, love.' He came across the room in three fast strides and wrapped his arms around me. 'I'm so proud of you.' He stepped back to look me in the eye. 'You're doing brilliantly.' I could see that he meant it. 'I can only imagine how hard it must be for you.'

'It is hard.' I tried to smile but my head felt too heavy.

We sat down on the sofa together and he began. 'So, I was thinking about you when I was on the train and, about the drinking.' He stared down at his hands. 'There has to be a reason for someone to drink so much, doesn't there?'

I could have said no, not necessarily. That for lots of people it wasn't that simple, that alcohol sucked them in through no fault of their own. They started out their drinking journey as happy-go-lucky-let's-get-pissed-and-dance groupies and ended up with a crippling addiction.

'Your mum mentioned her cousin—' he continued.

'I told you already.' My patient tone was forced. 'Alcoholism doesn't run in the family.' Oscar hadn't had a drink problem. My mother was lying about that. 'If it did, I would have battled to stay sober all these years and you would have known about it.'

'Okay …' His eyes were worried and his voice shook when he asked, 'I wonder if moving here was the final straw?'

'It was the only straw.'

'Well, I wonder if there is more going on.'

'Like what?'

'Are you unhappy with your life?'

'No.'

He took a breath. 'With us?'

'Of course not.' I smiled. 'I love you, Zack.'

The worry was still there. 'Should we have tried harder for a second child?'

This was an old wound, one that never quite healed. 'Three rounds of IVF,' I said, meeting his sincerity with mine. 'It wasn't meant to be, Zack.' Both our hearts had been broken but we'd learned to look on the upside: Adam. Adam made us one hundred per cent more fortunate than many of the couples we met.

'I've started thinking about how I share some of the blame.'

'Blame for what?' I asked.

'For not showing more of an interest, finding out more about your childhood. I mean, I know your dad died when you were barely sixteen but that's about it.' He took a breath. 'I want to be part of fixing that, of helping you mend your relationship with your mum.'

Uh-oh. I saw where this was going and I didn't like it.

He kissed my hand. 'I think we need to talk about your mum.' My smile dropped. 'She'd like to get to know Adam. He's her only grandchild.'

'I've already said that's not happening.' My tone was gentle and I backed it up with a 'sorry' expression.

He was uncomfortable with that. 'I'm not sure that's the best way forward, Lyds. Surely it's better for us to include her in our lives so that she can see all is well?'

'No. That won't work.'

'Lydia.' He blew out a breath. 'She's your mother.'

'I know.'

He changed tack. 'Sometimes when a parent dies they become the hero, and the one who's left alive, who had to make the difficult choices, who had to work through the aftermath, ends up being punished.'

His eyes were wide and sincere as he said this. I wondered whether he'd been practising it. Whether she'd told him to practise it so that he got it right. 'Did my mother tell you this?' I asked.

He looked sheepish for a moment. 'She said that you adored your dad, that she did too, and that you were both lost without him.'

'And?'

'That your grief was overwhelming, and that you blamed her.' He was wide-eyed again, shaking his head at the truth of it. 'You went to live with your aunt in London for a couple of years and your mum has never been able to mend the fences with you.'

'That's not the whole truth,' I said. 'She's rewriting history.'

He was expecting me to say this and he had an answer ready. 'She understands that you might feel that. She admitted that her own grief was so overwhelming she was unable to care for you.'

That was too much. 'Bullshit!' I gave a short laugh. She was no more grief-stricken than the birds in the trees. 'She wasn't kind, Zack,' I said, my tone light. 'She hit me. She pulled my hair. She pinched me.' I said each sentence with a forced flatness to my expression.

Zack was visibly shocked. 'What? Why?'

'She's controlling. And she's crafty. She only hit me when my dad wasn't there.'

His face paled and then reddened. 'That's awful.' His chest heaved several times as if he was running. 'Lydia, I … Did you tell your dad?'

'No, because she told me that I was wicked and that he wouldn't believe me.'

I knew that Zack couldn't conceive of an adult being cruel to any child, let alone their own flesh and blood. He started pacing, his tread light and quick as if he was ready to give chase. 'I wish you'd told me this before.'

'It's okay.' I followed him across the floor. 'I had a great dad so that made up for it.' I brought his hand up to my cheek, felt the warmth from his palm seep through my skin.

'I'm going to go and see her.' He tried to walk away but I held his hand tight. 'She needs to know that she's not getting away with it.'

'No, Zack. You mustn't do that.' My voice was quiet but strong. 'Trust me, it will make matters worse.'

His chest sagged. 'I can't bear that your mum was cruel to you. She needs to explain herself.'

Explain herself? She would never do that. I'd revealed enough. 'Let's go upstairs.' I nudged his knees with mine. 'Do what we do best.' I leant into him then, persuading him with my lips and my hands that we were okay. Before long we were kissing on the stairs, in the bedroom, clothes pulled off, skin on skin, the rush of desire.

Afterwards we lay entwined, limb pressed on limb, heartbeats in tune. It was almost time to collect Adam but Zack had drifted into sleep, his weight increasing as tension left his body. I gently moved from half-beneath him, inching to the edge of the bed until I was able to stand up.

She'd been working on Zack for a while, insinuating herself back into my life. I'd seen her do this when I was a child. She would tell an aunt, a neighbour or a colleague something about a loved one, create an element of doubt in their mind and then set out to deepen that doubt. It gave her control, allowed her to wield her upper hand. And she did all of this with a gentleness, a faux sincerity that had people believing her. She would know that I'd tell Zack about the physical abuse and she would have a comeback. I was sure of that. She wanted to drive a wedge between me and him, and now that I was about to lose my licence, it was the perfect time for her to strike.

I couldn't let her make all the plays. I had to stop her in her tracks. I found my mobile and reread her text. **I expect to hear from you today.** Short, not sweet. There was threat in the subtext.

I replied with **We should meet.**

We were long overdue for a face-off.

Tess

She was determined to do better for Bobby. His team had a match today and there was an extra practice session afterwards. Normally, at weekends, her dad took him along to the club but she knew that this time it had to be her. She had to show her face. Most of the parents would have seen the video by now. She was on the back foot and it was all her own doing. Staying home wouldn't change that.

She was in the kitchen with Rose when her dad came downstairs. They both sat at the table with cereal and coffee. 'So, what's on the cards today?' he asked.

'I'll take Bobby to football this morning. Would you be able to look after Rose for a couple of hours?'

'I can take her with me to the football,' her dad said. 'I like watching Bobby play.'

'I need to get out there, Dad,' she said quickly. 'For Bobby's sake.'

He took a sip of his coffee before saying, 'Is this because of that video?'

She put down her spoon and prepared herself for her dad's disappointment. 'You've seen it?'

'Me and five thousand other people.' He shook his head, eyebrows raised. 'I must say, I was surprised that you lost your temper, Tess, but I said to the blokes down the social club last night that you would have had good reason.'

'Thanks, Dad.' She smiled and nudged his shoulder. 'I appreciate you sticking up for me.'

'Of course.' He nudged her back harder. 'You're my girl.' He waved his arm. 'Give it a few days and it'll all blow over.'

You're my girl. That felt good. 'I hope you're right. Bobby was really upset after school on Tuesday. I want to help him somehow. Invite a couple of his friends back or take them on a trip to the cinema.' *And there's something else.* It was on the tip of her tongue to tell him about Oscar but she couldn't bring herself to say the words.

'I could help with that.' He suggested tenpin bowling the following weekend. 'Pizza afterwards. That'll do the trick.' He took a loud slurp of his coffee. 'So, what's going on with you and Lydia?'

'She pretends not to know me and it makes me feel …' She trailed off. *Sad? Hopeless? Angry?*

'Why would she pretend not to know you?' he asked, frowning.

'I'm not sure. Maybe I wasn't such a good friend.' She covered her face with her hands. 'I really thought we were best friends when we were young.'

'You know, sometimes people change, Tess,' he said gently. He tipped more cereal into his bowl. 'Look at me! I was barely around when you were growing up, something I'll always regret—'

'How come you weren't around, Grandad?' Bobby called out from the kitchen doorway. He was wearing a lurid green onesie with gnarly monster feet, the oversized hood pulled down over his forehead.

'I had to work away a lot,' her dad replied, gesturing Bobby towards him for a hug. 'But I wish I'd tried harder to be there for your mum.'

Tess blew him a kiss. 'Love you, Dad.'

Bobby took some cereal through to the living room to watch cartoons and Tess poured them both another coffee. They sat in companionable silence. It was still on the tip of her tongue to tell him about Oscar but she couldn't get the words out. She knew he'd ask her *Why this man? Why after all these years? Why are you so afraid of him?* She'd have to explain herself, tell him everything. And she couldn't do that. Partly because she didn't fully understand what everything *was*. She hadn't feared Oscar back then – not really. But now the thought of him back in the village filled her with a sickening, visceral fear. And she didn't understand why. Her memories were incomplete. Great chunks of time and experience seemed to be lost to her. It was frustrating. Especially as she didn't know how to refind the missing pieces.

She stared down at Rose who was making high-pitched, chatty sounds as she watched the shifting light on the trees. Her legs and arms waved and kicked as if she was having a whole body conversation with the outdoors. 'Fairies,' Steve would say about Bobby who was very similar at that age. 'Babies see spirits, you know? They're far more in tune with the world beyond the veil than we are.' She smiled at the memory, saw Steve's return smile in her mind's eye and felt warm inside. She jiggled Rose's baby legs so that she turned her face towards her, eyes wide, her smile gummy and full of wonder.

'What are all those messages coming into your phone?' her dad asked suddenly.

Tess was reluctantly pulled back to the present. There had been a steady stream of beeps, all of which she'd ignored. She picked up her mobile and glanced at the screen. Loan payments. She was lagging further and further behind with payments and was being hounded. And there were a couple of emails from clients too, one of them a cancellation. 'Just work,' she said.

'Bit rich on a Saturday, isn't it?'

'I'll answer them later.' She moved the button to silent but her moment of calm was lost. She wanted to stand up and shout, *I can't always be the person who has to be strong. I can't always be the person who knows the answers. I am terrified that the worst man in the world is back in the village. And if he is, then I am in way more trouble than I'll ever be able to handle. Money will be the least of it. And it isn't fair! It isn't fucking fair! Because I never sowed this. Not now and not when I was a teenager.*

The words screamed inside her head. She heard them but she didn't speak them. She was safe in her kitchen, her children and her dad close by. For now, that was enough.

She found a parking space close to the clubhouse and Bobby ran off inside to change. She had decided to bring Rose with her – pushing the buggy gave her something to hide behind. The playing field had been in use all through the autumn and now, with the wet December days, the grass was trampled on and tired. There were huge muddy puddles in front of each goal and some smaller patches close to the centre of the pitch. She stopped the buggy between the playing field and the clubhouse. It was a good spot; Bobby would see them when he came running out of the changing rooms.

'We might be lucky,' one of the dads next to her said as they both stared up at the overcast sky. He wasn't someone Tess had seen before. Most likely he was a supporter from the opposing team. 'But I'm not holding my breath,' he added. He glanced down into the buggy. 'Who's this little one?'

'Rose,' she replied. 'She's come to watch her big brother play football. If she can stay awake long enough.'

'We're expecting to take a beating,' the man told her. 'You've got a great team here.'

'We do. And our star player is a girl.'

'Equal opportunities.' He smiled. 'Not before time either.'

His eyes were kind and Tess had a few seconds of imagining what it would be like to date again, a man like this who would make her smile and wouldn't expect too much too soon. But then his wife appeared and the moment faded. 'Let's stand under the trees,' his wife said to him, pointing to a spot several metres away, and without a backward glance, they walked off.

She felt an ache for something lost but it didn't last long as Rose gave a throaty babble. She was waking up to the world, tuning into what was happening around her, entranced by a liver-spotted spaniel with an impossibly waggy tail sniffing for all he was worth. 'What do you think, Rose?' Tess crouched down beside her. 'Is the dog funny?'

Rose turned wide eyes towards her and made earnest, agreeable cooing sounds before her attention was caught by a sudden rush of activity beside them. The club-house doors were thrown open and the home team came running out, wearing their blue and white striped tops and navy shorts. Bobby gave them an enthusiastic wave then stopped to retie his laces. When he was finished, he jumped up and down on the spot a few times before joining the others in the centre of the pitch where their coach was gathering them together.

211

She looked over her shoulder for signs that she was being watched but there was no one there. And she wasn't just worrying about Oscar. She watched people's expressions when they caught her eye, waiting to see whether there was a spark of recognition and they'd turn to the person next to them to say 'that's her in the video!'

And suddenly there was Genevieve – again! 'We must stop meeting like this!' Genevieve said, laughing. 'Shall we go inside for a cuppa?' She slipped her arm through Tess's, not waiting for an answer. 'We'll get Rose out of the cold.'

'I've not seen you at the football before,' Tess said. *But I have seen your cousin, Oscar.* It wasn't the right moment to say this, but fate had brought her to Tess and she would ask her as soon as the time was right.

'I don't normally come but … well.'

There was a leak in the clubhouse roof and Tess dodged two buckets, carefully placed to collect the drips, before walking into the seating area. She had a choice of seats and plumped for one by the window again, close to where she'd sat with Vanya. Rose was content in her buggy and Genevieve went up to the counter for the tea. Tess was drifting in her thoughts when a voice said, 'You've really let yourself down, Tess.'

Tess jumped and looked up. It was Romilly, Harry's mum. 'Hi, Rom—'

'Throwing the wine at Lydia.' Romilly folded her arms. 'I'm—'

'It's all over the internet, too.' Her eyebrows were raised in a sceptical arch. 'I hope you've apologised.'

'I have.' Tess felt her cheeks redden. 'By voicemail.' She'd also meant to say it in person but when Lydia came to collect Adam, she was full of accusations; Tess couldn't get a word in to defend herself never mind bring up the incident with the wine.

'All our children have seen it,' Romilly said. 'What sort of message do you think that sends to them?'

'I know, and—' Her shoulders slumped in defeat. She wished she had prepared something to say but short of agreeing it was wrong and she was sorry, what could she do?

Romilly gave her a weighty stare and walked away just as Genevieve came across to the table carrying a tray with two mugs of tea and a plate piled high with a variety of traybakes. 'I got far too many so that you can take some home for Bobby and your dad.' Her eyes followed Romilly's retreating back. 'What was she saying?'

'Just ...' Tess glanced across at the photo of child-Steve. *What would Steve do?* He would be honest. 'I did a stupid thing.' She wiped her eyes with the back of her hand. 'To Lydia.'

'The video?' Genevieve asked, sitting down opposite. Her expression was a question mark but not an unkind one as Romilly's had been.

'Yes.' Even Genevieve knew. Was there anyone in the village who wasn't a witness to her shame? 'I feel really bad about it. And to make matters worse, one of my clients cancelled her contract with me this morning. I think it's because she saw it.'

'Tess.' Genevieve gave a weary sigh. 'I know my daughter. It's clear to me that she goaded you until you snapped.' She pursed her lips. 'People like Romilly are so quick to judge.'

'I'm ashamed of the way I behaved.'

'And I'm sure you've apologised.'

'I have but I need to do more. I need to cover the cost of the damage to her clothes, but I'm not sure how to go about it. Lydia doesn't want anything to do with me and no wonder.'

'Lydia's changed, Tess. She's grown very acquisitive, always wanting more. A bigger house, a new car.' She shook her head and then brightened again. 'Zack is a wonderful man. Have you met him?'

'No.'

'She wouldn't even take his surname, and I know that's the modern way, and I applaud that because it's important for women to have careers.' She gave a wry smile. 'I certainly missed the boat there, but with Lydia it's all part of a bigger problem.' She paused, staring down at her hands. 'I don't want to be talking out of school, Tess, but you know me. I'm not malicious or cruel.' She took a breath. 'Lydia would have Zack believe that I'm not a nice person.' Her frown was pained. 'I think alcohol causes paranoia. I didn't know it could do that but I looked up the symptoms and low and behold, it's Lydia to a T.' She leant in closer, her voice low. 'In Lydia's eyes, I'm not allowed to care about her or Adam. But I think her problem is far worse than either of us knows.' She sat back again and took a bite from a piece of shortbread, chewing slowly before she said, 'Enough about me.' She took another breath and focussed on Tess, her eyes kind. 'When I saw you outside just now, I remembered that it's not even a year since Steve passed away, and I know how hard it is, Tess. A year is nothing.' She shook her head sadly. 'After Adam died, I wasn't myself for a good three years and I can still have my bad days.' She took a sip of her tea. 'And people forget, don't they?' Tess nodded. 'They think you should just move on. As if you wave a magic wand and the man you loved is in your rear-view mirror and you're speeding along the highway towards a new relationship.'

'I miss Steve so much,' Tess said, grateful for this opening. Sometimes a full day could go by without her saying his name out loud. But not today. Genevieve listened as she told her about his illness and how hard they had tried to find a cure.'

'It was like that with Adam,' Genevieve said. 'We tried conventional medicine and all the alternative therapies we could lay our hands on. I remember buying the best vegetables and mixing juices for him. But sometimes, death just can't be cheated.'

There was a tug somewhere at the back of Tess's mind, a smudge of memory that made her question this. But she couldn't grasp hold of the thought.

'Life is all about family, isn't it?' Genevieve said, glancing down at Rose who was being her sweetest baby self. 'How I worry about young Adam.' She paused again. 'Zack does his best but ...' she trailed off. 'Let me know if you hear or see anything, won't you?' Her eyes widened. 'And when I next speak to Zack, I'll make sure he knows how sorry you are about the video.'

'Thank you.' Tess swallowed some more tea before saying, 'I'm glad we've had time to properly catch up, Genevieve.'

'We mustn't leave it so long next time.' She slid what was left of the traybakes into a brown paper bag. 'You take these.'

'Thank you. Bobby has a sweet tooth.' Tess placed the bag in the bottom of the buggy. 'And a savoury tooth for that matter. He's forever eating. Hollow legs, my dad says.'

'They're growing so fast at this age aren't they? But wait til he's a teenager!'

Rose started to make impatient noises and Tess moved the buggy with her foot but she didn't stop so she stood up and put on her coat. 'I think she needs a nappy change, or maybe a change of scenery.'

'She's been an absolute poppet.' Genevieve smiled down at her.

'Thank you.' Tess gave her a hug. 'It's been great to see you.' Now was the moment. She had to ask her about her cousin otherwise Genevieve would be gone and Tess would be annoyed with herself again. She took a breath and said brightly, 'How is Oscar? Does he ever visit?'

'Oscar?' Genevieve stared at Tess, surprised. 'What makes you ask that?'

'I just remember him being around a lot back then.'

'Yes, he was, wasn't he?' Her eyes held fast to Tess's. Beyond the surprise there was a hardness about them that made Tess move back a step. 'I'll keep your interest in mind,' Genevieve said, and then she abruptly walked away.

Tess didn't know what to think.

Lydia

It was Saturday and I'd yet to hear back from my mother. I continued with my life regardless. Adam was going to Harry's for a sleepover but he'd left his coat in my car so after I'd visited my dad's grave, I found a parking space, grabbed Adam's coat and walked towards the clubhouse. A toddler had fallen over and skinned his knee and his yells filled the air. I gave the teenager who was with him a sympathetic smile. 'I have a first aid kit in the car if you'd like a plaster?'

'That's so kind of you.'

I fetched the kit from the boot and opened it for her. She reached for a wipe and tended to the child's knee with tenderness, reassuring him as she did so. When she'd applied the plaster, she stood up and said, 'Maybe next time he'll wear trousers but it's difficult to get any clothes on him at all.' She gave me a quizzical look. 'You look familiar.' She thought for a second and said, 'OMG, the video! In the restaurant!'

'My five minutes of fame.' I shrugged it off.

'I'm Sadie.' She held out her hand for me to shake. 'I babysit for Tess.' She pointed to the little boy who was sitting on the frosty grass trying to pull off his welling-tons. 'Archie's not Tess's child, though.'

'I know,' I said. I started to walk towards my car to put the first aid kit back. 'Enjoy your day.'

'Hang on!' She took hold of my arm. 'Please,' she added. 'I just want to say that Tess is really nice.' Her eyebrows furrowed. 'She's been through a lot, and she was really upset when she came home. She pretended she'd had a good time but I could tell that she hadn't. And then I told her about this guy who came to the door and she went white and I thought she was going to faint. She thought he might be called Oscar and I—'

'She thought he was called Oscar?' I asked quietly.

'Yes. I'm not sure why. She looked scared.'

I took a breath. Every single one of my muscles had tensed at the sound of his name. 'Scared?' I asked lightly.

'Like I said, Tess has had it hard.' Sadie looked wary all of a sudden, as if she'd just remembered something. 'I talk too much. It's my worst thing. My fatal flaw. You know that's when—'

'I know what a fatal flaw is.' I smiled at her. 'I don't think talking too much could ever be fatal.'

She laughed. 'Not according to my mum.' Archie started to run off and she grabbed for his hand. 'My parents got divorced and I've said *way* too much to my dad's new girlfriend.'

'Yeah, well.' I laughed. 'I can see why that bothers your mum.'

'You won't sue Tess, will you?' She bit her lip. 'I mean I understand why you'd want to make a point but—'

'I'm not about making points,' I assured her. 'It's water under the bridge.'

'That's good because it would be the final straw for her, I think.' Archie started pulling at her hand so that she had to break into a jog. 'Bye!' she called out over her shoulder.

Oscar? Why on earth was Tess thinking about Oscar? It didn't make any sense. Except that maybe it did. It could be that I wasn't the only one who had time-slipped thirty years.

I could see Romilly in the distance looking at her mobile and I walked quickly towards her. 'Romilly, hi!'

She glanced up. 'I didn't expect to see you here.' She slipped her phone into her back pocket and kissed my cheek. 'Did you forget I was collecting Adam?'

'No, but his coat was in the back of my car. I thought he might need it.'

'Brilliant!' She took it from me and wedged it under her arm. 'How are you? After the …' she trailed off. I wasn't sure whether she knew that I'd been caught drink driving so I waited until she added, '… the video.'

Romilly wasn't a friend. I hadn't actually made a good friend in the time I'd been here. All my friends were in London still. It wasn't that none of the women here were welcoming and interesting. It was more that I'd changed. I was guarded, preoccupied. I wasn't the person that I had been in London. That woman had faded away into the shadows and friendship wasn't on the agenda for the woman I was now. While I hoped to bring the real me back into the light one day, it wouldn't happen while I was living here at the mercy of my mother's scheming.

'What are you going to do about it?' Romilly leaned in closer. 'It's had thousands of views. I'm sure you could sue her. I know she's had her troubles, but it really was out of order.'

'We all have our troubles,' I said softly.

'She's inside the clubhouse.' Romilly pointed towards the café window. 'I'm not sure who she's with but they've been deep in conversation for ages.'

I glanced across, blinked and narrowed my eyes to see better. It was my mother. That's who Tess was with. They were holding hands across the table, my mother leaning in towards Tess in an intimate, conspiratorial manner. I guessed that she would be manipulating Tess, but the fact that Tess was stupid enough to fall for it only cemented my dislike of her. *Did she remember nothing about our teenage years?*

'I've said to Harry that Bobby won't be included in sleepovers in the future. I know that's punishing the child but I just don't think Tess should get away with behaving like that.'

'Don't punish Bobby,' I said, my eyes still on my mother. Heat was climbing into my cheeks. She shouldn't be here, spreading poison.

'I guess it's not his fault his mum is out of order.'

Tess smiled at Genevieve with an openness that made me want to go inside and rip their heads off. *Fuck this.* 'Zack and I have discussed the video,' I said flatly. 'We're considering suing her for assault.' Even though I'd said the opposite to Sadie, let that rumour take off, see how Tess liked it.

'Exactly!' Romilly's eyes were wide with the kind of meanness that took very little feeding. 'I know a good lawyer. I'll share his details with you.'

I went back to my car to wait, mulling over what I had just seen. I kept coming back to one single detail. My mother must somehow have known that Adam was going to be collected by one of the other mums and that there was no chance she would bump into me, otherwise she would never have met Tess there. She wasn't one for public arguments; she always controlled the narrative. But what could she want with Tess?

I waited for ten minutes before Genevieve came out of the clubhouse, walking quickly towards the car park. I got out of the car, hanging back until she was a few feet away and then I stepped out in front of her. She was startled to see me and drew back, dropping her car key onto the ground. When she bent to pick it up, I placed my foot over it. 'We should talk,' I said.

'I'm not ready to talk to you.' She pulled herself upright, her stance haughty. 'Not here and not now.'

'How did you know to target Zack?' I asked flatly.

'I beg your pardon?' She looked behind her to check that no one was within earshot before adding, 'This is *your* doing, Lydia. *You* are the one who has kept your husband in the dark.'

I shifted my stance, deliberately relaxing my shoulders and fists. 'I know you set me up.'

'You're my daughter! I have a grandson!' She laughed. 'Why would I not take an interest?'

'So you knew Zack was my husband?'

She lifted her eyes to mine. 'Zack and I have grown very friendly over the last few months. I'm sorry if he's recently been made aware of your weaknesses but that wasn't me either.' She thought for a moment. 'Actually, Lydia, I'm not sorry. You've brought this on yourself.'

'You need to leave me and my family alone,' I said softly.

'Or else what?' she scoffed.

'Or else I'll tell the police what you did.'

'Will you now?' She licked her lips. 'And what did I do, Lydia?'

Holding her eyes was strangely satisfying. I felt completely calm from head to foot and at all points in between. *I'm not afraid of you any more.* That thought

221

was spooling through my mind, repeating ad infinitum. It was a revelation. I wanted to raise my arms and cheer. Instead, I simply removed my foot from her key and walked back to my car.

When I arrived home Zack had just been in the shower and smelled fresh when he kissed me.

'How was the gym?' he asked as he opened the fridge.

'Fine.'

He frowned, his eyes on the cans in the fridge door. 'Did you go?' There was a half-smile on his lips when he glanced across at me. 'Really?'

'Why do you ask?'

'Crofty left his mobile there yesterday, so we dropped in on the way to our run in the forest.' He chose a can of mineral water. 'I didn't see your car in the car park.'

Right. It was truth-telling time. Again. We'd had our heart to heart, made love, ended on a high, but every day was a new day. With every sunrise I would have to prove myself all over again. 'I didn't go to the club.'

His jaw tightened. I kept letting him down and it was beginning to get to him.

'Would you have liked it better if I said I'd parked round the back because there were no spaces out front?' My tone was light.

'I'd like it better if you told me the truth.' He popped open the can and took a long drink.

I reached out and touched his upper arm. 'I changed my mind about the club. I went to my dad's grave instead and then I went to the clubhouse to give Romilly Adam's coat.' I added false cheer to my voice. 'And while I was there, I had a conversation with Genevieve.' I smiled, determined to find out whether she'd had advance warning that Adam was going home with one of his friends. 'When did you speak to her?'

He didn't even hesitate. 'This morning.'

'Did you tell her Romilly was collecting Adam?'

'Yes.' He shrugged dramatically. 'Why? What's the problem with that?'

I couldn't look at him. I stared at my feet instead and walked around in a small, neat circle. I tried to take a breath but my lungs refused to fill. 'So what did you talk about?'

He pursed his lips. 'After what you told me about her hitting you, I had to speak to her.'

'And did she deny it?'

He was raising the can to his mouth again and he stopped midway. 'Not exactly,' he replied before taking another drink.

'What then?' I pushed.

'Just that—' He thought for a second. 'The gist of her argument was that recollections vary.'

'She's mimicking the Queen now?'

'Lydia.' His voice was tight. 'She wasn't the one who drove our son to school when she was over the limit.'

'Ah, I see.' I nodded. 'That's your trump card and I'm sure you'll play it over and over again in our marriage, but as you've been speaking to my mother for some time—'

'Yes, I have. But I didn't know she was your mother!' He threw out his arms. 'And whose fault is that?'

I steeled myself not to lash out at him. 'She's already convinced you that I'm a liar.'

'Lydia, your own actions have sunk you. Stop blaming her!' He steadied his breathing before adding, 'She has *one* child and *one* grandchild who live a mile from her and she doesn't see them.' He waved the can in the air.

'If you find her dogmatic or tiresome or just plain boring, I get it! But she's your mother, Lydia. Your *mother*. And your son is surely entitled to get to know his grandmother.' He stared down at the floor before looking back at me. 'Will you lose your licence?'

'Yes.'

I had been in touch with a solicitor and knew what would happen. 'You're not a high risk offender so you should expect to lose your licence for one year,' he'd told me. 'And it's important that you apologise. Don't try to justify what you did.'

I had no intention of trying to justify my behaviour. Now that I was sober again, I looked back on what I had done – *Driving Adam when I was drunk? What was I thinking?* – I knew that I would live with the shame forever.

'So maybe your mum could help with school pick-ups—'

'No. NO. NO!' I said with increasing volume. 'She's not worming her way into Adam's life!'

'This makes no sense!' His arms were outstretched.

'You have to trust *me* not *her*.' I gave all my energy to staring him in the eye so that he could see how important this was to me.

'I want to, Lydia. I really want to.' He shook his head at me, frowning. 'But you have to be truthful with me.' The sensible Zack, who struggled to see the wrong in anyone, had reinhabited his body and at that moment, he was more inclined to believe her than me. It took every ounce of mental strength I had not to grab the can from his hand and throw it across the room.

'What if I had a good reason for Adam not to spend time with her?'

'And what is that reason?'

I opened my mouth to speak but my voice was gone. I wasn't ready to say it. I couldn't bring myself to say the truth out loud because I knew that if I did, my chest would crack open.

Tess

She woke in the middle of the night, a scream in her throat. She'd had the dream again, the one where she was running through the forest being chased by a man. She felt his hand on her hair as he caught up with her, pulling her back towards him. She knew dreams like this were common. She'd looked it up on Google and it told her she was 'avoiding something she'd rather not face', and that it was associated with 'ongoing stress'. *Tell me about it*, she thought. But there was something about this dream that made it feel real, as if she was preparing for an event. A showdown? A once-and-for-all reckoning?

Oscar. He was the man chasing her. That was what her gut was telling her. Was it a warning that she had to be careful? She should never be out on her own in the evening. She shouldn't clean any of the larger houses without Vanya. She should log her concerns with the police as soon as possible. She wasn't sure whether she'd read about it somewhere or seen it on television, but she knew it was important to speak up before it escalated.

Because she knew it would escalate. She felt it in her bones.

'Morning! Another Monday!' Vanya said brightly. 'Everything okay?'

Tess held the door open just wide enough for her to come in without the meagre heat escaping. 'Three of our customers have cancelled on us.'

'What?' Vanya's eyes were wide. 'Who?'

Tess gave her the names.

'They're no great loss,' Vanya replied with conviction. 'Especially Romilly and those boys of hers.'

'It's *money*, Vanya,' Tess snapped back. 'We can't start haemorrhaging clients! I can barely keep house and home together as it is.'

'I know. I'm sorry.' Vanya gave her a hug. 'That came out wrong.' She hesitated, biting her lip before adding, 'Erica and I have watched the video a few times now—'

'Why?' Tess interrupted, her arms tightening across her middle.

'Well …' Vanya took her mobile from her pocket. 'Erica noticed that towards the end, the face of whoever filmed it is reflected in the window and she thought you might know who it was.' She glanced at Tess. 'I completely understand if you don't want to watch it again.'

'I don't. But I want to see who filmed it.' She shrugged. 'It's probably someone random, but why not.'

'I'll show you.' Vanya pressed the screen until she found the place. 'It's not super clear.'

Tess took the phone and stared at the screen. She heard traffic noise but couldn't see anything except herself throwing wine at Lydia. She shivered. It wasn't any better on the second viewing. 'I didn't see a face,' she said when the video finished.

Vanya restarted it and pointed to the bottom of the screen. 'Don't look at what's happening inside the restaurant. Remember, the person was standing on the pavement, filming through the glass. Keep your eyes focussed on the lower right-hand corner.'

Tess did as she was told. Several seconds went by and when the camera moved slightly, the direction of light changed and she saw a face. Or part of a face, because a cap was pulled low on his forehead. But she could see his mouth. And that was enough.

'Fuck.' Her hands shook as she passed the mobile back to Vanya. 'Fuck! It's the guy who's been following me.'

'Someone's been following you?' Vanya's eyes were huge.

'I think it's Lydia's mum's cousin.' She pulled at the worry band on her wrist. 'Sadie told me he came to the door when we were at the restaurant. She must have told him where I was.'

'*What?* Why?'

'Sadie talks a lot—'

'No, I mean why would he be following you?'

'I don't know! Maybe Lydia set him after me!' She twisted the band around on her wrist, tighter and tighter until there was no feeling in her hand. 'I wouldn't put it past her.'

Vanya frowned. 'But why would he—'

'He used to follow me and Lydia when we were teenagers!' Tess shouted, agitated now. 'He was a creep!'

'Did he ever hurt you or …?'

'No, I mean, Lydia always chased him away. She wasn't scared of him.' The wristband snapped and she threw it on the floor behind her, rubbing at the sore spot. 'I wasn't afraid of him either! But now I am. I don't know why!'

'Tess.' Vanya took hold of her shoulders and said softly, 'Take a breath. Please.'

Tess hadn't realised she was holding her breath. Her chest felt tight, her vision blurry, but it wasn't until Vanya told her to breathe that she did so, her inhale loud and ragged.

'If you're being followed,' Vanya said slowly, 'then you need to contact the police.'

If you're being followed. Tess knew that Vanya didn't fully believe her. 'I don't have any evidence,' she said. 'He was banging on the door the other night but instead of calling the police, I lay on the floor! Curled up like a frickin' mouse!' Tears gathered in her eyes. She blinked them away rapidly, as if she was on fast-forward. She couldn't break down again. Not after what happened when Rose was born. *Imagine if social services took her children away?* 'It's fine. I'll sort it.' She waved her arm. 'You should be cleaning by now. We can't risk losing any more customers.'

'Tess, I—'

'Hang on …' She handed Vanya the keys she needed.

'Tess, I really want to help you.'

'I'm fine, really.' She forced a smile. 'You know me …' She rolled her eyes 'Nothing if not emotional.'

'If you know who this man is, and you feel that he's targeting you, Erica can help,' Vanya said, her expression concerned. 'She doesn't deal with stalking, but she can point you in the right direction.'

'Great. Thank you.' Tess opened the front door. 'I'll meet you later for the clean at West Field, yeah?'

'Sure.' Vanya hovered for a moment on the doormat before walking to her car. Tess closed the door and placed her hands over her mouth to stop herself from screaming. Oscar had filmed her in the restaurant then put the video online. He was everywhere. All the time. Stalking her as if she was his prey. How? *Why?*

Lydia had hated Oscar just as much as she did. She wouldn't have sent him after her, would she? It seemed unlikely. The Lydia she knew wasn't spiteful. Forceful, opinionated, sometimes stubborn, but never spiteful.

So how had he found her, then? And what did he want?

The dream came back to her, rising through her body in a merciless wave. She gripped the banister at the bottom of the stair as the wave washed through her. Her heartbeat increased. She could smell the stench of him; she could feel his hand on her hair. She began to shake. She felt for the wristband but it wasn't there. She remembered it had snapped and she lurched across the hallway to pick it up from the floor but the edges were torn and she couldn't fix it. She had another one in a drawer in her bedroom. She tripped over twice as she climbed the stairs. Her legs were jelly again, her hands shook as if she was a drug addict coming down from a trip. She emptied the drawer, haphazardly pulling at her clothes until she found the band. She put it around her wrist and lay down on her bed.

'Breathe,' she whispered. 'Just breathe.'

When her heartbeat returned to normal, she looked at her watch. She had ten minutes before she needed to leave for the first clean. Rose was with her dad at the park. Bobby was at school. She closed her eyes but her mind wouldn't let her rest.

Perhaps she should just walk into a police station and tell them about him?

But what if social services became involved again? The fear of her losing her mind for a second time lingered on and fed into her anxiety. She knew she could trust herself now. She *knew* she could. But could she expect anyone else to? What if Bobby and Rose were taken into care?

There was no way she could risk that. She'd rather commit murder than risk that.

She opened her eyes and stared up at the ceiling, her thoughts revolving on a merry-go-round. And when she widened her scope to include Lydia, she began to realise how selfish and self-centred she'd been back then. She was all about Steve, Steve, Steve. After the holiday in Wales, she never saw Lydia again. She didn't even go to Lydia's dad's funeral. She'd meant to, but Steve had planned a trip to the cinema and she just fell in with it. He would have changed it if she'd asked him, but she didn't ask him. Lydia was out of sight and out of mind.

How could she have simply abandoned her like that? No wonder she didn't want to have anything to do with her. No wonder she'd pretended not to know her. Lydia lost her dad and her best friend in the space of one weekend.

The more she thought about the recent conversation she'd had with Genevieve, the more it unnerved her. She felt like she'd been played. Set up, even. Genevieve hadn't left the club with Adam – he'd gone off with Harry. Tess had never seen Adam with his grandmother, not once. So why was she there?

Genevieve had always favoured her and Tess had liked that. She found her own mum and step-dad embarrassing with their lack of class. They didn't read books or go to the theatre. It was all chip butties and soap operas. Genevieve made her feel as if she was different, better than them. Once she'd even said to her, 'You're a cuckoo, Tess. You landed up in the wrong nest.' She'd taken her arm and whispered, 'You should have been my daughter.' Tess was ashamed to remember how that made her feel – as if she belonged. Genevieve had appealed to her

231

insecurity, and her vanity, and Tess had fallen for it. What a vacuous, fickle teenager she'd been.

There was so much to regret.

Tess cleaned for Grace Linford once each week, and it was as close as she was ever going to get to a therapist. She wished that she could afford to see Grace as a client but she couldn't, and there was no point trying to get help through the GP – she'd tried that but there simply wasn't any help to be had.

When she rang her bell, Grace opened the door wide and Tess walked inside. 'Hello, Tess,' Grace said, her face serene.

Tess smiled; Grace didn't. That was normal for her. Tess had noticed that she didn't feel obliged to smile like she did. Tess was someone who smiled to put people at their ease – *Hi! I'm a nice, non-threatening person.* She said sorry for being in someone's way in the supermarket or taking up space in a lift. Steve used to tell her to 'Stop apologising! You're as deserving of the oxygen in the room as everyone else.'

'How are you?' Grace asked.

'Not too bad, thank you,' Tess replied. She followed Grace into the kitchen where she told her what she wanted her to clean that day. Tess was used to being in other people's houses and it always surprised her how many of them didn't feel like a home. They might be expensively styled and decorated but the look was generic, pleasing to the eye but making no connection with the heart. Possessions bore witness to the lives led, silent observers of day-to-day choices. Shoes took on the shape of the wearer's feet. The mug that had lost its handle but couldn't be parted with was repurposed as a vase for wildflowers.

Grace's house was a home. There was the light, the colours and the personal touches. There was her use of natural materials – the dining table that had seen decades of dinners. The scratches and rings on the surface spoke of family gatherings and times well spent. The table was proof of life in a way that the brand-new could never be.

A trio of small woodland fairies, arranged on a shelf above the sink, caught Tess's eye. They had scraps of material for clothing, tiny feathers for wings and coloured beads for crowns. They were exquisite, quirky and imaginative, and for a moment Tess smiled. 'My grandma made them,' Grace said, following her gaze. She poured herself a glass of water. 'Would you like some?'

'Please.'

She poured a second glass and handed it to Tess. 'I'm going to prepare for my client now but I'm expecting a parcel delivery at eleven. Would you keep an ear out? I'd rather he didn't ring the bell.'

Tess nodded. 'Will do.'

Grace left the room and Tess stood there for a moment, holding the glass tightly, before opening the door and stepping out onto the small brick-built patio. The morning had been stressful so far – Rose was fretful, Bobby couldn't find his football boots and her dad was tired with all the work he was taking on. He got up just in time to take Rose from her.

And then there was Vanya showing her the video. Oscar already loomed large in her thoughts and the fact that he had filmed her in the restaurant fed Tess's anxiety.

What would Steve do? Even better, what would Steve advise *her* to do?

She promised herself she would look at the letters in the shoebox when she got home.

Lydia

Monday, and I was back in the therapist's chair again. My second visit and I felt stronger than last time. The alcohol withdrawal symptoms were receding, and I was on the cusp of almost-calm. There was still the irritation, the craving, the anger, and the shame, but I felt as if I might just make it through the swamp of my addiction without being swallowed up whole.

'It's good to see you again, Lydia,' Grace said. 'How did you feel when you left last week?'

I thought for a few seconds. 'I felt confronted. It's hard sometimes being honest.' She nodded. 'But I know I have to do this.'

'And your weekend?'

'The weekend was tricky.' We weren't a couple who argued very often but now, it seemed, we were arguing every day. Zack and I had ended up going for a walk and it was an uphill climb, physically and metaphorically, neither of us breaking the silence, each of us waiting for the other to speak. 'I know that my secret drinking has pushed my husband to the limit.'

Grace gave an almost imperceptible nod of encouragement.

'I met Zack at just the right time in my life. I'd been sober for a few years and ...' I took a breath, '... the timing was perfect. I'd spent my twenties building a business and was ready to settle down.' I felt her unspoken question and added, 'Zack didn't know I'd had a drink problem. He thought I was teetotal through choice. I think I told him that I just wasn't a drinker. I didn't need to be truthful because I never expected this to happen.' I shook my head and stared up at the ceiling. 'That's what I told myself.' There was a central light, a beautiful chandelier made up of circles of colourful glass. I'd seen something similar in a shop in Venice and regretted not buying it. I looked back at Grace intending to ask her about the light but her attention was laser sharp. She was not about to be deflected. This was work, for her and for me.

I refocussed. 'As soon as I knew we were moving back to the village, I started drinking again. I can pinpoint the exact moment when I knew I needed a drink. We'd come down to visit Zack's mum and look at houses to rent. We stopped in the village for an ice cream and, well ... The shops are different but the same, you know? The village hasn't changed that much in thirty years, and we were in the queue. Zack and I had chosen Cornettos, Adam had an orange lolly, he's not a big fan of ice cream, and as we approached the till, I felt something drop inside me.' I touched my chest. 'I was fifteen, almost sixteen and I stood in that queue often with my best friend. One day in particular, I'd been to the hardware store to buy a lock.' My mouth felt dry and I licked my lips, tried to generate some saliva before swallowing. Grace had placed a glass of water next to a box of tissues on a table by my right hand. 'Is it okay, if ...' I lifted the glass. She nodded and I drank, deliberately lengthening out the time it took because I wasn't sure I wanted to unpack those memories. It would set off a tsunami of emotion that I would never be ready for. 'Yeah,' I said, sighing. 'Coming back here? It's a lot.'

I fell silent.

My thoughts darted off to nowhere in particular. I had learnt to create this place, this nowhere in particular. It was a safe space. A room in my mind where only good things happened. My happy place. My childlike space where I thought about the beach, about blue skies and hot sand. Salty water that cooled me down and kept me afloat as I lay on my back, my arms and legs wide as a starfish. And afterwards there was an umbrella to lie under, shade to seek and birds to watch. Seagulls drifting on the air currents, their wings wide and plumage ruffled. Their beady eyes alert for morsels of food on the beach or fat fish swimming just beneath the surface of the water.

'A phrase that has stuck with me since our last session,' Grace said softly, 'was when you said, thinking is the enemy.'

I came back into the room, back into the body I had briefly left, safe on the magic carpet of my imagination. 'That was my dad,' I said. 'He used to say that action was the enemy of thought, that we had to be careful not to think too much. Thinking can drive people crazy. It can make them believe things that aren't true.' I stared up at the chandelier again and wondered whether it moved in the breeze, whether the circles of glass sang when they knocked against each other. 'He was a policeman,' I continued. 'It's a strange job in some ways. It attracts the best of men and women who then have to deal with the worst traits in other men and women, and well, you are the company you keep, so they have to be careful not to lose their moral centre.' I nodded to myself. 'That never happened to my dad. He always knew right from wrong but sometimes I wonder—' I stopped. Bit my lip. Took another mouthful of water.

'You wonder?' Grace said quietly, not probing, not even nudging, simply knocking at memory's door with the gentlest tap.

'My mother,' I said quietly. 'Why didn't he realise what she was like? Why did the truth never dawn? Why couldn't he see her as clearly as I could? He was a policeman! He was trained to spot liars and deceivers! And there was one under his own roof!'

Even now it struck me as preposterous. We'd talked about her once, only once that I could remember, and he'd told me she'd had a difficult childhood, that she'd had to help raise Oscar, fend for them both, neither of them with a father, each with a mother who worked every hour just to pay the bills. 'Your mother has her good side,' he'd said to me. 'She loves you, Lydia, even though she might not always show it.' He'd taken my hand then, his expression sombre. 'But Oscar. He is not a good man and I've told your mum he must never be allowed in this house.'

'I should have told my dad about Oscar coming to the house.' My heart squeezed. 'But he became ill, and the moment was lost.' I continued to talk about the dynamics in my family when I was growing up. Mostly I was skirting the truth, dipping my toe into the water and then drawing back quickly before I was pulled under.

Tess

While she was upstairs stripping the bed, Grace's client arrived. She heard the soft murmur of voices and then the click of the therapy room door as it closed.

Her mood was low. She'd come to expect this since Steve died. She knew it was part of the grieving process but it wore her out. Sometimes she was overwhelmed with sadness and could barely lift one foot in front of the other. Today she was furious with him – how dare he die. Why him? Why *me*? Why was she the person who had to lose a husband? Why did she now have to cope with Oscar by herself? If Steve was still alive none of this would have happened.

She didn't have to scratch the surface very hard to feel the fear that lurked underneath. She was alone in the world. Sure there were her children, Vanya and her dad but there was no one beside her, no one to hold her hand and walk a parallel path. She was lonely yesterday, lonely today and she'd be lonely tomorrow. She saw no end to it.

As she remade Grace's bed, she felt a stab of jealousy. Tess knew nothing about Grace's husband except that he worked as a psychiatrist in the local hospital. She imagined him coming home that evening. They would share the significant moments of their day over a dinner of sea bream and samphire, a bottle of Chablis between them. Then they'd go to bed and read for twenty minutes before turning out the lights and making love with a natural, carefree intimacy.

And she felt jealous of their lack of children. Children were such a worry. They were a worry of impossible magnitude. *Perhaps Grace and her husband want children but can't have them,* a small voice inside said, counteracting her deep dive into misery. But she was having none of it because life was a game and they were playing it wisely. Tess, on the other hand … She had to raise Bobby and Rose without Steve to share the ordinary days, the ups and the downs, the triumphs and the hard times. Somehow, she needed to help them navigate from being children to grown-ups, cross the minefield of their teenage years and reach adulthood intact.

How could she even begin to make that happen?

When she was finished in the bedroom, she heard the van's arrival on the stone driveway, and went downstairs to collect the parcel from the driver as Grace had asked her to. She tiptoed quietly into the kitchen and left the parcel on the chair. She didn't normally come downstairs when Grace had a client with her, and her tread was light as she passed the closed door of the therapy room to return to her cleaning. She heard Grace's soft tones and then another voice. 'I didn't expect to be talking about my parents today.'

Tess's mouth fell open; she couldn't move her feet. They were stuck to the wooden floor, as if superglued. The voice was Lydia's.

'My dad's death ch—thing,' she said. 'Without him in the world, I fr— my —' Tess took a few steps and leant in, her ear closer to the door so as not to miss a word. 'No one really saw me any more.' There was a pause before she continued. 'I lost all sense of myself.' More silence. 'My dad wouldn't have liked the choices I made. I was a drunk who screwed around and regularly woke up next to men who meant nothing to me.'

'From what you've told me about him, he doesn't sound like the sort of man who would pass judgement on you,' Grace said.

'You're right,' Lydia acknowledged. 'He would have wanted better for me, but he would have understood.' There was the scrape of a chair on the floor as she repositioned herself. 'The reason I'm here is because of my drinking but more than that ...' She trailed off. Tess knew she shouldn't be listening but she couldn't help herself. She pressed her ear right up against the door, holding her breath. 'I started drinking again,' Lydia said at last, 'because I knew we were coming back here. We should never have done it but Zack wanted to, and I honestly thought I'd be strong enough. But now the memories are closing in on me and I can't see beyond them.'

Silence. Tess counted the seconds: four, five, six, seven, until Grace repeated Lydia's words back to her, 'But now the memories are closing in.'

More silence, and then: 'My mother didn't protect me. She forced her cousin Oscar into my life when she knew he was a monster. He hurt me. They both did.'

Tess jerked her head back and moved away. She went into the downstairs loo and closed the door behind her. There was a howling wind inside her skull and her limbs were dissolving to liquid. *Oscar.* Hearing Lydia say his name was so shocking that she could barely stand. Within seconds, she vomited into the toilet. She hadn't had any breakfast so there wasn't much to come up. When the retching had finished, she rinsed out her mouth and sat down on the lid of the toilet seat. Her stomach was hollowed out but her head was heavy, so heavy that she needed both hands to hold it up. She felt the onset of a panic attack and opened the door to help herself breathe, but it was almost the end of Lydia's hour and she could come out at any moment so she hugged the wall and forced her legs to carry her along the corridor to the kitchen, and then outside into the fresh air.

Despite the December temperatures, the patio felt warm. It was a natural suntrap. Tess collapsed onto a chair and cradled her head in her hands. There was the distant hum of traffic and the sound of two people talking in a neighbouring garden but neither sound was intrusive enough to override the shouting inside her own head.

Lydia's mother knew he was a monster. He hurt me. They both did.

Tess tried to think it through. She tried to rewind back through the years to when they were fifteen and Lydia's dad was ill but there was fog inside her brain. She couldn't see clearly. All she could see was Steve. She had thought about him constantly. She remembered lying in Lydia's garden smoking dope and talking about boys. It was soon after that Steve asked her out.

'Your finger is bleeding,' Grace said.

Tess jumped at the sound of Grace's voice. She hadn't heard her come outside. Lydia must have left already. 'Sorry, I—' She followed Grace's eyes and saw that she'd been picking away at the skin around one of her nails. Blood had seeped out and was spreading along her finger. 'I'll run it under the tap.' She stumbled toward the sink, banging her hip on the table. 'Sorry.'

'It's okay,' Grace said, her tone soothing. 'No rush.'

'Sorry,' Tess repeated.

She watched the blood circle the plughole and disappear, then she let Grace dry her finger and cover it with a plaster. When she was finished, she gently touched Tess's shoulder. 'Are you all right?'

'I was preoccupied with Steve,' she whispered. 'That's why I didn't know, I didn't see.' She pressed a hand against her chest and felt her heart pound inside her ribcage. Shame flooded through her. Lydia was right to have ignored her all this time. It was no wonder she hated her. She had left her as prey for Oscar and then she had been gutted by her father's death. And where was Tess? How could she have called herself her best friend?

And then a thought struck her. Soon after she started going out with Steve they went to Wales. Lydia's dad was too ill to travel and so the three of them set off, leaving him to be looked after by his sister. Genevieve stopped at the first motorway service station and Oscar jumped into the front seat. Lydia went nuts. She insisted that he get back out again but Genevieve said something to her that made her get back into the car.

The memory of what happened next was hazy because Tess spent most of her time in the phone box calling Steve and when she wasn't doing that she was drinking in the tent. But something happened when they were there, she could feel it in her gut.

'Tess?' Grace was staring at her. 'Are you okay?'

'I have to go.' She ran past Grace and up the stairs, grabbed hold of her cleaning products and was out the front door before Grace could say anything else.

Lydia

I went straight from therapy to watching my mother. My visits to my dad's grave were being replaced with spying on her. Visiting his grave was always about being close to him. I kept none of my feelings hidden when I was there. But how could I go to the churchyard now when I knew he would disapprove of what I was doing? In my mind I could hear him say, 'Nothing good will come from this, Lydia.'

He was right – nothing good would come from it. But I wasn't looking for good. I was looking for a resolution, an end to it. I couldn't wind back time. I couldn't prevent my dad's cancer. I couldn't make Genevieve a better mother – that was her choice, not mine. My dad believed in redemption. He was of the mind that people could change, no matter how entrenched their character flaws. He'd seen it, he told me. Criminals who turned their lives around. Could I really be sure that my mother hadn't changed? The answer that came back to me was a resounding YES. If I didn't fight back she would steal my family. I had to be smarter than her. I had to take the reins of the runaway horse before she ruined me completely.

I raised the binoculars and focussed on the large living room at the back of the house. My dad had never liked conservatories so when they extended the bungalow, it was to build a proper room with a large, long, low window that let in the light and allowed a view over the garden. My mother had been in and out of the room a few times during the twenty minutes I'd been watching, but now there was no sign of her. My limbs were already feeling stiff, despite all my cladding. I stood up and did some star jumps. The temperature had dropped again, and it was colder than ever. It was almost midday, but a weak sun had had no effect and the frost was still thick on the ground. The weather forecasters were predicting snow.

As I jumped up and down on the spot, I thought about what Sadie, Tess's babysitter, had told me. A man had come to the door and Tess was alarmed because she thought it was Oscar. Oscar, here? Now? It made no sense. I wondered what was going on in Tess's head. She'd always been someone who could get lost in her imagination but this was a step beyond.

My mother came back into the room. Someone was with her. I squinted, then picked up the binoculars and refocussed them, zooming in until I felt as if I was in the room alongside them. It was Zack. He removed his coat and sat down in a chair opposite her. She did most of the talking while he nodded at intervals, taking it all in. Lies told with sincerity can be more convincing than the truth. I got that. And she was the mistress of deceit. She was good. Boy was she good.

After an hour, they both stood up and hugged. It was prolonged. And when Zack stepped back, there were tears on his cheeks.

I lowered the binoculars and laid them on the bench. I had a queasy feeling in my stomach. I began to imagine, to plan, just exactly how I would settle this. The small voice inside my head tempted and teased me into action. Made suggestions, ever wilder, ever more extreme. *I couldn't do that.* I had no intention of doing that, but there was a certain thrill in allowing my imagination to sprint off in every forbidden direction.

Tess

She drove a short distance and sat in a layby. She should never have eavesdropped on Lydia's therapy session. But she had, and now she wasn't sure what to do next. She kept coming back to the fact that Genevieve wasn't to be trusted and Oscar had hurt Lydia. Did she know that he was back? Should she warn her?

She had to. It was the right thing to do. She would stop by Lydia's house after she'd been to the next clean. She sent a text to Grace, apologising for her hasty exit and drove to meet Vanya at a huge, modern made-to-look-older home that they cleaned twice a week. Mrs M was out which was always a blessing. She talked constantly about herself and was in the throes of her third marriage breakdown. She had three children, one to each of the dads. This week she was having work done on her face in one of the London clinics. She'd left them a note asking them to clean several of the rooms.

Tess and Vanya climbed the stairs to the first floor and Vanya talked about her mum's birthday party that had taken place at the weekend. Maisie was over her sick bug and the whole family had enjoyed themselves, although every get-together was tinged with sadness because her mum had multiple sclerosis and was able to do very little for herself. 'I wish I could help her more,' Vanya said. 'But apart from visiting regularly and trying to keep her cheerful, there's really nothing we can do.'

Tess was quiet as they worked their way through the children's bedrooms before going upstairs to the attic playroom. A bespoke Noah's ark took up most of the space. A carpenter had spent six months building the ship and then painting each of the carved wooden animals. They were lined up in their pairs on the open end of the boat, the giraffes as tall as a man. Vanya and Tess spent time inside the boat, picking up old sweet wrappers and the odd sock, and marvelling at the quality of the workmanship. 'This should be in a school or a nursery where more children can play with it,' Vanya said, polishing the curved wooden bow.

Their final clean and tidy-up was downstairs in the family room. Butter-coloured walls and perfectly placed soft furnishings, in pale yellows and blues, were artfully arranged to make the space feel inviting. 'Mrs M can lie down in here when she's had her face done,' Vanya said, plumping up the cushions. And then she stopped, hands on hips. 'You've barely said a word, Tess.' She took hold of her shoulders and gave her a hug. 'I don't want you to think I didn't believe you when you said that earlier about being followed.'

'It's okay.' Tess shrugged. 'I know it sounds ridiculous.'

'And I meant to say that, if it's any help, Erica doesn't think throwing the wine would necessarily classify as an assault, bearing in mind there was no actual injury.'

Tess felt a surge of annoyance. Vanya was her friend, and she was most likely being oversensitive, but she had the feeling Vanya was almost enjoying this. Something for her and Erica to discuss of an evening. *Poor Tess has done it again. Will she never get back on her feet? Aren't we so lucky to have each other …*

'I heard Lydia's husband was mad and that they were considering suing,' Vanya continued. 'That's why I'm mentioning it.'

'I have no money! They're welcome to my debt,' Tess said. She gave a dry laugh. 'And let's hope Maisie hasn't overheard you talking about me being sued. Bobby cried for long enough the last time she told him what she heard.'

Vanya took a step back. 'What do you mean? Was Maisie mean to Bobby?'

'She was only repeating what you and Erica said.' Tess told her what had happened when she collected Bobby from school. 'He was upset because you said to Erica that I'd been the one who made the phone call to the police.'

'I didn't say that!' She flushed and her hand went to her throat. 'Why would I say that?'

'Because you believe it?' Tess suggested.

'Oh, come on, Tess! That isn't fair. Maisie must have got the wrong end of the stick.'

Tess's phone rang and she glanced at the name on the screen before answering. 'Dad?'

'Just to say I'll need to be off to work in a minute and Sadie's running late her mum tells me.'

'I'll be back in ten.' She ended the call and said to Vanya, 'I have to go.'

'Anything I can help with?' Vanya asked. Tess shook her head; she was busy texting Sadie. 'Tess, I really—'

'I can't talk now,' Tess said, not even looking at her. 'Let's get going.' She gathered together her cleaning products and waited outside for Vanya, locking the door behind them both. And then she went quickly to her car, not even saying goodbye.

'Sorry, Dad.' She kissed his cheek. 'It's probably me. I expect I got the time wrong again.' People loved to talk about baby brain but her problem was double that. She also had a bad case of grief brain. She lifted Rose up to change her nappy and by the time she'd done that, her dad had left and Sadie had joined her. She was her usual chatty self but Tess's mind was still on Lydia. She wanted to get going as soon as she could.

'I'm wrapping all the Christmas presents in scarves this year,' Sadie said as she carried the dirty nappy over to the bin. 'Because we're not allowed to use paper.'

'Why's that?' Tess asked, gently bending Rose's knees to get her legs back into her tights.

'It's my mum's idea. She's saving the planet one metre of wrapping paper at a time.'

'Good on her.'

'I'm scouring the charity shops for scarves. If you have any you don't want, you know who to give them to.'

'Will do.' Tess handed Rose over to Sadie. 'There's a bottle made up in the fridge.' She glanced at her watch. Time was tight. 'I'll be back after I've collected Bobby.'

'No worries.' Sadie smoothed Rose's cardigan down at the back. 'Oh! And I'm really sorry, Tess. I'm going to be away at my dad's when term ends on Friday until Christmas Day. Aren't I, baby?' She smiled at Rose before bringing her up onto her shoulder. 'My mum says I have to go because he won't help me with university expenses unless I make more of an effort to see him.' She rolled her eyes, sighing. 'I mean, it's not that I don't like his girlfriend. She's nice enough and she wants to be friends with me because we're only ten years apart in age but …' Another sigh. 'I can't relax when I'm there.'

'Families, eh?' Tess kissed Rose's cheek and gave Sadie a hug. 'Who'd have 'em?'

She drove within the speed limit, but only just, until she reached Lydia's. She parked outside the front door and rang the doorbell, dropping back down a step to wait. She had no clear idea what she was going to say. She just knew she had to let Lydia know about Oscar.

Zack opened the door. They'd never been introduced but Tess knew it was him because she'd seen him at the clubhouse. 'I'm sorry to bother you,' she said. 'I was wondering whether Lydia was here? My name is Tess and—'

'I recognise you from football,' he said, unsmiling. 'And from the video, of course,' he added.

'Yes.' Tess sighed. 'I'm sorry about that. It wasn't my finest hour.'

'Why did you do it?' He had kind eyes, but they were red-rimmed as if he'd recently been crying. 'It was a verbal and physical assault.'

'You're absolutely right.' She shook her head, genuinely regretful. 'I don't have an excuse.'

He sighed and stared down at his feet. She could see that he wasn't committed to being unfriendly. 'Lydia isn't here.'

'Do you know where she is?'

'I don't. But if I was to hazard a guess, I'd say she was at the health club.'

'Thank you.'

Lydia

I drove around for a while after I left the back garden. I found myself down by the sea where the waves were stormy against a rust-grey sky. My dad had loved his coastal walks and I'd often gone with him. He used to say walking was a great way to work through his problems. 'Legwork,' he'd say, 'gets the job done in more ways than one.'

When I arrived back home, it was already after five and the house was quiet. Adam was staying for an after-school club and wasn't due to be collected until seven. I lay my car key on the hall table and hung up my coat, placed my shoes in the rack and slid my feet into my slippers. The living room sofas were inviting. The artwork on the walls was tasteful, eye-catching without being provocative. People said that if you were going to be miserable, you were better doing it in comfort. I wasn't cold or hungry. I was comparatively rich and privileged. But no amount of extravagance on the outside could fix the way I felt inside.

And when I walked into the kitchen, I knew there was trouble ahead. On the counter were four half-full bottles of alcohol. Two were vodka, one gin and the fourth was port. It was a brand of port I had never bought, never drunk. This was my mother's drink of choice. Always port, always this brand. In my mind's eye I could see her with a glass in her hand, and my dad with a beer in his, sitting in the garden enjoying the sunset. They only drank on a Saturday. Neither of them were big drinkers so the bottle lasted a long time.

This was my mother signalling to me, hoisting a great big flag that said, 'I've got you.'

When I turned around, Zack was standing behind me with his hands in his pockets. 'Oh!' I moved forward to kiss him. 'Where did you come from?' I went up on my tiptoes to land the kiss on his lips but he drew his face to one side. My lips met the air. 'Everything okay?' There was a look on his face I'd never seen before – sad and disappointed, as if he was taking his dog to be put down. 'What's up?' I pointed behind me to the bottles. 'Where did this lot come from?'

'You know, Lydia.' His teeth were gritted so the words sounded low and flat. 'You know where they came from.'

'How would I know? I've never seen these bottles before in my life.' I glanced round at them again and felt saliva fill my mouth. I would happily have upended each one of them and drunk the lot.

He sighed. 'I found the gin bottle in the airing cupboard behind the towels. One vodka bottle was under the kitchen sink, the other was under the sink in our bathroom. The bottle of port was in the back of the wardrobe in Adam's bedroom.'

His face told me that this was the one that offended him the most. My mother was bold. She must have come to my house to plant evidence against me. My limbs twitched. I wanted to pound the floor, kick out, make fists. But I held it in. 'Why were you looking in the airing cupboard?' I laughed. 'I'm surprised you even know where it is!'

His grim expression remained. This was a level of discomfort that he hadn't signed up for. He was a naturally happy, straightforward bloke and so I'd kept him ignorant of the dark side of my life. I hadn't told him about my mother and Oscar because I wanted to move on from the fear and the anger, not breathe more life into it. I'd always believed that a secret was only a secret if your mind kept returning to it. And if you shared it? Then it was out of your control. Sorting out my own life was ingrained in me from a young age and I'd behaved in a similar way with Tess. I didn't tell her how much of a predator Oscar was because she would have been terrified and my impulse was to protect her.

'Really, Zack?' I pressed. 'What made you look in all those places? Did my mother tell you to go on the hunt?' I pretended to think. 'You went to see her today, didn't you?'

He took a step back. 'You're going to blame this on your mother?'

'Why did you go to her house?'

'Because she asked me to, and from what I know of her, she deserved to be listened to.'

'Ah! And she turned out to be right.' I widened my eyes and mimicked her voice. 'I'm worried Lydia might still be drinking. Have you checked for hidden bottles? I'd hate for anything to happen to Adam.'

His head dropped. I watched his chest move up and down with his breath. I desperately wanted this to stop. I willed him to look at me and say, 'I don't trust her'. I wanted him to hold out his arms and kiss me until all her power was gone.

But that didn't happen. 'When are you going to take responsibility for your own behaviour?' he said quietly.

I sighed.

'She's concerned for Adam, and frankly, so am I.' He took a breath. 'You brought this on yourself,' he continued. 'I don't want you to drive the car any more. Not when Adam's in it.'

'Legally I'm allowed to drive until after I've appeared in court.'

'And what about morally?' he said forcefully. He pointed to the bottles on the countertop. 'You know what, forget morally. You're obviously past that. What about the safety of our son?'

'I would never put Adam in danger.'

'Lydia, you did *exactly* that.' He leant in towards me and gestured towards the bottles again. 'And you're still doing it. I think you should consider checking in to a clinic.'

'*You* think that or *she* thinks that?' My tone was light.

'I think that.' He jabbed a finger into his chest. 'The Priory has a good reputation. They have individual care plans for every resident.'

I walked across to the window and stared out into the garden. Frost lay on the grass beneath the bushes, shimmering like sequins in the moonlight. It was a beautiful winter scene, perfect for the lead-up to Christmas. Adam wanted a new bike. I'd ordered it a few weeks ago and it was due to be delivered very soon. I wasn't going into any Priory. My son would not visit me in a place like that. I was already sorting out my alcohol problem. And I'd sort out the problem of my mother too.

'The Priory isn't so far away,' Zack continued. 'Adam and I would be able to visit—'

I turned back to face him. 'Did you give her a key to this house?' I asked. We had triple-locked doors and a fully functioning burglar alarm. She would never have got inside to plant the bottles without a key and the code. 'And the alarm code?'

'What?' He shook his head, exasperated. 'No, of course not.'

Maids of Honour, then. There was the *Je Reviens* scent when I came inside on Thursday. Had Vanya let her in? Or was it Tess? I wouldn't be surprised if Tess had given her the keys to our house. *Fuck.* As usual, I was playing catch up.

'Does it ever cross your mind how betrayed I must be feeling?' He blinked very deliberately several times, as if he was holding back tears. 'You've lied to me our whole marriage.'

For the first time a small voice at the back of my mind asked me whether I'd got it wrong – maybe it wasn't Tess who had called the police on me? More likely she'd called my mother to say she'd seen me, and my mother had reported me. Concerned citizen. She'd be good at that. They were in it together, the pair of them. Hence the cosy little chat in the clubhouse while the boys played football.

'You're often emotionally distant,' Zack said. 'It's something I've noticed before. It's as if you can switch off your feelings. You're doing it now.'

I couldn't argue with that. I went to the front door and put on my shoes and coat.

'And now you're going out!' He threw up his arms. 'For fuck's sake, Lydia. This is serious.'

'Just for the record,' I stood in front of him, 'my name is Lydia Green and I am an alcoholic.' I held his eyes, paused to let that sink in. 'I have a drink problem, Zack, but I am dealing with it.' I pointed behind him. 'I have not drunk any alcohol since the police station. *None* of those bottles are mine.' His jaw tightened. 'I'm not in denial. It's the truth.'

'Where are you going?' The words came out on a sigh. 'We haven't finished talking.'

'Talking?' I stared into his handsome, stubborn, innocent face. 'I guess she told you that alcoholics lie and that they'll do anything, say anything, to save their own skin. I expect she told you that she knows this side of me, she knows how difficult it will be for you, and she wants to help. That's all. Just to help.' I wrapped a scarf around my neck. 'You have a choice to make,' I said slowly. 'You can believe me, the woman you've been married to for fifteen years, or you can believe my mother.'

'I want to believe you, Lydia. I really do. But there are too many secrets.' He took a shaky breath. 'It's difficult to get past that.'

'She killed my dad,' I said bluntly. As soon as the words were out of my mouth, my breath caught and my legs shook.

His face blanched. 'Say that again?'

'You heard me.' There was no way I could say those words a second time.

Zack rallied quickly. 'You told me your dad had cancer.'

'He did.' Sadness swept through me. 'But that's not what he died of.'

I told him how it had happened, just the bullet points. I watched the shock – and a shadow of disbelief? – cross his face. I let him hold me and say he was sorry. Did I have any proof? I shook my head. 'It would be my word against hers,' I said.

I let him make all sorts of suggestions about my aunt and the police and then he said, 'But why? Why would she do that?'

'To punish me,' I said.

'To punish you for what?'

I shrugged. 'For being me,' I said.

Lydia, summer 1994

My mother drove back from Wales in a fury, her mood matched by the rain that poured down from a thunderous sky so that the wipers moved with frenetic speed across the windscreen. Not one word was spoken on the entire journey. Oscar had gone missing the night before and she was convinced I had something to do with it. Tess slept the whole way home, oblivious to everything: what had happened at the caravan park, what happened immediately afterwards, and now, the atmosphere in the car. I woke her up as we drove into her street and there was Steve waiting for her. As soon as he saw the car, his face lit up and for the first time I thought their feelings for each other might be more than just a teenage crush. Tess fell out of the car and into his arms. She looked back to say a quick thank you, and my mother drove off immediately. No small talk this time. 'We need to get back to Adam,' she shouted to Tess's mum. 'Got to rush.'

As soon as we drove onto the driveway I ran inside to find my dad. He was barely awake. 'There you are, Lydia Jane.'

Four days had taken their toll. He was starting to not look like himself. His face was gaunt, cheekbones angular as the softness of his face disappeared. His voice was barely above a whisper. We'd recently been informed that the cancer was everywhere, stealing into his bones and his brain, his lungs and his throat. I summoned up every ounce of enthusiasm inside me and told him about the holiday, making it sound so much better than it was. And no mention of Oscar, of course.

He watched me with tired eyes, lids closing every now and then so that I frequently stopped my storytelling, but then he would say, 'Keep going, Lydia. I'm enjoying listening to you.'

After about fifteen minutes I had exhausted him and he fell into a deep sleep. My aunt Flo was preparing to leave and I went to say goodbye to her. She hugged me for the longest time and I knew that this was her way of supporting me. Neither of us could voice the truth that my dad, her brother, was close to passing away. When she let me go there were tears in her eyes. 'Darling Lydia.' She stroked my hair back from my face. 'You are your dad's pride and joy.' She kissed both my cheeks. 'You know where I am. Call me any time.'

My mother was standing beside her, pretending to be sad. But I knew what would happen as soon as Flo left. We waved her away in her car and as my mother closed the door behind her, she turned and landed a hard slap on my cheek. My teeth rattled and I bit my tongue. Normally she didn't hit my face – too visible. But now she was too furious to care. I could have locked myself in my room but she would only threaten to punish my dad so I stayed downstairs and tried to deflect her anger.

'What happened to Oscar?' She grabbed for my neck and caught hold of a fistful of my T-shirt, pulling me towards her. Her teeth were painfully gritted as if she was holding something back. Venom probably. She was more like a snake than a human being, although that was insulting to snakes. I hated her with an intensity that shocked me. I had never felt such feelings of loathing in my entire life.

'He must have gone home,' I replied, my tone flat. *Ask about me!* I wanted to scream. *Ask about what he did to me!*

She slapped me again. 'He would never have gone home without saying goodbye to me.'

'I didn't see him yesterday evening. Tess and I were at the disco.' My cheek was aflame and my jaw ached. 'Maybe he met someone.'

'Did you tell anyone about him?'

'Tell them what?' I ground out, defiance rising inside me.

She squashed my cheeks with her hand, pressing and pressing until my eyes watered.

'I will find out.' She shivered with a cruel excitement. 'If it takes me the rest of my life, I will find out what you said or what you did.' And then her head jerked back on her neck as she considered a thought. 'But it doesn't have to take that long, does it?' She laughed. 'Because I have something you want.'

She dragged me through to the living room by my hair. I tripped and banged my head on the sideboard but she didn't stop. She forced my chin up to look at her and I cried out in pain. 'I will give your father a fatal dose of morphine,' she said loudly. The dizziness inside my head was so acute that I started to retch. 'You will be killing your father unless you tell me.' She paused to let this sink in. 'His *death* will be on your conscience.'

I should have fought harder. I should have knocked her out, grabbed a heavy pot and hit her so hard over the head that she ended up in a coma. I should have scratched at her face and bitten her hand. I should have punched and kicked her. Her body should have been unrecognisable. I should have done all of that rather than let her approach my dad with a syringe of morphine. I would have been sent to a kids' prison but at least my dad wouldn't have died that evening.

I didn't think she would do it. It was one thing hitting me. It was another actually *killing* a person, wasn't it? My dad. Her husband. The man she professed to love.

But she did it and he died.

Because I wouldn't tell her. I wouldn't tell her what had happened to Oscar.

Tess

After Tess had spoken to Zack, she drove to the health club to look for Lydia. The club was set in over one hundred acres on the edge of the forest. The mansion house had been built in the mid-nineteenth century and was the country retreat for one of Queen Victoria's statesmen. In the 1980s it had been turned into a country hotel and health club, the latter used by hotel guests and by members who lived locally and could pay the premium rates. Tess had only been inside twice, both times with Bobby who'd been invited to children's parties in the pool.

She passed a small herd of deer grazing close to the driveway, the sun highlighting the warm red in their winter coats, and parked in one of the spaces outside the main door. She couldn't see any signs of Lydia's four-by-four but maybe there was parking elsewhere. She looked at her watch. Half an hour before she needed to collect Bobby. She would have to be quick.

There were two men wearing tracksuits and carrying tennis rackets ahead of her. One of them used his fob to enter the club and she followed them both in, walking with confidence past the café and the changing rooms and along the corridor to the swimming pool and gym. On one side were large glass windows with views over the golf course, and on the other, a dance studio and yoga space. She looked through the glass panes in the doors and saw multiple women in leotards but she couldn't see Lydia, so she continued on to the gym and swimming pool. She wasn't in there either. The changing rooms then.

She retraced her steps and pushed open the door. The room smelled of expensive shampoos and lotions. The lockers were clustered in groups of eight around a dressing area. There were piles of towels neatly stacked on the wooden counters, large mirrors above. There were boxes of free tissues and indoor slippers, hairdryers and period products. She felt momentarily jealous of all this luxury. She could never afford to be a member of a place like this, not in her wildest dreams.

She left the changing rooms, and it was as she was walking through the foyer again that she heard a voice. 'Tess!'

She looked round, startled. It was Genevieve. Again. 'Everywhere I go you seem to be there,' Tess said to her, resisting the older woman's hug.

'What a strange thing to say.' She gave Tess a cold smile. 'I didn't know you were a member here?"

'I'm not,' Tess said.

'Then perhaps it's you who's following me?' she suggested.

They were standing close to the desk and from the corner of her eye, Tess saw the receptionist's head swivel their way.

'I would be very happy to put you forward for membership,' Genevieve said. 'And I'm sure Lydia would be delighted to second you.'

For the very first time, Tess looked at Genevieve with eyes that were wide open. How had she never noticed before how phony she was? She remembered how she'd behaved around Oscar, the way he could do no wrong in her eyes. She brought him into their home when she must have known what he was like. What sort of a mother did that? Tess would *never* allow a man like that to hang around her kids. 'Why didn't you protect Lydia?' she asked.

'I'm sorry?' Genevieve shook her head as if shocked by such a question. 'I *always* protected my daughter.'

'No, you did *not*,' Tess bit back. 'Your cousin was a creep and you let him harass Lydia, follow her around, make rude comments.'

'Lydia flirted with him!' She laughed. 'You were *both* very flirty from what I remember.'

'Neither of us *ever* flirted with him.' Tess leant in towards her. 'And the next time I see him, I'm calling the police.'

Instantly, Genevieve's dark eyes met Tess's. They were so dark that they were almost black as coal. As night. As death, Tess thought. For the first time in what felt like weeks, she knew what to do. She was an adult. And a mother. She could take on Oscar.

'If you see him, feel free to let him know,' she told Genevieve, and then she walked away with her head held high.

She met Bobby at school and they had just climbed into the car when her mobile rang. It was one of her long-term clients. 'Hello, Mrs Janion.'

'I'm not looking for you to clean today, Tess,' she said. 'It's just that David and I have decided to go away for the next few weeks, very last minute, and the fridge is full. I expect some of it can be frozen but the freezer is also full. Would you mind awfully stopping by and taking anything you want?'

'That's very kind.'

'You'd be doing me a favour,' she told her. 'I do hate throwing food out. And you have a family to feed.'

'I'll be about ten minutes.' She ended the call and turned to Bobby. 'Guess what? We're going to Mrs Janion's house to raid her fridge.'

'Really?' His eyes lit up. 'Will she have orange juice?'

'I expect so.'

'And bacon?'

'For sure!'

Steve used to say that when the universe took with one hand, it gave back with another.

Mrs Janion's fridge was enormous. Bobby opened both doors and stared inside. It was full to the brim with food, most of it perishable. 'Here are some carrier bags.' Mrs Janion handed them to Tess and Bobby. 'We were expecting friends to stay but they can't come now so we thought we'd fly off to see them instead.'

Tess looked at Bobby. He had a wide grin on his face. They'd be eating like royalty: smoked salmon, blueberries, avocados, apples, broccoli, four types of cheese, a marmalade ham and a beef Wellington. They filled the carrier bags and went home to Rose and Sadie. Bobby helped carry everything inside and unpacked the bags on the kitchen table.

'Take some for your mum, Sadie,' Tess told her. 'It'll save her cooking tonight.'

'Are you sure?'

'Of course. There's more than enough.'

Sadie chose some vegetables and fruit. 'We're on a healthy eating kick at the mo.'

'I'll let grandad know that we're going to have beef Wellington for tea,' Tess told Bobby, lifting Rose from her seat to give her a hug. Rose was watching Bobby put everything in the fridge. He was her favourite person to focus on.

'With roast potatoes?' Bobby asked, holding up a pre-packaged foil tin of them.

'Defintootley.' She texted her dad with the news and a reply came back almost immediately. 'He's running a bit late so he's asked us to keep some warm for him.'

'He'll be happy because he really likes meat. I mean, he likes lentils as well, but meat's his first choice, especially beef,' Bobby said. His expression was so earnest, so like Steve, that her heart squeezed.

When the food was cooked, Bobby snuggled up next to his mum on the sofa and they ate like kings while Rose nodded off in her chair beside them. They watched Bobby's favourite movie and laughed at all the funny parts, their bellies full to bursting. Tess regretted not inviting Maisie and Vanya to come and share in the food. Erica was on late shifts all week. It was mean of her. Vanya was her best friend and her most reliable worker. She would take a share of the spoils round in the morning and apologise.

Tess's attention constantly drifted back to Genevieve and Oscar. Something was going to happen. She was sure of it. But she was determined not to be afraid. She'd spent too much time worrying and not enough time fighting back.

And then the doorbell rang, and all her resolve fell away.

Lydia, 1994

After my dad died, the next few days were a blur. I couldn't stand up. I had to crawl on all fours to the toilet. I'd never experienced grief before and I was completely overwhelmed.

The day of the funeral, Genevieve put a tranquilliser in the carton of milk before I poured it over my cereal. I should have known, I should have been wary because she'd done it before, but I was too tired to be careful. The milk tasted funny but I thought that was because I was grieving. There were rows and rows of policeman at the funeral and I wanted to tell them that a crime had been committed and that my dad's body should not be buried yet but I could barely stand, never mind speak. I heard my mother telling the mourners that, 'Unfortunately, Lydia is grieving so very badly that she missed her footing on the stairs.' She held me next to her, her grip vice-like.

I kept expecting to see Tess. If only I could see Tess. Without her, I was cast adrift. My dad had died and now my best friend had dropped me. And there was what happened with Oscar. I couldn't pick over the memories, not out loud, not even in my head. They held far too much power to be spoken of.

A few days after the funeral, I went to Tess's house and knocked on the door. Loud music was playing in one of the rooms and I had to knock several times until, finally, Saskia opened the door. She was pretty in a vacuous way, a body without a personality. Her face was unsmiling as she said, 'She's not here.'

Gary followed her to the door, rubbing at his eyes. He looked like he'd just woken up. 'Sorry, Lydia. She's gone out with Steve again.' He turned to his daughter. 'Where has she gone this time, Sas?'

'I dunno.' Saskia walked away. 'I don't speak to her.'

'Girls, eh?' Gary gave me a hopeless look. 'And sorry about your dad, love.' He frowned, his eyebrows meeting in the middle. 'He was a sound bloke, your dad.'

'Thanks, Gary.' I tried to smile. 'Will you tell her I was here?'

'Will do, love.'

I knew as I walked away that Tess wouldn't call. She'd moved on. I couldn't blame her. She was in love and I wasn't fun any more. The rest of the summer holidays stretched ahead of me, a wasteland of loneliness and fear. I couldn't spend any more days in my mother's house. I needed to tell someone about what she'd done but I knew that her public face was so well established that no one in the village would listen to me.

I walked back home, entering the garden from the path at the rear of the bungalow. I sat in the summer house and waited until she'd gone to the shops then I went inside. I packed a bag and caught the bus to East Grinstead and then a train to London. When my aunt returned from work that day I was sitting on her doorstep. 'Lydia! Darling.' This time when she hugged me, I cried and cried until I was completely empty. She sat me down on her sofa and fed me toasted cheese sandwiches and hot chocolate.

Then, when I was composed, I told her that my mother had given my dad an overdose of morphine.

'Darling, he was dying.' Tears of grief and sympathy ran down her cheeks. 'Your mum loved him, Lydia.'

'She didn't. Well, maybe she did but she loved—' I hesitated. 'She *loves* her cousin Oscar more.'

'My darling girl.' She took my hand. 'Grief makes us imagine all sorts of things that aren't true.'

It was at that moment that I realised she wasn't astute. She was kind and empathetic. She had a loving nature, not a suspicious one. And she had no idea what my mother hid behind her mask. She hadn't seen into the dark of those eyes as I had.

'Can I stay with you?' I asked. 'Please, Aunty Flo. I can't go back there.'

'Are there too many memories of your dad in the house?'

I nodded.

'But you'll miss your mum.'

'I won't,' I said at once. 'But she can visit,' I added, because I wanted my aunt to know that I was thinking it through. 'I just don't want to be in the village. And Tess has Steve now so …'

Flo called my mum and she reluctantly agreed. She demanded that I come to the phone and said to me, 'I am watching you, Lydia Green. I will always be watching you. You remember that.'

Lydia

When Tess came to the door she was wearing an all-in-one outfit that even had a hood. 'Lydia.' She pulled the door in tight behind her back. Her eyes widened in panic before she said, 'Did Zack tell you I came to the house?'

'No.' I climbed up a step. 'Why?'

She brushed her hair under the hood, her movements jerky. 'I wanted to tell you that I've seen Oscar. He's back in the village.'

I didn't know what to say to this. It was so absurd. I could see where her fear was coming from – memories of Oscar and all his weirdness haunted her – we weren't so different in that. But what I couldn't understand was why she thought he was back in the village.

'I know that he—' Her face twisted. 'He hurt you?'

It was a question, not a statement. Her words landed on a soft spot beneath my throat. I clenched my fists.

'I tried to speak to your mum about it—'

'Was that when you were having a tête-à-tête in the clubhouse while the boys were playing football?' I asked coldly.

'What?' She frowned and then shook her head. 'No! We met there by accident and had a cup of tea together. It was nothing. But I saw her today at your country club—'

'There too?' I almost laughed.

'But Lydia ...' She grabbed my forearm. 'I feel like something's about to happen, and I wanted to warn you. That's all.' She started to sway from side to side. I didn't steady her; I let her collapse against the door so that it fell open, and she slid down onto the floor in the hallway.

I stepped inside. 'I've come for my keys.'

She turned round onto her knees and stood up, her hand rubbing at her hip. Her face was unnaturally pale when she looked at me. 'You don't want us to clean for you any more?'

I laughed. 'Look, let's just cut the pretence. I know you let my mother into my house.'

'No.' Her mouth hung open. 'I wouldn't do that. But. Oh, God.' She briefly put her hands over her mouth as she remembered something. 'I cleaned your house on Thursday because Vanya couldn't do it.'

'And you let Genevieve in?'

'She came to the door. She was dropping off flowers for you and snacks for Adam.'

'Well, she didn't. She hid four bottles of alcohol in various places around the house and then whispered into Zack's ear. So he thinks I'm still drinking.' I folded my arms. 'You've given her a way back into my life. Thanks for that.'

'I don't—' Tess frowned as she tried to think that through. 'What?'

'For the last time,' I said loudly, 'please give me my keys.'

She opened the door to the understairs cupboard, and it was then that I noticed Bobby in the doorway to the living room. He was wearing a teddy bear all-in-one and held Rose in his arms. 'Hi, Bobby,' I said. 'I'm sorry for interrupting your evening.'

'Have you come here to shout again?' he asked, shifting Rose's position so that her head rested on the crook of his arm.

'No. And I'm sorry about last time.'

He nodded. 'That's okay. Sometimes people get mad but they don't really mean it.'

'Here are your keys,' Tess said. 'Thank you. I'm sorry.'

I took them from her outstretched hand and turned to go.

'I know the way this looks,' she called after me. 'But I swear on my children's lives that I would never willingly help your mum.' Her voice cracked. 'I was an idiot. I didn't know how awful she was to you when we were kids. She's not a good person, Lydia.'

I turned back to glare at her. 'And you've only just realised that?'

As I drove away, I noticed there was a man at the end of the street. He was wearing jeans and a leather jacket, a cap pulled low over his face. The resemblance to Oscar was there, even from this distance, and suddenly I knew who Tess was talking about. I shivered, and continued driving.

Next stop the hospice.

It was late to be visiting Paula but luckily she was still awake, propped upright in her bed, the pillows artfully arranged behind her head.

'I was hoping you would come.' She reached for my hands, as she always did. 'Stephanie will be here tomorrow and then I'll be off on my hols.'

I gave her a weak smile. 'I'm sorry I haven't been in recently.'

'It's okay.' She squeezed my hand. 'Tell me what's been happening.'

I pulled up a chair and sat down. 'You'll have heard about Jenny?'

271

'Oh, yes. I've heard all about it. But let's be clear, Lydia.' Her eyes widened. 'I've known you a lot longer than I've known her, and if my son is too blind to see that you'll have had your reasons for keeping shtum, then it's because he's hurting inside.' She patted my hands. 'Give it time. The hurt will fade, and he'll remember who he's married to.'

'I hope so.' I cleared my throat. 'Did he tell you I have a drink problem? And that Adam—' I hesitated. 'I was caught driving over the limit.'

'I know.' She nodded. 'And I also know how sorry you'd be for doing that. And I'm absolutely sure you won't do it again.'

'Thank you.' My smile was wider this time. 'I appreciate your support. I really do.'

'I'm team Lydia all the way.' She shifted her head on the pillows. 'Now apart from reminding my son where his loyalties lie, how can I help?

'Well …' I sat up straight. 'I'd like to find a way to prove to Zack that none of this was an accident. Jenny knew you were my mother-in-law. She knew Zack was my husband.' I told her about the online articles in the various business magazines. 'She'll have known that I married Zack Purdew and that he came from this village. All the stuff she's drip-fed him about her estranged daughter will have been deliberate.'

'Let's think about it.' Paula stared up at the ceiling. 'She wasn't volunteering when I was first admitted here. It was a week or so before she appeared on the scene.'

'Okay.' I leaned forward on the chair. 'Is there any way she could have found out you were in the hospice? Do you have friends in common?'

Paula thought some more. 'I wouldn't say friends, exactly, but you know I support, or I used to support, children's reading at the primary school?'

'Yes.'

'Well, I had to stop when I got cancer, and the secretary there is one of your mum's neighbours. I know that because when she came to visit with some drawings from the children, they got chatting about the deer problem. They're always coming into the gardens along that road, apparently.'

'So that's a connection.' I walked up and down by the foot of the bed. I felt both restless to get on and prove Genevieve's deceit and cautiously optimistic that I could do it. Team Lydia. I smiled. It felt good to have Paula onside.

Her voice was quiet when she said, 'I'll take your secrets to my grave, Lydia.'

My eyes flicked towards her.

'No pressure. Only if you feel that telling me would help get the secrets off your chest.' She paused, unhurried. 'Sometimes, we need to hear our thoughts and feelings spoken out loud. It helps to bring them into some sort of order.'

'You'd make a great therapist,' I said quietly.

She gave a wry smile. 'I'll save that for another life.'

I allowed myself to consider her suggestion. Should I? *Could* I? 'Are you sure? It's—' I sighed. 'It's not a cheerful story.' I bit my lip. 'Far from it.'

She tilted her head towards the chair. 'Spare me none of the details.'

And so I told her. All of it. From the beginning to the end, doubling back on myself when I realised I'd missed some of the details that helped make sense of what came next. The dam had burst and the words poured out of me. I didn't pause, I didn't allow myself time to think. I let the truth flow without fear or favour. Twice, Paula sobbed, her hand flying up to cover her mouth, and a curse under her breath. She asked two questions. 'Have you spoken to Tess about this?'

'No. She seems to have blocked it out.' I shrugged. 'It's not her fault.' As I said the words, I knew it to be true. 'I protected her from the worst of Oscar, and from the truth about my mother. I always did, from the moment I met her.'

'You were both teenagers,' Paula said. 'Your parents should have been protecting *you*. That is quite literally a parent's job.' Her second question, 'What are you going to do now?' was more difficult to answer.

'I'm going to gather evidence. Like we've discussed.' Even as I said it, I knew that anything I could find was unlikely to be enough. 'It's thirty years since she killed my dad but …'

Paula's expression was doubtful. 'I think proving the part she played in your dad's death would be incredibly difficult. Not that I'm saying you shouldn't do it, but—' She took a shaky breath. 'I think you need clarity, Lydia. Would your dad want you to focus on avenging his death? From what you've told me of his character, I would say not. Are you in any personal danger? I don't think so. The way she will hurt you is by turning Zack and Adam against you.' Her expression grew fierce. 'Zack can look out for himself. It's *Adam* you need to protect. Your boy is more precious to you than any other living being on this earth. Bar none.' She winced and rubbed her hand over her abdomen.

'Are you okay?' I asked, concerned that I had tired her out. 'Are you in pain?'

'I'm fine.' She waved my concern aside. 'I need to say this, Lydia.' She took another breath. 'If that son of mine is too blind to see what's going on here then you *make* him see. And if that doesn't work—' Our eyes locked.

'Then you *do* whatever it takes to protect Adam.' She delivered the sentence with intensity and then she gave a small whimper and her head fell back on the pillows.

'Shall I get a nurse?'

'No, I'll give myself some morphine.' She had a pain-relieving pump implanted beneath her skin. She pressed the button until it clicked and the dose was delivered. I waited while she took several shallow breaths and then the morphine started to work, her facial muscles relaxed and she breathed more deeply. 'That's better.'

'I'll leave you to rest now, Paula.' I kissed her forehead and her eyelids immediately closed. 'Thank you for helping me.'

As I was turning away she reached out for my arm. 'You know, there's one funny thing that happened last week. Some medicines went missing. Two bottles. Diamorphine and a tranquilliser.' Her words slurred a little as she drifted towards sleep. 'There was a hullaballoo but nobody could find the bottles and the nurse in charge was blamed.' She let out a relaxed sigh. 'It happened when Jenny was on shift.'

Tess

'I think Rose needs changing,' Bobby said, sniffing the air around her wriggling body.

'Let's take her back into the living room,' Tess said, her hands on his shoulders. 'I'll put another log on the fire so it will be nice and warm.'

'We can't afford it, Mum!' Bobby said, his voice urgent.

'You know what, Bobby? Sometimes we just have to be kind to ourselves.' She added the log to the fire and they both watched as the dying flames were reinvigorated, licking at the edges of the log.

'That was weird, Adam's mum coming round again,' Bobby said, bringing the changing mat and wipes across to the sofa. 'Why is she so mad all the time?'

'She had a point, Bobby. I didn't help her when we were young, and I've made things worse for her now.' *But, back then, my eye was elsewhere because I fell in love with your dad.*

Timing. Timing is everything.

'But she's a grown-up now.' He settled back on the sofa and covered his knees with the blanket. 'This is a good bit,' he said and was immediately sucked back into the film.

Rose was at her most cooperative and let Tess change her nappy without making a fuss. When Tess had finished, she settled the baby back in her chair and took the nappy to the kitchen bin. She stayed in there to tidy up, thinking about what Bobby had just said about being a grown-up. Was anyone ever really grown up? It seemed to Tess that her childhood self, teenage Tess, lived just beneath her skin, ever ready to leap out and control the narrative. When she was in her twenties and living with Steve, her mum and Gary had moved to Australia to be near Saskia who had gone there for a gap year and never returned. Within months of them leaving, Tess's dad had appeared back in the village. It seemed he needed her mum out of the country before he could be a regular part of her life. He'd been so absent when she was a teenager that she'd found it difficult to get along with him at first. She never let him forget how much she'd longed for him to be there for her. She remembered shouting at him, 'I needed you, Dad! I bloody needed you!'

'What you need is to drop it!' he'd shouted back. 'You're not a child any more. Those days are behind us.'

'When is childhood ever behind *anybody*, Dad?'

'Of course it's behind you!' His mouth had turned down. 'Years have gone by!'

'But the fact that you were never around hurt me!' She'd banged her chest. 'It shaped the person I became. That's my point!'

She recalled what she'd heard Lydia say at her therapy session. *My mother didn't protect me. She forced her cousin Oscar into my life when she knew he was a monster. He hurt me. They both did.*

Tess didn't want to speculate about what Oscar had done to Lydia. But deep down she knew.

All day long she cut her memories of Steve short in case they floored her, but when she was in bed she allowed herself to remember him, to imagine his presence next to her, the comfort of his bulk, the way his love and support made her happy. She tested the weight of each memory, held it at the front of her mind and tried to only explore the ones that were more sweet than sharp. They had been good at doing nothing much together: she'd be tidying up and he'd make one of his curries; they'd both be out in the garden planting bulbs; he'd wash his car while she prepared an apple crumble or steamed puddings, which were his favourite. She didn't imagine that she'd ever find as good a relationship again, but she counted her blessings to have had him in her life.

Often, she found herself believing in the afterlife; it was just a matter of time until she was with him again. Or she would get lost in magical thinking – he wasn't really dead, he was just out of the room, and any minute now he would be back beside her. He'd tell her wonderful tales about where he'd been and then they'd fall asleep together.

After Bobby and Rose were settled down for the night, she'd pulled out the shoebox of letters from under the bed. If there was ever a time when she needed advice it was now. When Steve gave her the shoebox, he'd laughed; 'This way I'll always have the last word.'

She tried not to open a new one unless she really needed to. Once, in a fit of isolation and misery, she'd opened four, one after the other. She was about to give birth to a baby girl whose dad was already dead, and she found the reality of that almost unbearable, for her baby more than for herself.

Mostly, she opened one of his letters at a critical time, and she knew that this was one of those times. She'd already spotted a letter entitled, 'When you don't know what to do next'. That was the one she'd opened tonight.

My dear Tess,

I know you. You're smart - always smarter than me. When you're at a crossroads and you don't know what path to take? Trust your intuition.

Do you remember the first time I went to the doctor? I came back to you pleased because he said I was okay. But you knew that wasn't true. You knew in your gut that it was something serious.

Remember when Saskia went into labour four weeks early with the twins? You knew before your mum even called us.

So, if you're at a crossroads now and you don't know what you should be thinking or feeling or doing, then be brave - and trust your intuition.

You've got this.
Love always
Steve xxx

She'd read the letter twice and then put it back inside the shoebox and under the bed. The advice was simple; she could hear his voice saying it to her.

And that had to be enough.

Lydia

When I arrived home from seeing Paula, Adam was sitting at the table; Zack had made dinner.

'You're just in time,' he said. 'Cauliflower, broccoli and cheese and fish fingers.' He used a spatula to load the fish fingers onto the plates. 'I'm not sure it goes together but I'm keeping my fingers crossed.'

He said this almost every time he made dinner, and every time I said, 'I'm sure it will be delicious.' I kissed his cheek and washed my hands at the sink.

'Did you hear we're going to Grandma Jenny's on Saturday?' Adam said. He poured tomato ketchup over the fish fingers. 'Dad's arranged it.'

'How lovely,' I replied, my voice overly bright. I'd told Zack that she'd hit me as a child. I'd told him that she gave my dad an overdose of morphine but somehow, he trusted her more than he trusted me. I wasn't sure whether that made him especially naive or my mother especially powerful. Probably a bit of both. And as Paula had said, his feelings were hurt and it was clouding his judgement.

I dried my hands and stood beside him. 'We're going to employ another cleaning company from now on,' I told him. 'I've taken our keys back from Maids of Honour.'

He accepted this with a nod. 'I'm not even sure we need a cleaner,' he said. 'Maybe we could just have a company come in and blitz the place every three months or so.'

'Sounds good to me.'

He smiled and I smiled back.

We were both behaving so well.

All too soon the weekend came around and a farce was about to play out. We would go to my mother's house. She and I would pretend to be like any other mother and daughter. It would be as if there were no unspoken secrets between us, no reason for hatred.

I could do that. I could do it for my son if not for myself. The alcoholic inside me was screaming for a drink but I wasn't giving in. I was holding fast – almost three hundred hours and counting. I'd given up alcohol before, and I could do it again.

Speaking to Paula had helped me focus on what was important. She was right about my dad. He wouldn't want me to dwell on the manner of his death. He would want me to live in the present. And today, I was going to my mother's to play the game. With any luck she would make missteps and Zack would begin to see through her pretence. And Adam, like most nine-year-olds, would take his lead from his parents. If we suddenly stopped seeing her, he would accept it.

And if that didn't work? Then I would take Paula's advice and do whatever it took to protect my son.

'Come in! Welcome!'

We all walked in. I didn't speak. Zack handed over a bouquet of roses and a bottle of alcohol free wine. My mother accepted the gifts with thanks and turned her attention to Adam. She had bought him an enormous Lego model from the Star Wars range. 'Wow! Look Mum! Look Dad!'

They went into the living room to lay the pieces out on the floor. I stared at the photographs in the hallway. They were in matching silver frames, a dozen of them, arranged in groups of four across the wall. Nostalgia blew through me like a draught. In the first photo, my dad had his arms around me and my mother, and we were all smiling at the camera. I remembered the exact moment the photo was taken. We had just moved into the bungalow. It was a new beginning, a happy day. The other pictures were taken in Wales on the beach, running, doing cartwheels, swimming, and there was one of my dad in his uniform on the day he received a medal from the Queen.

Three of the photographs were of Adam: one from school sports day, another from Christmas two years ago and the third was taken in our back garden. Zack must have given them to her. I felt the sting of betrayal and wondered whether we'd ever get past what we were doing to each other. Perhaps there could be mutual forgiveness and we could move on.

Perhaps not.

I walked into the living room and found the three of them sitting on the floor, the Lego in the centre. Adam was holding up the instruction booklet while my mother laid out the bags of bricks and Zack smiled at them both. I could see that he was happy to have brought them together.

I didn't sit down immediately. It was a shock to be here after so many years. The walls were a different colour, the curtains were changed and the television was a newer model but otherwise, it was much the same as I remembered it. I stared across at the place where my dad's chair used to be and closed my eyes. *Forgive me, Dad.* Then I sat down on the sofa in the place where I had always sat and watched the three of them interact. I felt as if I'd landed in a parallel universe where happy families was the name of the game.

'I didn't know Mummy was good at hockey,' I heard Adam say.

'Why, didn't she tell you?' Genevieve looked triumphant. 'She could have been *very* good but she was never too keen on applying herself. Not like you with your football.' She stroked his hair and stood up, walking over to the drinks cabinet. There was a bottle of champagne chilling in an ice bucket. She poured a glass for herself and Zack. 'Of course, not for you, Lydia,' she said cheerfully. 'Here you are.' She handed me a glass of the alcohol free wine. 'And what would you like, Adam?'

He stood in front of the array of drinks, his eyes popping. It wasn't like this at home. 'I'll go for that one, please.'

'Now that I know your favourite, I'll be able to keep it in the fridge for when you come round.' She smiled at me. 'Come and help me in the kitchen, Lydia.' I followed her through wordlessly, a timid child. 'This is the way it will be from now on.' She passed me some vegetables to tip into serving dishes. 'I take it you've called the Priory?' She took my silence as consent. 'You need to leave your family to me for the foreseeable. Sort yourself out.' She brought the roast out onto the work surface. 'Your dad would want the same.'

The table was laden with food. I was managing. I was cutting up the chicken and potatoes on my plate, loading them onto the fork, lifting it up to my mouth. I could chew; I could swallow. I reached for sips of fizzy water. I was smiling in all the right places, joining in when I could.

We were just finishing pudding when a dizzy sickness crept up on me, filling my head and my stomach with panic and dread. 'Excuse me.' I held a napkin over my mouth and ran for the downstairs loo. I retched over the pan multiple times, everything I'd eaten coming straight back out again. Zack, Adam and my mother were outside the door expressing concern. 'I'm okay,' I said between bouts. 'Please just leave me for a minute.' I tried to stand up but my legs were unsteady and I fell against the sink.

'Let me help you, Lydia,' Genevieve said, opening the door, her tone kindly, her grip on my elbow not so much. I caught sight of a look that passed between her and Zack – a worried look, an oh-no-I-hope-she-hasn't-been-drinking look. Here I was drawing attention to myself again. It couldn't be the food – no one else was vomiting. Therefore it had to be something I had done.

I let her lead me out of the toilet. 'If I could just lie down,' I said. I didn't need to fake my trembling limbs or shaky voice. 'I'm sure I'll be fine soon. No, I won't manage the stairs,' I told her as she led me to the bottom of them, so she took me to her bedroom instead. I lay down on the top of her bed and she placed a blanket over me, then pulled the door almost shut.

I lay there for a couple of minutes gathering my wits about me. This was all a little too convenient. What was more, this feeling was familiar to me. I recognised it from when my mother had drugged me as a teenager. I sat up slowly; my head was heavy, my stomach churned.

'I'll fill up the bird feeder!' I heard Adam shout, and I rose to my feet, holding on to the furniture as I crept to the door and out into the hallway.

Zack and Genevieve were in the living room. 'I think she must have swiped some of this vodka,' I heard Genevieve whisper. I peered through the crack between the door and the frame and saw her holding up a half empty bottle.

'I don't think she would do that, Gen,' Zack said. I was pleased to hear him stick up for me. 'She's been trying very hard to stay sober.'

'She went into the garage at one point. I'd stored all the alcohol out there so as not to tempt her.' She looked stricken. 'Might I have made a mistake with the champagne?'

'No.' I watched Zack's confidence in me waver. 'I don't think so . . .' he trailed off.

'I don't want it to be true,' Genevieve said, a tremor in her voice. 'But there's no other explanation. This was a new bottle. And sadly, this sort of behaviour is not uncommon with alcoholics. Has she booked herself in to the Priory yet?'

'I know she's seeing a counsellor,' he said.

'Good as that is, and I hate to say it, but I still think she needs to be free of all the daily pressures, stay some-where away from temptation where she can concentrate on getting *well* again.'

'Perhaps you're right.' I could see he was completely out of his depth. Why couldn't he tell her to back off? Mind her own business? Take her suspicions and shove them where the sun don't shine?

'Dad!' Adam shouted.

'Let's join Adam,' Genevieve said, taking Zack's arm. 'I expect Lydia will need to sleep it off.'

I crept back into the bedroom and steadied myself against the back of the door, my eyes taking in the room. Thirty years hadn't changed it much. While the curtains and covers were new, the furniture was the same or similar and positioned in the usual spots. And if she'd kept the same hiding place, then I knew where the drugs would be. I'd found her stash one day when she was out with Oscar, and my dad was in hospital. It had taken me hours. I'd gone through the whole house room by room, cupboard by cupboard, until I'd come across it. The panel at the back of one of her wardrobes gave way at the lower corner when pressed, and behind it, was the hiding place.

I moved as quickly as I could, dizzy headache permitting, and found two medium-sized brown bottles hidden in the space. I looked at the labels. One was morphine and the other temazepam. Both were prescribed to Edward Gibson. I'd noticed his name on the door of the room three along from Paula's. Genevieve had taken the drugs from the hospice. This was evidence, wasn't it? I could take it to the nursing staff now. But there was a warning voice in my head. *Would she say that I had stolen the bottles and planted them in her house?*

Possibly. Probably. Most likely I wouldn't be believed.

I tiptoed out into the hallway and took my water bottle from my handbag. I set my mobile on the bathroom shelf and activated the camera to film what I was doing. I held the brown bottles in front of the camera so that the labels could be read. I poured the contents of the water bottle down the plughole and filled it with the liquid from brown bottles. Then I half-filled the brown bottles with water and returned them to their hiding place.

When my water bottle was back in my bag, I stood at the kitchen window and watched the three of them in the garden. They had walked down to the summer house and gone inside, my mother talking all the while. I expect she was promising Adam that she would turn it into somewhere for him and his friends to hang out. No doubt she was promising him all sorts of things. And with me out of the picture, there was nothing to stop her taking over completely.

I was a liar, a secret-keeper, the one who was losing her driving licence. It wouldn't matter if we moved town – she'd only invite herself to stay. It wouldn't matter if we divorced; Zack would allow her to see Adam. She would be there forever at my back. Worse, she would be at Adam's back, directing him, subtly belittling him. And when he didn't cooperate, would she drug him like she did me? Would she undermine him, gaslight him, until he doubted his own sanity?

Over my dead body.

'Or hers,' I said out loud, my words rising softly into the air, melodic, like birdsong.

Tess

Saturday morning and Tess was up just before six as usual. Her dad appeared soon after, dressed in his work clothes.

'You're not working today, are you?'

He glanced at the kitchen clock. 'Pete's on his way to collect me. There's some work come up in Dartford this time. Kitchen needs fitting and the chippie's let him down. It'll be more money for Christmas.' He took hold of her hands. 'You're freezing, love. You put the heating on. I'll make at least two grand. Let's push the boat out. No more hardship. Not this year anyway.'

She stood up to hug him. 'Honestly, Dad, you're a godsend.'

He smiled. 'Better late than never, eh?' As he walked away, he turned back to say, 'And don't you be thinking that I don't know about all those loans you took out.'

She flushed red. 'Dad, I—'

'Don't worry.' He winked at her. 'I've got a plan.'

After she waved him off, she came back inside and switched on the heating. A luxury, but with the money her dad would earn, maybe they could afford it. She smiled at the thought of a happy family Christmas where she would be able to forget, if only for a short while, that she had to scrimp and save. And he'd known all along about the loans? She shook her head. She would be surprised if he knew the extent of the debt but she was relieved that now the truth was partly out in the open.

There was frost on the inside of the windows in the living room so she stayed in the kitchen. She made another coffee and sat down on the chair where she had a view over the back garden. It was already eight o'clock and the sun was up but, unusually, both children were still asleep and she could take a moment. She closed her eyes and enjoyed the luxury of the air warming around her. The feeling was short-lived. It wasn't long before she felt the warning pulse of her raised heartbeat. She sat up straight and stared outside into the garden. She knew it would happen one day, and now it had. Oscar's face was visible through the gap in the fence. He was staring directly at her, no cap this time.

She jumped to her feet. *You've got this.* It was Steve's voice. *Tess, you've got this.* There was no time to think. She grabbed a knife and opened the back door. Her breath froze instantly as it hit the air in front of her. Crusts of ice had formed on the fence and on the overhang from the garden shed. She walked towards him unafraid, her head up. 'What the fuck do you want, Oscar?' she shouted. 'Do you think I'm still the naive teenager I used to be, is that it? You think you can intimidate me?'

When he lifted his eyes to hers, she stopped. Her jaw dropped. 'What? But you look ...' She trailed off. It wasn't Oscar. 'You sound like him.'

'We're calling in the debt,' he said, shifting from one foot to the other. 'You've been ignoring emails.'

She walked closer. He was almost Oscar's double but without the grey eyes. This man's eyes were a deep brown. 'You're a debt collector?'

'Working for Jim MacKay,' he said. 'He wants his money.' He pulled out his mobile and pressed a button, briefly turning his back on her while he talked. Tess waited, the wind beginning to chill her to the bone.

When he passed her the phone, she listened as MacKay told her that he wanted what was owed. 'I don't have it,' she told him.

'Your car,' he said loudly. 'That'll be worth a mint.'

Steve's car. She'd never wanted to part with it because to do so would be like saying goodbye to more of Steve. But selling it made sense. It was a classic. She'd be able to buy a second-hand car for a third of what it was worth. *Steve would understand.* And there were so many more of his possessions that she could treasure.

'Okay. I'll sell it,' she said, ignoring the sharp pain in her heart. 'I'll get you your money.' Steve had a friend who had already offered to buy the car when she was ready to sell. She'd call him later, and that would be one loan paid off, at least.

'I'm going to hold you to that,' McKay said. 'You have a week.'

She returned the phone to the Oscar lookalike and said sharply, 'I don't appreciate you filming me and putting it online.'

'I had to do somethin'.'

'Well, it caused me problems, but I expect that was your intention.'

'You threw the wine, not me.' He gave a lazy laugh. 'You and them posh bitches. Serves you right.'

'Your mum must be so proud,' Tess said, then turned on her heel and went back inside. She stood next to the radiator, warming her hands, her legs, her back. Her teeth were chattering. Her nerves were vibrating, as if the electricity inside her had dialled up a notch. She didn't know whether to laugh or to cry. She'd been worried sick for two weeks that Oscar was back in her life. But it wasn't him! It wasn't Oscar.

So what did the dream mean?

Lydia

When we returned from lunch with my mother, Adam went to play outside. 'I'll join you in a minute, Buddy!' Zack told him. 'I'll go in goal.' He turned to me. 'Do you need to lie down?'

'No.' My stomach was still queasy, but I was determined to have one last try with Zack. 'I didn't drink anything. I heard her telling you that I did, but I didn't.'

He sighed. 'Lydia.'

'She drugged me.'

He threw out his hands, laughing. 'How? With *what*?'

'I'll show you.' I told him what Paula had said about the missing medicine, and about the brown bottles I'd found in the wardrobe. He watched the video I'd made. He saw the name on the labels. 'Edward Gibson is a patient in the hospice.' I took the water bottle out of my bag. 'Smell it,' I said, removing the lid and holding the bottle out towards him.

He sniffed it. 'Doesn't smell of anything.'

'Taste it, then.'

He took a small sip. 'It tastes of nothing.'

'Do you believe me?' I asked tightly.

He bit the edge of his thumbnail. 'I want to believe you,' he said. 'I really do.'

292

'Your mum would believe me.'

'My mum?' He sighed again. 'Lydia, my mum loves you. She always has. From the moment she met you. She's always thought you were smarter than me – which you are. And she's always thought you were a better judge of character than me, which you probably are.' He shrugged. 'Of course she's going to believe you because she isn't standing in my shoes.'

I waved my phone at him. 'You think I'm capable of stealing meds from the hospice, drugging myself and then setting up a video?'

'I don't know what to think! I feel very let down by you, Lydia. I know you want to blame all of this on your mum but she didn't start it! You did! You were caught drunk-driving. You've been keeping secrets. It's very difficult for me to get past that.'

I walked away, went upstairs to my bedroom and had a shower. When I was finished, I opened the photo app on my mobile and scrolled through photos of Adam, stopping at one where he had a medal round his neck and was grinning at the camera. He had a smile as wide as my arms, and eyes as kind as my father's. Just looking at him allowed me to breathe more freely. If my life was just about me, I'd leave Zack. I'd move away to one of the world's major cities, where life was a twenty-four-hour party and there were bars aplenty. I'd spend my waking moments on a high stool at the counter, making superficial chat with the bartender or the people perched on stools next to me. I would drink myself into sweet oblivion. I would only eat occasionally: bar snacks, olives, maybe some chips. Mostly I would drink.

There was an inevitability about what I had to do. I was an adult and this was an adult decision. My mother had never protected me. I doubted that she had ever even loved me. She loved Oscar and she loved herself. She would continue to undermine me and slowly edge me out. For all Zack said that he wanted to believe me, he didn't. Our bond was not unbreakable. His love for me was not unconditional. I understood that.

Next day, I drove to the forest car park and hid my car at the far end as I always did, making sure it wasn't visible from the road. It was close to two o'clock and I knew that my mother would be home because she'd told me so. She'd come into the bedroom while Zack and Adam were still outside. 'You'll visit me tomorrow so that we can make arrangements for Adam,' she'd said. 'I'll expect you at two.'

Snow had been falling since mid morning, large wet flakes swirling down from the sky to land on paths and people, trees and grass, turning the landscape to a scene from Narnia. I watched my step as I jogged along the path and, as I had done before, approached the house from the rear. I could see my mother reading in the living room. I knocked on the patio doors and she looked up.

'Well, well, well.' She opened the door. 'Why the back door, Lydia?'

I ignored her question, wiping my feet on the mat before walking into the house.

'I'm pleased you've shown up.'

'May I remove my coat?' I asked. She inclined her head. I took that as a yes and slid my arms out of my jacket. She immediately took it from me and went to hang it up. When she returned, I looked her straight in the eye. 'I've come to apologise.' My lip trembled. 'I'm willing to share Adam with you. All I ask is that you don't alienate Zack. I want to stay married to him. We're good for each other.'

She nodded. 'He does seem to love you, right enough.' She thought for a second then gave me a lizard smile. 'This calls for a celebration.' She walked across to the drinks cabinet and opened the glass door. 'You'll have to watch me drink.' She poured herself a port and smiled again. 'Nothing alcoholic for you, Lydia. Would you like an elderflower cordial?'

'No, thank you.'

She sat back down. I watched her relish her power. 'Everything that's happened to you, you've brought upon yourself.' I nodded and she smiled again, glad to see me weakened. 'Of course, your father ruined you. Always letting you have your own way.' She glanced across at the spot where his chair used to be. 'But I'm glad you've come round at last. I'm sure we can work together.'

'Actually, Mum.' I made an attempt at clearing my throat. 'I would like a drink of water if that's okay.'

'Of course.' She stood up and left the room. The second she was out of sight, I took the water bottle from my bag and walked swiftly across to her chair. I took a large swig of her port and topped it up with the mix of morphine and temazepam from the water bottle. Colourless and tasteless, it blended easily with the deep red port.

By the time she returned with the water, I was sitting down again, my expression reflective. 'So, let's make some concrete arrangements.' She took a sip of her drink. 'I'll collect Adam from school on Mondays, Wednesdays and Fridays. I want him to get to know his granny properly so he will stay Friday nights with me, and I can take him to football on weekends.' Another sip. She had it all planned. 'That will give you time to check into the Priory, and then repair your marriage.' She gave me a stern look. 'Zack's a good man, Lydia. He doesn't deserve to be treated as badly as you've been treating him.'

Another sip. 'Your dad would be disappointed in you.' She thought for a second, her eyebrows rising. 'Ashamed of you even.' Another sip. 'Yes, he'd *definitely* be ashamed of you.'

I let her talk because I knew she was a dead woman still sitting in a chair. She underestimated me. I'd watched her from when I was knee-high. I knew how to have two faces. I could pretend if I needed to, just like she did. I kept my body language dejected. My shoulders were slumped, and my mouth was a flat line. She was sealing her own fate. I had watched her murder my dad to teach me a lesson. And I knew that, at some point in the future, she would come after my son. Maybe not for a few years. But it would happen. I knew it with a certainty that kept me in the seat, in the house, watching her drink herself unconscious.

'I know you blamed Tess for calling the police,' she continued. 'But she had nothing to do with it. She was simply in the wrong place at the wrong time. You never treated that girl well enough. You were always taking the limelight. Showing off.' A larger sip this time. She was warming to her theme. 'I had my eye on you and by reporting you to the police, I did what any responsible person would have done.' She sniffed. 'I've been watching you since you moved back here and I saw at once that you were a drunk.'

'I do my best but it isn't always good enough.' My voice was barely a whisper. So Tess hadn't been involved at all, and that made me feel relieved. I didn't want to be suspicious of her. Quite the opposite. 'You're right. I didn't treat Tess as well as I should have.'

'It's a pattern,' she stated. She gave me what should have been a sharp look but her eyes were beginning to close. The drugs had started to take effect but she hadn't noticed yet. She was too enamoured with her own victory. She tried to stand up but immediately fell back onto the seat.

'We are all the authors of our own demise,' I said.

'What's that?' She squinted across at me.

'If you hadn't let your cousin loose on me, if you hadn't killed my dad, if you hadn't reported me to the police, if you hadn't planted alcohol in my house or drugged me at your dinner table. If you hadn't poured yourself a celebratory port ...' I stood up and walked closer to her. 'There's only one thing left to say now, isn't there, Mum?' I whispered.

Her right eyelid twitched and then her left did the same as if in conversation. 'You ... li ... le ...'

My heart was pounding. 'You made one mistake, Genevieve. You forgot that I'm your daughter.' I paused. 'Remember when you said to me that if it took the rest of your life you would find out what happened to Oscar?' I moved in closer and smiled. 'I think it's only fair to tell you that Oscar is dead. Thirty years dead.'

Anger flared in her eyes. 'You ...' She raised a hand to strike me but it fell back down onto her lap. Then her eyes closed and her head slumped forward.

I moved away from her, my breathing rapid. There was still time for me to walk out the door. If I left now, she'd wake up at some point and wonder what the hell had happened. Most likely she'd remember that I'd visited her and then she'd put two and two together and realise I'd drugged her. And she'd make my life hell. She'd put all her energies into destroying my marriage and teaming up with Zack. Then Adam would be hers.

But if I killed her, it would haunt me for the rest of my days. I would be even more haunted than I was already and it would be an even greater feat for me to stay teetotal

– because blocking it out with alcohol wasn't an option, not if I wanted to be Adam's mother. And I did want that. I wanted that with every part of me.

I had to move quickly. I wasn't sure how long I had before she woke up, the mix of drugs made it hard to tell. My mother always put her car in the garage. She cared for her possessions, made sure that they lasted, and a garaged car was less likely to suffer from the elements. Strange to think that it was this detail that made her easier for me to kill her. Suicide by carbon monoxide poisoning was surprisingly common. Hanging was violent and pills were risky – sometimes death didn't happen immediately; liver damage led to a slower death.

I found her car keys in the drawer in the kitchen where they had always been kept. Another drawer held the disposable gloves she wore to chop onions and garlic. I pulled on a pair and wiped down every surface I had touched. I washed both glasses, dried them and put them in the cupboard then I opened the door to the garage. I was pleased to see that the driver's door was closest to me. I opened it as wide as it could go and retraced my steps back to the living room, making sure my way through the house was clear. I didn't want her knocking into walls or wedged in a doorway.

She was slight, no more than eight stone, but carrying a dead weight wasn't easy. I bent my knees, and with some huffing and puffing, managed to lever her up and over my shoulder – a fireman's lift. My knees almost buckled as I made my way to the garage. Her arms were swinging at my back and I slowed my pace to make sure they didn't knock into the walls. I lowered her gently into the car seat, holding onto her head to prevent it from hitting the side of the car. Unexplained bruises weren't part of the plan. I didn't think that there would be an investigation but it was important to be prepared, just in case. I wrapped her limp hand around the garden hose. I made sure there were fingerprints on the ignition switch and on the keys. Then I found a pair of pliers and shortened the other end of the hose before I put it into the exhaust pipe. I started the engine and at once the exhaust fumes travelled along the hose pipe and came out of the end I was holding. I opened the driver's window a couple of inches and fed the hose through so that it lay on her shoulder. Her eyelids flickered briefly, like a faulty electrical circuit sparking on and off.

I stood back and watched the fumes fill the car. Thoughts ricocheted around inside my skull, making me dizzy and breathless. *I should save her. I should let her die. I would end up in prison. I'd get away with it. My son would find out I was a murderer. My son would never know.*

I wasn't sure how long it would take for her to die. I could have looked it up on the internet, but I didn't want there to be a record of me googling it. I was tempted to open the car door and drag her out. I should, shouldn't I? My hand rested on the handle ready to pull but I couldn't do it. I wouldn't save her.

I didn't want to watch her die so I closed the garage door behind me and I went inside.

Tess

By Sunday afternoon, Tess was beginning to feel angry. How dare Genevieve manipulate her like that? Coming into Lydia's house when she was cleaning. Planting bottles of booze all over the place? What the fuck? She'd used Tess as a pawn in whatever cruel and deceitful game she was playing. It was too much, and she wouldn't allow it to go unchallenged. Now that she knew that she wasn't being stalked by Oscar, she felt stronger. She could look at everything with fresh eyes.

Snow was falling steadily, and the kids were with Sadie and her mum in their back garden. Sadie wanted to spend time with them before she went off to her dad's the next day. Genevieve lived close by, and Tess decided she could do with the walk. She dressed in multiple layers and pulled on her snow boots, trudging along the road to the bungalow. She passed several families enjoying the beginning of the school holidays dragging their sledges to the park. Traffic was light as the road became dense with ice and snow. By the time she arrived there was at least three inches underfoot, and despite her layers, the cold was beginning to bite.

She rang the doorbell and waited. She knew what she was going to say. She would be short and to the point.

She would leave Genevieve in no doubt that she was on to her, and then she would go back home and warm herself by the wood burner in the living room. She'd make toast and hot chocolate for Bobby and Sadie, and she'd start to plan for Christmas Day.

The air was quiet and still, snow landing soundlessly on her jacket, crystals clumping together to form great lumps that she brushed off onto the ground. She rang the doorbell again and tuned into the only sound – a car's engine turning over. It was coming from the garage. Surprising, because one look at the weather would surely stop most people from going out.

She moved across to the garage door and pulled on the lower edge. It didn't budge. Most likely the door was electric and was activated remotely. She walked round the side of the house and into the back garden. The landscape was like a scene from a fairy tale: tall trees, the summer house, hedges and bushes all bedecked in snow. She stopped to admire the white crystal shimmer before peering through the patio doors and into the living room. There was no sign of anyone inside. She pulled at the patio door and was surprised when it opened. 'Genevieve!' she shouted. 'Are you home?'

There was no reply. She pulled the door wider and stepped onto the mat, removed her boots and coat, and walked on to the carpet. She knew she was taking liberties, but in her defence, Genevieve should not be going out in her car. The roads would be treacherous. She was right to warn her of that.

It was over thirty years since Tess had been in this house, but she remembered the layout and she walked confidently to the door next to the kitchen that led into the garage. She reached for the handle and turned it, jumping with fright when a hand came from behind her to hold the door closed. 'Fuck! Lydia?' Her breath was ragged. 'You gave me a fright!'

Lydia's expression was stony. 'What are you doing here?'

'I came to speak to your mum. Is she in the garage?'

'You should go,' Lydia said. 'She has a doorbell with a camera. You need to be seen leaving. *Go.*'

'What?' Her stomach did a backflip. 'I don't understand.' She stared at the garage door and whispered, 'Is your mum in there?'

Lydia didn't reply but then she didn't need to because Tess began to read the truth in her eyes. 'You can't allow this to happen, Lydia,' she said softly. 'If your mum is ...' she hesitated ' ... taking her own life then you have to stop her.' Their eyes were locked. Tess felt a chill settle next to her heart. 'Take your hand away from the door, Lydia. Please,' she pleaded. Lydia leaned in harder. 'You can't let her do this. You can't have this on your conscience! Jesus, Lydia, you won't get away with it!'

'Why not?' Lydia asked. 'You did.'

There was a rushing in Tess's ears and her head flooded with vertigo as she was pulled back into her past.

Lydia and Tess, Wales summer 1994

'There's a disco in the rec room tonight,' Lydia told Tess. 'It should be quite good.'

'Okay.' Tess was lying on the camp bed reading a magazine and eating toffee. 'What time does it start?'

'Sixish.'

It was day three on their holiday-that-wasn't-a-holiday in Wales and Lydia had to work hard to keep Oscar away from them. Every which way she turned he was there – on the beach, outside the toilet block, ordering coffee from the on-site café. She was counting down the hours until she got home to her dad. She should never have come. Her dad was dying. He was *dying* and she was stuck in the caravan park with her mother whom she despised, her pervy cousin Oscar, and Tess, who only wanted to be with Steve and was spending all her pocket money on tokens for the phone box.

'I'll call Steve just before six then,' Tess said, pushing herself up into standing position, her neck bent against the roof of the tent. Oscar and Genevieve slept in the caravan while Tess and Lydia slept in the tent. 'What are you going to wear?'

'I'm not sure,' Lydia replied. She didn't care. She just wanted to go home.

Tess started rummaging through their bags, pulling out multiple items, like scarves from a magician's sleeve. Soon their camp beds were covered in tops.

'This maybe?' Tess held a skimpy T-shirt in front of her. 'Shows off my assets.'

'You should wear a jumper,' Lydia said, choosing one for herself. A long slouchy one that covered her boobs and her bum.

'You've turned into my mum,' Tess said cheerfully. 'But I suppose you're right. No point in drawing unwanted attention.'

When they were dressed, they went into the caravan to see if there was anything to eat. Neither Genevieve nor Oscar were in there which to Lydia felt ominous. She liked to know where they were at all times. They found a tin of tomato soup and heated it up, dipping white bread and butter into it. Tess talked at length about Steve and what she was going to buy him for his birthday. Lydia counted off another hour.

At six o'clock they went to the phone box and Lydia stood outside smoking a cigarette while Tess giggled and whispered her way through the call. About half an hour in, she pushed open the door with her foot and called out, 'Lydia, you can go into the disco if you want!'

Lydia moved to the alcove to give Tess some privacy but kept a sideways eye on her.

Another hour passed. Tick. When Tess finally finished talking to Steve, Lydia had smoked five cigarettes and drunk a quarter of a litre bottle of vodka that they'd persuaded an older boy to buy for them from the campsite shop. Tess drank the same in one go, coughing and shaking her head against the taste. They hid the bottle under a bush and went into the disco. The hall was fairly basic but the music got them going and they danced solely with each other for almost two hours, sneaking outside between tracks to drink some more. The room was full of kids, parents popping their heads in every now and then to check on their sprogs.

When Lydia's favourite song came on, she was elated. She turned around in circles, eyes closed, arms waving above her head, singing along loudly. She would be home with her beloved dad tomorrow, and now, in this moment, she felt carefree.

When she came back down to earth, Tess wasn't there. 'For fuck's sake.' She felt the onset of panic. She ran outside and up the hill to the phone box but there was no one in it. The caravan, then. As she ran back there, Oscar came out of the shadows and made a grab for her, pulling her behind the campsite shop which was already closed for the night. His breath stank and his hands were everywhere. She slapped his face and poked him in the eye, and when she started to scream, he covered her mouth with his hand. She was pinned against the cold stone wall unable to move, his forearm across her neck as his free hand pulled at his trousers and then hers. When he forced himself inside her, she felt as if she were being split in two. It was painful, humiliating, more terrifying than anything she'd ever thought possible. She tried to disassociate, to imagine that this was happening to someone else, but she couldn't. She was completely in the moment, each second lengthening out into a pain so acute that she knew she'd never recover from it.

When he was finished, he grinned at her. 'One down, one to go.'

He pulled up the zip of his trousers and left her there. There was blood running down her leg. She grabbed a dock leaf to wipe it away. Her hands shook so much that she spread the blood further. She gave up and pulled up her pants and her trousers, wincing at the pain between her legs. As she struggled with the zip, she lost her balance, pitching forward onto her face, clumps of grass pushing into her mouth and eyes. She righted herself again, pressing her weight back against the wall as if she were standing on a ledge. 'I'm in shock,' she told herself. 'I'll be all right in a minute.'

'I'll be all right. I'll be all right. I'll be all right,' she repeated, tears running down onto her neck.

And then her heart stopped. *Tess*. Where was she?

While Lydia was dancing, Tess went outside to be sick, retching onto the grass multiple times. She must have drunk too much. Her brain was fuzzy so she wasn't entirely sure. Avoiding the patch of vomit, she collapsed down on the grass and stared up at the stars. She and Steve were growing really close. There'd been heavy petting, as Gary would have called it, had he known. She just about managed to keep her mum and Gary in the dark about her feelings for Steve otherwise they would be embarrassing her at every turn. Perhaps she would have sex with Steve soon. She wished Lydia was at the same stage so that they could discuss it.

'And look who it is!'

Oscar's voice came out of the shadows. She hauled herself to her feet and shouted, 'Back off, creep!'

He lunged towards her, his foot slipping on the patch of vomit on the grass. Tess started to run. She should have run towards the caravan but she lost her sense of direction. She was running through the woods, gulping in air that stung her throat and made her want to cough. She felt him behind her and her heart doubled in speed but her legs couldn't go any faster. When he caught hold of her ponytail, she screamed, yanked herself free, then pushed back into his chest. He grunted several times, sounding so much like a pig that she had to stifle the hysteria wedged tight against the fear in her chest. She pushed him again and he lost his balance, slithered down the bank to one side of them. There was the crack of twigs, the dull thump of thighbone and elbow, the scrape of flesh on stone, and all the while he was cursing, howling her name into the darkness like a wolf to the full moon.

Seconds of falling, and then a loud splash as his body came to rest in the stream.

She waited, her heart ticking, her knees shaking. A huge shiver passed through her. Wide-eyed, she held her breath and listened, tuning into sounds beyond herself: the soft shuffle of small mammals and insects, the breath of wind trailing through the leaves and lifting single strands of her hair.

When she was satisfied that enough time had passed, she followed his fall down the bank, not sliding as he did, but carefully placing one foot in front of the other, stretching out blindly to grasp hold of tree roots and rocks to keep her steady.

She reached the bottom and blinked into the gloom before spotting the body-shaped lump in the stream. She shivered again when she imagined him crawling towards her, silent as a snake, to wrap his hands around her ankles and pull her underground. But as she edged closer, she saw that he couldn't crawl, that movement would be impossible. His limbs were twisted, his pelvis raised at one side, the angle unnatural. She felt sure his left knee had popped from its socket. There was the dark stain of blood on his temple. His eyelids fluttered open then closed again as he hovered in the space between the conscious and the unconscious.

The air was heavy here. *Off the beaten track.* Where dangerous possibilities lurked. She felt this significance move through her in a wave of heat. Here, chance and opportunity collided. No one was watching.

With quick, rough hands she dug aside the pebbles beneath his head. An inch more depth and his head dropped further back, his ears, his cheeks and finally his nose and mouth sinking under the water. He breathed in the stream and coughed. Startled, his eyes opened fully this time and she caught his panic, her indrawn breath stopped short as her hand flew to her throat.

Should she? Shouldn't she?

She stood away from him, watching as he tried to lift himself up. He almost managed, gave a growl of desperation when he failed. She hesitated for a split second before placing her foot high up on his chest, leaning in until all of her weight was over this one foot. He gurgled, tried for the last time to lift his mouth to the air, his bloody-knuckled hands failing to grasp the shoe pressing down on him.

When he was quiet, she watched him for a full, unconscionable minute before blowing on her hands to warm them. Then she retraced her steps up the hill, the moon's glare highlighting her flushed cheeks.

Lydia caught up with her as she came up the bank. 'Tess!' she called out. 'Are you okay?' Tess briefly looked back, but it was as if she didn't even see her. 'Tess, wait!' Lydia ran after her, grabbing her arm. 'Where is he?'

Tess swayed on her feet. 'Who?' She gave a drunken burp and staggered away. 'It's okay. He won't bother us any more.'

There was a heavy feeling in Lydia's chest. It had been there since – well, she wouldn't say it, wouldn't even think it. She shone her torch down the hill. She could see a body at the bottom of the bank. She slithered down, crying out as her ankle twisted and her hand was scraped by brambles. She approached him cautiously, sure that at any moment he would rise up like a vampire and pin her against a tree this time.

But he didn't move. She stood at his side and let the torchlight creep up his body. His face was under the water. His eyes were open. They were dead eyes, glassy and opaque. She hated this man, but still she was shocked to see him dead. When she looked closer, she noticed that his head was lower in the water than the rest of him. It looked as if the stones around his head had been dug out from underneath him. Tess? Did she do that? There were small piles either side of his ears. Lydia moved the torchlight to his chest which was above the water. There was a muddy footprint on his shirt.

Fuck.

She stood up and tried to keep breathing. Tess had done this. She'd killed him. *She'd killed him.* It was both believable and unbelievable, welcome and unwelcome. She switched off the torch and when her eyes adjusted to the gloom, she paced around his body, the moon her only witness, silent and heavy in the sky above her. Despite all the reading she'd done, there was only one forensic law that she could distinctly remember – every contact leaves a trace. There would be DNA traces of her and Tess all over him. She briefly considered honesty – adults, the police, the lock on her door, the fact he'd been following them all the time, the r— She tuned into the pain between her legs and cried out, smothering the sound with her hand. Tess could go to prison – and for what?

She scooped handfuls of water from the stream and threw it over him to smudge the footprint. She closed his eyes and pushed the stones back under his head again so that his face was out of the water. She took his wallet and his lighter from his pocket. She climbed up the bank and walked back to the campsite, praying for rain with every step. It was two o'clock in the morning and she saw no one, neither man nor woman, only a watchful fox, bright eyes gleaming in the dark.

Lydia

'The dream I've been having,' Tess said quietly. 'It's not a dream, is it?'

I shook my head.

'I thought it was something that was *going* to happen,' she said, her voice stilted. 'It never occurred to me that it had actually happened.' Her eyes were huge and fearful when she looked at me. 'How could I not remember?'

'We'd had a lot to drink,' I said. 'That, and the hippocampus shrinks after trauma. It doesn't always store memories.' *If only that could happen to me.* 'We read about that in the library once. Do you remember?'

'I think I do.' She sat down heavily on the bottom stair. 'I killed Oscar.' Her hands were shaking, her eyes huge and red-rimmed. 'And all this time you knew?'

'There was no point in telling you.'

'Lydia, you've carried this. All this time.'

'It rained the day we left Wales. The heavens opened and it poured down,' I said, my tone businesslike. 'It was almost biblical. He would have been swept out to sea. I'd taken his lighter and wallet out of his pockets and threw them into a bin in the service station we stopped at when my mother drove us home.' I smiled at her. 'You slept the whole way.'

'Fuck!' She groaned into her hands.

'I scanned the news for weeks but I never found any record of a body. I suppose, if he was found, then he was just another missing person.' I clenched and unclenched my jaw. I wouldn't share Genevieve's revenge with her. My dad's death would be forever on my conscience.

'Your mum, Lydia.' Tess gestured towards the garage door. 'What are we going to do?'

'You should call an ambulance. Say you found her here.' I walked towards the patio doors. 'Then call me.'

The hospital corridors widened out into an atrium where there was a coffee shop and rows of seating for waiting relatives. Tess was standing in the corner away from the main doors. She must have heard my footsteps as I walked towards her because she swung around, her eyes wide. She was wearing an intense, hypervigilant look as if she expected to be ambushed by men with machine guns. 'I'm a murderer,' she whispered.

'Don't say that.' My tone was urgent. 'You didn't know what you were doing.'

'Your mum's dead.'

I nodded. I felt numb. I felt nothing. Neither dread nor relief.

Tess shivered. 'I'm sorry, Lydia. For everything.'

'Me too.' I took her hands. She was freezing even though the building was heated. I took my gloves from my pockets and gave them to her.

'Lydia!' I turned to see Zack running towards me. 'What's happened? Where is she?'

'She's dead,' I said. 'Suicide.' I took a ragged breath, not because of the stark words I'd just spoken but because of the look on his face. He wasn't only shocked. He was disbelieving, confused, suspicious.

'Why would she do that?' He shook his head at me. 'She was happy yesterday. She loved having us there for lunch.'

'She suffered from depression, didn't she?' Tess piped up. 'I remember that.'

'She'd had her problems, on and off,' I affirmed. It wasn't true but I knew what Tess was doing.

'When I saw her in the clubhouse café the other day, she was quite down.'

'She rallied round when we visited yesterday, but—'

'I know from having problems myself that I can have days when I disguise it well, and others when it feels overwhelming,' Tess finished.

We were playing our little game. The one we'd played at school, where we backed up each other's stories. 'I went to see her to thank her for a gift she'd given Bobby,' Tess continued. 'And that was when—' She broke off and started to cry. I held her tight and stared at Zack.

I think he almost believed us.

Lydia, six months later

Grace held open the door and I walked inside. I knew Zack had arrived before me because his car was in the driveway. I went into the room and sat down on the chair next to him. Neither of us spoke. We were chipping away at the secrets and lies between us, still living in the same house, trying to keep everything as normal as we could for Adam's sake.

The first three months were the worst, but then Paula passed away and something in Zack softened. He'd spent the last few days by her side, and I knew she'd remained on Team Lydia throughout. She'd kept my secrets, just as she promised, even though I was sure that when she heard about my mum's suicide, she would have wondered whether I had anything to do with it. I held my breath for a week or more, but there was no suspicion surrounding her death. No police investigation. No hands raised to question her decision. Just the fearful beat of my own guilty conscience.

Zack and I had started coming to therapy as a couple a month or so ago. It was torturous at times. Zack expressed his hurt and anger and I was mostly silent until I gradually accepted that it would never end unless I told my story with as much truth as I could safely share. So far we had covered everything up to the point where I moved to London to live with my Aunt Flo. Everything, that is, except Oscar's death. When Zack asked what had happened to him I simply said that I never saw him again after the trip to Wales.

I waited until Grace was seated and then I took up where I'd left off. 'I joined a sixth-form college close to my aunt's house. I wasn't expecting to make any friends. I tolerated my life. I managed to wake up in the morning and get myself out the front door. I missed Tess and I missed my dad, and I kept the R-word out of my mind because I was terrified that it would come to define me. I'd done everything I could to keep him away but still he'd managed to get to me.'

Zack shifted in his chair when I said this, his hand going up to his face. I knew he found the rape difficult to cope with. 'I'm sorry.' I glanced across at him, moving my head to different angles as I tried to catch his eye. 'It gets better soon.'

He stared across at me then, the hurt on his face so acute that I winced. 'Keep going,' he said quietly.

'I managed to come up with every excuse I could think of not to see my mother. I felt betrayed and let down by her. I hated her for what she'd done to my dad, and for what she'd done, and let happen, to me.' I didn't add that I was afraid of what I might do if I was left alone with her. My mind had been travelling to strange and unfamiliar places. I spent even more time in the sixth-form library than I had in the library at the grammar school. I knew how to murder someone without being caught. I relished all the different ways that I could end her life and she would never see it coming.

'Had I loved my dad too much?' I said to the room. 'Was his death the universe's way of telling me it was time to grow up? I thought about children in concentration camps. Children who had never been loved. I was lucky! I had been loved by my dad for fifteen, almost sixteen years. That had to be worth a lot. I tried my hardest to place my loss in a context that included the wider world, but I couldn't do it. Every hour of every day I knew what I was missing.' I paused for a drink of water before saying, 'And then one of the girls in my English class asked me why I was so miserable all the time.' I gave a short laugh. 'It wasn't deliberate. I just couldn't smile any more.' I stopped talking again because I remembered the feeling well and it made me want to cry. All of my happiness had relied on my dad being alive, and without him, there was a fist of pain squeezing my heart and never letting go.

I cleared my throat and continued. 'What the girl said helped me to see my life from my dad's point of view. I knew that he would want me to thrive. He loved that I was curious. He loved to hear me laugh. He loved to know that life was good for me. I had to try to lean into that, and when I did, I fell for one of my classmates. He was called Liam. His parents were Christians and so we had to keep our relationship a secret. That was fine with me. The first time I slept with him I was drunk enough to be able to dissociate.'

I sipped some more water. I still hadn't touched any alcohol since I'd been caught drink-driving. (Apart from a mouthful of my mother's port before I spiked it with the drugs she'd stolen. Yes, there was that. There would always be that.) The physical cravings were gone but the emotional ones lingered on, sometimes biting me when I least expected it.

'It occurred to me that I could dilute the R-event with more sex,' I went on. 'I counted every time I did it. By the time I'd had sex two hundred times, that meant the

R-event was only zero point five of the whole. Surely, I'd diluted it enough by now? I learned that it didn't work like that, but still, I carried on counting.' I turned to Zack and reached for his hand. 'When I met you, you made me feel as if everything was simple.' I remembered his exact words and quoted them back at him. 'You breathe in and you breathe out. You smile. You feel happy because … why wouldn't you? Life is good. The sun rises and sets for you, Lydia Green. Just for you.' My voice caught. 'And with you, Zack, I didn't have to count any more.'

He stood up then and pulled me out of my chair, hugging me so tightly that I thought I might stop breathing.

Tess and I had come full circle and were back to telling each other everything. We were often in each other's houses, not least because Adam and Bobby were best friends. I helped her reorganise her business so that she could maximise profits and secure enough money to live on. And as expected, I lost my licence for a year so she helped me with school drop-offs and pick-ups while I was no longer driving.

On a sunny day in June, we sat outside on the grass, Rose on a blanket beside us, while the boys played football. Tess rummaged in her bag and brought out a photograph. 'Look what I found.' She handed it to me. 'I always loved this picture.'

It was Tess, me and my dad in Oxford, when we'd gone to visit the university. 'Look at us!' I smiled. 'We were gorgeous. We had so much potential.'

'Didn't we just.' Her expression was wistful. 'If you could give your fifteen-year-old self some advice, what would it be?'

'That's a hard one.' I stared at Rose who had raised herself up onto her knees and was rocking backwards and forwards, yet to work out how to crawl. 'I think I would say … I dunno … be cautious, don't go to Wales!' I tried for a laugh. 'Ask for help. You don't have to manage everything yourself.' I bit my lip. 'What about you?'

'Be a better friend.'

'Tess.' I smiled at her. 'You weren't to know how much I was keeping from you.' I stood up and held my hand out to her. 'My dad used to say that the truth is what everyone can agree upon. And I think we can agree that we've got each other's backs. Don't you?' She accepted my hand and stood up alongside me.

'Forever,' she said. 'And then some.'

Later that night, when Tess had gone home with Rose, and the boys and Zack were asleep, I drove to the grave-yard. The waning crescent moon cast a meagre light, but with the absence of clouds, the stars were bright and I could easily find my way to my dad's grave. Since my mother's death, I had kept his grave spotless. She was buried in a plot close by and I tended to that too, although only as a mark of duty rather than love.

Matricide: the killing of one's mother.

Secrets are ghosts. And I knew that what I'd done would haunt me until my last breath.

Adam Green
12.12.1950 – 30.07.1994
Beloved husband to Genevieve and father to Lydia
May he rest in peace

'I killed her for Adam, Dad,' I whispered. 'I did.' But even as the words came out of my mouth, I knew I was lying. I hadn't killed her for Adam.

I'd killed her for me.

318

Acknowledgements

A sincere thank you to my editors at Hodder & Stoughton, Bethany Wickington and Cara Chimirri, for helping me hone my ideas and improve each draft. The novel is so much better for your input. Cari Rosen for her expert copyediting, and my agent Euan Thorneycroft for his ongoing interest and support.

My daughter-in-law Cristina for spending hours talking through the whole plot with me and coming up with the one line that helped sharpen my focus.

Sean for his advice on police process – any mistakes are mine!

Peta Andrews for reading the first draft and giving me invaluable feedback.

My friends George, Neil and Mel for their enthusiasm and love of all things writing.

Carmen Marcus who is, quite simply, a genius – her Zoom courses on the writing process are unparalleled.

Teacher versus pupil.

It's your word against hers.

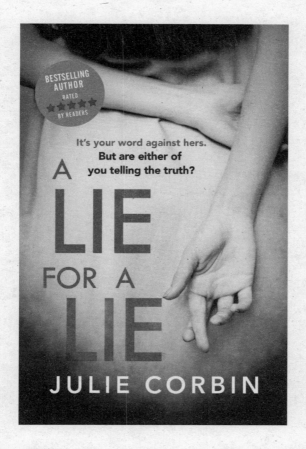

Read Julie Corbin's gripping suspense thriller now!

When an anonymous note is left in a child's schoolbag, scandalous accusations are made.

The school playground becomes rife with rumours, leaving friends Nina, Bel and Rachel to wonder who could be revealing their secrets . . .

Small secrets grow into...

Whispers of a Scandal

JULIE CORBIN

Julie Corbin's addictive psychological suspense thriller is available now!